AI/DNA

ARTIFICIAL INSEMINATION

DEOXYRIBONUCLEIC ACID

by
Peter Wilkinson

Published
by
NETWORK PUBLICATIONS (Scotland)

First Published 1998
Network Publications(Scotland)
6th Floor, 34 West George St.,
Glasgow, Scotland.

Copyright 1998 Peter Wilkinson

First printed June 1998

ISBN 1-899651-01-2

Characters or reference to any person in this book are based on fiction.

Printed and bound by Caledonian International Book Manufacturing Ltd.
Bishopbriggs, Glasgow

*DEDICATED TO THE MEMORY OF MY FATHER,
AND THE ONGOING ENERGY AND ENCOURAGEMENT
OF MY MOTHER*

Chapter One

It was a particularly cold night, dark. The street looked dark, the car was dark and if you looked very carefully into the interior, you would have seen a dark lady. Her motives for being there were not bright.

The car had been there a while. A casual observer might not have realised, but there was a distinct covering of dew forming on both the hood and the roof. The occupant had been there a while, too, and a passing police officer would have been suspicious. There was condensation on all the windows, apart from the area of the windshield that benefited from the last remnants of heat from the fast-cooling block. Those minuscule droplets of pure water made her feel more secure, like a child, hiding behind it's fingers. This lady didn't need to look out. She was listening, imagination racing. Her breathing matched her pulse.

She checked the lock. It was central locking, but her eyes touched every door. At least the doors were secure. She checked them again. There were many checks, but not as many as usual. She was more alone than she had ever been, but now she was focused, pre-occupied.

Yes, she'd been there sometime. But there were no police officers, it was a smart neighbourhood, without controversy, only one property at the end of a cul de sac, no need for patrols, because this house was hardly open plan, it had a high, high brick wall and imposing gate, that said keep out and money in equal proportions.

You would have been forgiven for being mistaken. Cold car, cold night, cold lady, but no, she was far from cold, she was the sort of temperature you would have expected in passionate love making, but dry. In a way she was making love, or at least, she was ready. It was a new experience. She'd been ready for some little while. She sat still with expectation, the expectation and hope of being taken by the man that she wanted, but this wasn't the first time she had sat here and not the first time she was expecting sex. Would this be the night, she mused, but mused, would be an inadequate description, her thoughts possessed an intensity that had long been absent.

She could hear the lover, calm, relaxed, confident, but unhurried. He could have most women, she thought. He knew it, she wasn't keen on that, but this time and for a long time to come, it would be her. He was inside her head, he would be inside her body. She could smell him, the atmosphere, see his nakedness . . . but there was another man inside her, inside her head, very annoying, but necessary, and he was impatient, but for other reasons, the reasons were poles apart, north and south, she hated him, yet needed him badly. He and his type revolted her. She pressed the smooth plastic button of the lock again. It was a reaction, she had no control. Perhaps, even . . . the thought process, the justification, wound through her mind . . . perhaps there was something inside her head that also told her that if she was not careful and positive at this time in her life, she would be more like this cretin than her lover. She had never been more positive.

You could also be forgiven for thinking that she was a music lover, expensive little set of headphones fitting snugly, discreetly. But of course she was a music lover, it wouldn't have been this evidence that would have given that fact away, though. Hadn't she spent years staying at home, listening to the classics, content and excited by their tones, yet lulled into wasted years? Still a blasted virgin at thirty eight, still! A virgin. A virgin. Her sister, Beatrice had called her that, and certainly not in any tone of endearment. It used to be a virtue, now it was an accusation.

One of the phones blasted noise in her ear above the background of the other. Yes, just one. It was a perverse kind of stereo, she thought in a millisecond, not the high fidelity from Sweden that she had imported specially and had grown moodily accustomed to, and reliant. It was crackly and shrill. Admittedly, the sound in each ear was different, but it came from totally different sources and totally different worlds.

"It's Ian, I'm freezing my balls off here, how long are we going to sit here tonight, Lady?"

"Shut up you bastard," she hissed, with the elongated accent firmly on the first 'a' of the swear, "It's tonight. And soon. Just be patient." God knows, she thought, I've been patient enough, but tonight was the night and she had felt for the first time that feminine intuition, that feline certainty of a cat, on heat with it's back arched and it's tail in the air. Tonight would be the night all right.

Dalton stood by the window, looking out in a sort of . . . well he couldn't put his finger on it, but, again there was a millisecond in it, just too long to be normal. Intuition comes in very short bursts, but is rarely recognised until after the event. It could take months.

He knew it would be cold enough out there for dew on the windows, if he were still in his teens, living in that cold cladding house in Virginia, with single glazing, but he'd moved in many more ways than one since then. He'd made it. He'd arrived. He produced films. He was a 'Film Producer', and he liked the sound of that. But he could still see the glint of the dew on the immaculate lawns under the security light, through the double glazed windows. He was attuned to things like that, nature. Country boy of forty, living in the city, but he still had hardwood frames, none of your city plastic rubbish for him. Keep in touch, was one of his favourite sayings. He'd inherited that from his Daddy.

Keeping in touch was what he was good at, he knew every aspect of his business, in the broadest sense, that was why he was so successful in his endeavours, and women were just one of them. Dalton made it look effortless and that made it easier. He was proud of the way that he looked, not an ounce on him, just muscle, slightly tanned and slightly grey at the sides, but Sarah liked that. Sarah was much the same, perhaps her breasts were slightly heavy, but he liked that. She had a deeper tan, with 'no white bits', a saying that irritated him. She was confident, perhaps over

3

confident, moneyed and thirty eight, but no husband . . . no children. Nor did she ever admit to wanting either, it just wasn't a subject that Dalton liked, not that he ever mentioned it, but they could all tell, every last one of them. Patience was the only game-plan open to them.

In this particular case, patience was not one of Sarah's virtues, they had had a good night out, the end of season yacht club dinner and dancing had been fun, a time to dress up, black dress, short, sequins, narrow straps and backless. The decollage was low enough to sink the ocean's finest and was bound to result in bed. Now it was lying on the floor, next to the bed, intermingled with the nautical attire that Dalton looked so cool and clean in, new flannels and blazer, though the confidence of his position allowing no tie, just an open-necked polo shirt, in white, contrasting with the blue deck shoes, a must in the club, and a sinful thing to omit if there was the slightest likelihood of going aboard any one of the super yachts, moored on the first pontoon, next to the club house. Arriving with shoes that left marks, was akin to exposing oneself, and bare feet were equivalent to bending over.

Sarah had hit the 'champers', not in an extravagant way, it was far from polite, things might slip and Dalton never drank, only fresh orange. If she had been out with the 'girlies', it would have been a different matter altogether, but that would be her little secret and he would never know. (In your dreams, Sarah). Even the little she had was enough to give Sarah a tinge of worry, in case Dalton would mention the smell of alcohol on her breath when they inevitably kissed. "Alcohol on her breath and Chanel on her breasts", he'd once quipped. She knew that he would log it, even if he couldn't be bothered to mention it, so she took the precaution of going to the bathroom and cheekily using his toothbrush. She was very cautious. Priscilla, heard her.

The reality was that he would not only notice the alcohol, but he'd also notice the brushing and the distinctive taste of his toothpaste, when they did kiss. He would log them both. Not that it really mattered, he would even try his hardest to see it as her being considerate.

He was careful too. He would always shower before bed, and always use protection. Sarah heard the cabinet open, the rustle of the box and glimpsed a couple of tiny silver parcels in his hand, before putting them on the table at their . . . his, bedside under the lamp. "Two," she thought, and smiled inwardly at his optimism.

Priscilla had heard it all too, she didn't know how many, but she knew they were there. It made her slightly shiver, not with cold, but Priscilla's face whitened further in expectation and, if it were light enough, the contrast between her pale complexion, turning paler, against the immaculate, slightly harsh lines of her shoulder length, auburn hair would have been further pronounced, leaving that thin line of unostentatious pink lipstick almost invisible. It was, after all, her first time.

There was no tan for Priscilla, not that she disliked a tan, but it was a sure sign of trying to attract a mate, a come on, I'm available, like red lipstick or neon lights.

If Ian spoke now she might miss something, but she dare not call him and tell him to keep quite, just in case she indeed did. She had blanked out the reality of the act, from her mind, caught up in the logistics of the operation, the risks, the risks that she were taking and the risk that he was running, though his care was to be his downfall and her gain. Interesting concept, she thought to herself, but was too pre-occupied to think through the logistics of the balance between risk and counter risk, who was gaining and who was loosing. Priscilla was gaining, and she liked to think that Dalton would be gaining, too. Sarah wasn't part of the equation, only the agent, not even the receptacle, as it turned out, an irony that Priscilla never wasted a millisecond on, but would have liked, had she thought of it. This was Priscilla's occasion she'd been second long enough, she was moving to first fiddle, the conductor, but still in the wings. Being in charge was not what she was accustomed to, but now was her time, she was taking charge. Permission was not being sought. She liked what she felt and the feeling was strong, stronger than she'd imagined, but not stronger than her imagination.

It was a coming together on equal terms, the initial embrace being mutual as they rolled down onto the bed, as one, well suited, with a similar desire for passion and relief, the smell of the champagne and the taste of the toothpaste being dismissed the moment it was registered, the smell of her hair and expensive, lingering perfume overcame that, and the mustiness of her body after all that dancing, this evening, as he kissed her from her neck to her breasts, just passing gently, the soft area beneath the shoulder, but not quite under her arms. Dalton pulled at the back of her hair revealing her slender neck and throat, where, until a few minutes ago, loosely hung the double row of natural pearls, the most feminine of adornments, for the exclusive use of women.

There were no words and Priscilla was thankful for that, she wanted him for herself, no intrusion, her thin, white hand, cupped round the earpiece that connected them, her knees pressed together. They still shook.

Sarah was squeezing him tightly, the body was hard, just how she liked, manly, the right amount of hair, but a gentleness of touch and manner and cleanliness, which women liked for themselves and deep down preferred in a partner, a bias toward the feminine side of masculinity, without passing that fine and hallowed line. She felt an urgency to take him, a recklessness, before carefulness overtook him and maybe herself. It heightened the passion. She slipped down to take him in her mouth before he was sheathed and he groaned, half rolling onto his back, legs half bent, wanting to close his eyes, yet keep them open to take in her form and sex, her small bottom . . . he could wait no more, she hesitated as she felt his move and simultaneously heard the tearing of that small packet, letting go, to kneel between his legs, staring and impatient, feasting on his familiar form. He was prepared, she slid over him with a glorious ripple that sent a shudder of pleasure through them both as they moved together, opposing forces, yet synchronised, with the unhurried assurance of two people who knew each other well. There was no groping or gasping, just a quiet enjoyment culminating in a satisfying release, as she slumped forward , her hot breasts spread on his heaving chest and their faces relaxed together, wet with Sarah's golden hair sticking to the moist, salty, skin.

It was almost time for Priscilla's climax. But not quite. Timing was absolutely everything, there would only ever be one chance and she could hardly wait, her finger poised rigidly over the transmit button of her radio. She had held her breath for long enough.

"Don't speak now, Ian, you . . .", but she heard Dalton moving and that girl roll to one side. There were the footsteps across the Italian marble floor, bare feet and hardly discernible, "Dalton had imported it himself," Priscilla's sister, Beatrice, had crowed. And then she heard it. The tiny noise of her imagined object dropping into the bathroom basket was hardly audible, but unmistakable. Give him another few seconds to return to the bed. She heard the tap run for a few moments and then the returning footsteps, warm flesh being pulled from cool stone.

Priscilla had been holding her breath again, the thumping of her heart, pumping the biggest rush of adrenaline it had ever experienced, seemed so loud, that she had had to turn up the volume on her receiver to full, occasionally making it squeal over the noise of the static sent out from the tiny transmitter hidden in the plug of the table lamp. One last deep breath, as much an effort to calm herself as prepare for speech, and out it came, not a loud command but a soft, firm, simple word that was to change everything. "Go."

What had seemed like minutes to Priscilla had seemed like ages to Ian and in fact had been over three hours that night. It had been over an hour since the radio had made a sound, but there again, he was being paid by the night and an end result bonus. He didn't understand what was going on, but didn't care that much, the longer it took, the more he got paid, although, fundamentally he would describe himself as slightly impatient and whatever the price, he would prefer action. Inactivity gave him time to think and he wasn't too good at that. His general description masked the real character, that is, he had a very short fuse.

Anyway, that solitary word suddenly entering his head through one ear made him start, and slightly annoyed him momentarily, because, although he wasn't doing anything active, he was over a rich man's wall, secreted in the shrubbery in the dead of the night with a gun in his pocket, and a boy could get slapped wrists for that, as Priscilla had , in her own way, at odds with his own style, reminded him. Unnecessarily, as it happened.

"They're in the bed, get in there now", was the next thing that he heard.

Even before he had time to move, and as he stepped out into the bright lights, he briefly wondered how she was so certain. He knew nothing of the transmitter. He was a big man of over six feet, broad shouldered, lightly bearded and with the remnants of a hair lip, and the six paces he took to reach the French windows created an appreciable amount of energy. The doors stood no chance and they both flew open, half off their hinges followed by the panes of glass and splinters of wood, all over the off-white , deep-pile carpet with a pale blue surround following the outline of the wall, for the first two metres of the room, then onto that expensive Italian marble, which when reached, caused some awful tinkling noise. It's funny how these details could be taken in so quickly, by someone who was basically a dim-wit, in such detail in such a short space of time, but he did. When the juices flowed, they always did. He had details from other adventures etched on his mind, some of them, most of them, he wished that he hadn't. They often came back to him in the night and like his projected mass, they were unstoppable.

He came to a halt at the end of the bed and with an unusually fluid motion for a man of his size, raised the pistol and took his finger away from the safety position, wrapping it around the trigger, pointed it at the horror struck occupants of the bed, and, as it was his turn for command, said, "Freeze, you bastards or you'll get a bigger sensation than you bargained for." They eyed each other for a little more than a moment, which was too long for Priscilla, she couldn't resist saying, "get on with it, Ian," but Ian heard nothing. It wasn't the rushing sound of blood pumping in his ears, but the earpiece had gone for six as he burst through the doors and it was swinging too and fro at the end of a fine black wire, like a pendant over his heaving barrel of a chest. He was in charge now, he was here, on the spot, and it was quite definitely his department.

He allowed himself the luxury of admiring the line of Sarah's single, visible, breast as she instinctively pulled the covers up, but that could easily have been his downfall. Dalton regained his footing, so to speak, and said "what the fuck do you think you're at."

That could have been Dalton's downfall. Ian was in no mood to be usurped from his position of dominance.

"One more fucking word," he menaced, but it was obvious neither of the parties in the bed would be doing any such thing.

"Get in the bathroom," he ordered, with a leer, and as they made to get up he added, "leave the covers." This afforded him the extra luxury of seeing Sarah's naked body pass by, but his macho psyche robbed him of any pleasure he might have derived, by the presence of a naked man, forced into parading in front of him, by his own direction, and his eyes seemed to be drawn to the man's buttocks, destroying any hope of derived pleasure. He realised and it annoyed him.

"Get back against the wall, and, Lady, push the waste bin out of the room." Sarah glanced at Dalton for confirmation and he gave her a half nod, before she pushed it across the floor with her trembling left hand and out of the door, at full stretch, keeping as far away from this lunatic as possible.

"Now stay there, against the wall and lock the door. Push the key under the door. Hurry, come on. Stay quiet and nobody will get hurt." He heard the door lock, the key came out, he kicked it across the room, with a further tinkle and tried the door, as a precaution. He's a smart guy I've got in there, he thought, but added, to himself, not smart enough and smirked. Nothing like getting one over these lucky bastards who had everything on a plate.

He heard the girl say something.

"Shut the fuck up or you'll see a bullet come through that door." Silence. Ian relaxed a little, stuffed the gun into his belt and took out a bin-liner, from his inside pocket. The safety catch was on. It was instinct. When he'd been in the army, one of the guys lost one half of his manhood forgetting that minor point. Nobody needed to be told again. Ever.

What he didn't know, was that Dalton took the two steps to the bathroom door, with the silence of bare feet on Italian marble and the developed grace of his tennis skills, bent down and looked through the key-hole. It was ridiculous, but Sarah fleetingly admired the look of

9

Dalton in this unaccustomed pose, even in the horrendous situation she was in. It didn't last long, but animal instincts have a strength of their own.

Ian's mind was on his allotted task, Priscilla was holding her breath longer than she thought possible, straining for every sound.

Ian emptied the meagre contents of the waste bin into his bag, followed by the contents of the bedside bin, neatly folded it and carefully slipped it back into his inside pocket. If that was what the Lady wanted, then that would be what the Lady got.

In the bathroom, Dalton was puzzled and uncomfortable, he daren't even blink, in case he missed something and illogically thinking the intruder would hear it, his eye remained glued on the scene, even with the draft from the key-hole trained into his eye, and salty wetness running down his cheek, following the man as he walked over to the dresser, pick up the double strand of pearls that had been lent to Sarah for the night, hair brush, his Rolex watch and the cash. The last two items were Ian's personal bonus, he felt that deserved it. The hair brush was placed in a separate bag of it's own. This was his precise instruction, she had repeated it several times. Scattered on the glass surface, there was a little under a thousand dollars, and if he had left it at that, it would have kept things simple, but he just had to pick up the loose change. This took both hands, one to scoop it over the surface and the other to catch it as it came over the edge, two hands were preoccupied and making a noise.   Physcologically, this was all the cover Dalton needed. He quickly stepped back one pace and sprang at the door. The whimpering Sarah knew instantly what he was about to do, and, in fact , in that split second, managed to get one, slippy, tear-wet hand round his left bicep, but it did nothing. His full fourteen stone frame took the lock out in one, but not the hinges. The hollow door banged back against the wall, shocking Ian to his socks. Three quick paces launched Dalton into a ballistic trajectory which would have permanently taken the wind out of Ian, had he contacted, but the handful of change which brought about the disaster saved the day, as he threw it hard into the contorted, oncoming face of his assailant. Dalton called out in pain as the coins hit him and he landed badly, just catching hold of one leg as he hit the floor, luckily in the carpeted area . With his free leg, Ian kicked out full in his attacker's chest and for the second time that evening, Dalton rolled onto his back with a groan. Ian had his gun out now, and in the worst kind of rage, brought on by shock and fear, he levelled his gun. He really did consider killing him there and then. The safety catch was already off.

Priscilla had heard everything and was hyperventilating, now.

"Don't," she screamed out, but, of course, her man heard nothing.

"One fucking move and I'll blow you away," with the emphasis definitely on the last 'a', of away. This time, he kept the gun in his hand and pointing in the right direction, his eyes flicking maniacally, between Dalton, laying at his feet, and Sarah, huddled in the corner of the bathroom, shaking and whimpering, fearing the worst. He walked slowly, backwards over to the bedside light, unplugged it, ripped the wire out, put the plug in his pocket and strode over to his wide eyed victim on the floor, hesitated for a moment and gave him one great kick. For the third time this evening, Dalton groaned and rolled onto his back, but this time, with his knees pulled up, in pain. Moving further, was not an option. The 'safety', was back in position. One last look around revealed the bedside phone. Ian's eyes met Sarah's. He knew what she was thinking. Two paces and he had the equipment in his hands. It came apart like a toy. Ian knew that it was of no practical use to break it, because there were bound to be more and the guy was bound to have a 'mobile', but it was the sort of thing they always did in films and Ian liked the role. He was sure that it impressed the girl. The 'big-man', crunched his way across the broken glass and he was gone.

Ian appeared at the top of the wall, just next to the gates. He was momentarily silhouetted by the glare of the security lights around the house, and, considering his bulk, dropped easily onto his feet with a practised and professional bending of the knees on impact with the ground. It spelt marines, to anyone who wanted to read it, but there was no one there apart from his temporary controller, and she didn't know the language. Her world was Chopin and hors d'oeuvres.

It was followed by a light rush of relief flowing over Priscilla, a faintness, not for his safety, although, in a way, it was. At this point, his safety, was her own. It was almost the end of this fleeting and pathetic bonding. She couldn't wait. He ambled over to the car, with a touch of nonchalance, which was enough to annoy her, and it did, although in reality, it wasn't designed to, that would have been beyond him. His measured pace was for his own safety, he didn't want to draw attention to himself, in case there were any prying eyes, but it was late and the street deserted. Nobody ever walked in this neighbourhood, anyway, but Ian didn't realise it, so any movement , observed, would have caused suspicion. Besides, he figured he'd earned a swagger, so he took the opportunity and awarded himself one.

Ian reached the car and put his hand out for the handle, but the window was already part down.

"Not in the front," was all he heard over the purr of the newly fired, four cylinders, (unlike the racy, six, of her sister Beatrice's).

Priscilla set off at a pace, her nervousness allowing a small squeak from the back wheels. Another first.

"Don't rush," said Ian, " it will take him some time to get his breath back before he can call the cops."

"What do you mean?"

"I gave him a good kicking."

"What? I specifically told you, no harm, you bastard."

"He tried to jump me," Ian said, with the sort of apologising tone that a school mistress might expect from her charges.

Priscilla clutched the wheel, her knuckles white, in a rage. Back to the business in hand, she took the bags from him.

"And the pearls," she said, glancing at him over her shoulder. He tossed them over onto the seat. She emptied the garbage onto the passenger seat and saw what she was after. She took out a small plastic bag and plopped the damp little parcel into it, with one hand, too preoccupied to take in the unfamiliar contents of her prize and slipped it up her tight black, short skirt, right between the top of her legs, where it was very warm and just as damp. She felt a rush of emotion course through her temples.

12

Ian had clocked what she had done, first, the pearls into her hand-bag and then the package. He'd seen the light from the street lamps through the rubber of that unmistakable gossamer as she dropped it in the plastic, and was going to say something, but she knew that he'd seen her and a look in the mirror was enough to keep him quiet. The hair brush, in a bag of it's own , was pushed into her hand bag.

They were passing through suburbia and presently reached the commuter car park. Not many cars, and she easily pulled into an empty area some thirty metres from Ian's, stone cold, waiting vehicle. She was eager to get rid of this association and get on with her main task, precious time was running out, it might soon all be in vain, although she was assured that if the temperature was correct, at least twelve hours would be safe, though the number of her irreplaceable charges was diminishing by the hour, but Priscilla's worry, verging on paranoia, was counting the decline by the second. She could imagine them dying in their hordes.

Ian was feeling more relaxed. He'd seen the car park approach, with his station wagon safely where he'd left it. He felt he was almost passed the finishing post, when they pulled up. No trouble from this lady. Strange job, strange character, just the pay to collect and get the hell out of the place.

"Nice job, eh, Lady?", he'd offered, not knowing her name, but was ignored, especially when he added, with the irony of ignorance, "satisfied?" He just opened the door and stepped out at the same time as his driver.

"That's novel, not used to being chauffeured by a woman, Ma'am, I hope that envelope's going to be scented, now," he quipped as he eyed her reaching into her bag, and placing her fingers around a small buff parcel. His eyes were on just one of her hands. It was a mistake. Had it been the NVA, back in 'Nam, he would never have been so stupid, but this was 'Peaceville', America and she was a house-wife.

He turned to pick up his discarded jacket, from the back seat, reached in. It had taken a moment, but then his world exploded. He fell back out of the car in spasm, sensing the gravel under his elbows and the back of his head as he ground them both into the surface involuntarily. South-East

Asia. He couldn't speak and his vision was a mass of flashing lights and greyness, his heart was bursting with a massive irregularity. There was something he hadn't seen in her other hand. Priscilla was clutching an electric hand-stunner, fitting in her palm, matt black with two stainless steel prods, sticking out, two inches apart. Oddly, it matched her handbag, in a way, but that finer point was wasted on Ian, who's breathing was laboured, to say the least. Priscilla had never used it before and this was the first time she had pressed the button, let alone jab it into the pink flesh of a bending man, in that vile area, between his trousers and shirt.

"Never could stand the sight of a man with his shirt out," she thought, as she lunged. She hadn't even been sure of the effect, as she had bought the thing in France and the shop assistant babbled on unintelligibly. Her French wasn't that good. She had got the general idea, though, and knew the word for 'incapacitation'.

"I take the safety of my baby's father very seriously, Ian."

(The irony of referring to her victim correctly, by name, was totally lost on someone of Priscilla's upbringing). It was also lost on the writhing man. She tossed the package of money onto him, and the fat envelope landed on his even fatter, stomach, which was not only bare, now, but protruded in a particularly vulgar way. His shirt was half-way up his convulsing torso.

The envelope wasn't a common brown one, but there again, it wasn't scented, apart from the unmistakable aroma of dollars and if Ian's brain hadn't still been scrambled, he might well have applauded the fact that he was still getting paid at all, but it is doubtful. Revenge would have been firmly on his mind, it was still there, but no way could it be described as firmly. He still could hardly think, was short of breath and his muscles, particularly in the chest, were still in spasm.

"I'll take the gun back," she said, reaching forward, "it's registered to me."

That was just enough to shake him half way to the real world, and with the strongest effort, born of revenge, that his large frame had ever made, he grasped the pistol butt, and forced his arm to pull it out of his belt, turning it on it's own axis.

"Now, lady," he rasped, but for the first time in her life, Priscilla stood with her legs slightly apart and squared up. Even Ian could see that the look of confidence was a little too strong for someone looking down the barrel of a gun.

She had her parcel tucked into the top of one stocking and was in a hurry, her thoughts were far from the welfare of this person, and, for the second time that night, and in her life, the stunner came back out of her bag. This time, Ian saw it all too well.

Complete fear overcame Ian making him instinctively pull the trigger. Not a thing happened, save the cocking of the hammer and a small, dull click, too low to be registered over the pounding of his brain, and a damn sight smaller than the percussion that he was expecting. From that range, it should have demolished her rib-cage and left through her back. Nothing. He loosed off another click in her direction, but he hardly had time to register that, when, another millisecond before he was bolted into unconsciousness, he felt the dual prods of her own weapon connect with the solid rib of his own, exposed, chest.

"Did you really think that I would have given you a gun with live rounds, idiot? That was your turn to be kicked," and at that, she turned on her squared heels, making an indentation in the gravel the same depth that Ian was doing, for the second time, except that he was drawing blood, and it was with his elbows. She wasn't.

It took her three minutes to reach the house that she'd always lived in, and until a few months ago, shared with her mother, open the front door and uncharacteristically kick off her shoes in the lobby (even this scene couldn't change the habit of never walking over the carpet with her shoes on), and switching off the alarms. She even ignored the two cats, sitting impassively on the stairs, four eyes following her moves, but knowing that this was not a good time for a stroke or a sound. Thirty six, thirty six, she punched into the panel. Just her sister's age, it repeated, her painted nails, not too long, clicking on the buttons, as the red light went out on the console and the green came on in it's place.

She was straight over to the less-grand bathroom and reached for the prepared, sterile brown bottle in front of the mirror, followed by running warm water over it under the basin tap. This was a precaution of her own making, and was taking the instructions of Dr Jack Jones very seriously. "Make sure your partner collects it fresh and keep it at body temperature for best results," he'd stated, in the serious tone that Doctors alone seem able to muster, designed to make you heed them. If he'd said warm, then warm, it would stay. She held the condom over the small bottle by the teat and squeezed down the full length three times. She was surprised by the lack of volume and was certainly not going to waste a drop of the valuable fluid. Screwing on the top, tightly, she held it up to the light, with both hands and kissed the warm glass, smudging the lip print off, with her thumb.

The navy blue silk blouse, with the single button open at the top, was quickly opened fully, revealing her lace bra, which matched those special panties. She neatly filled both cups, and mentally raised an eyebrow in a new found appreciation of her femininity and form. The blouse came off one shoulder and she picked up a roll of micropore tape, fixing the bottle firmly under one armpit, one quick look in the mirror and with a look of satisfaction, breathed, "there," followed by an involuntary, gentle pat. It was part of her, now. The top was quickly re-buttoned, but this time there were two buttons open at the neck.

There was just time to pick up the bag with the hair brush, open the seal and breath in the scented air from within, reseal it and with a reluctance to let it go, replace it in the cabinet and smile to herself. Had she been that kind of Lady, she would have punched the air. She wasn't.

Back in the hall, and giving her cats a return stare, she pressed the redial button of her mobile phone. "Jack, it's Priscilla, is it still all right to come over to your place now?"

"Yeah, course it is, Priscilla, just ring the clinic bell, on the main door and I'll put on the coffee."

She tried not to race, but travelled at about the same pace as her pulse, taking fifteen minutes, on a journey that would have taken forty in daytime. She felt good, the stockings felt good. It was the first time she'd worn them since high school, they were just part of her careful plan, but she could get used to the feeling and she felt more of a women then she had in a long time, alive and sexy. She was wearing her best panties, too, you could were anything with tights, but not stockings. With further irony, they were part of the set that her sister had bought her, three Christmas's ago, but she'd never worn them before, she'd always felt that they were a put down, a dare, an accusation, even. She could handle them now. Yes, she felt more alive, but a little anxious, with a feeling that every second was a minute, her chances dying by the thousand.

When she left the house, she pulled the door closed, against the lock. She was down three of the front steps before she even looked back. Her eyes rested on the lock. She didn't shrug, but she carried on down the steps. It was the first time that she'd not checked for years.

The outside light was on in the porch of the Clinic, and she could see the light behind the blinds as she pulled up and abandoned the car at the sort of rakish angle that would have created a torrent of tutting, about anybody else, with little thought for any possible reasons. Inconsideration was normally her sister's department. The lights flashed as the alarm and locks were cycled twice. She tugged the handle to make sure.

Dr Jones, 'Jacky', to his friends, was a genial sort of chap, broad face, white hair and something past retirement age, he wasn't married, but was dedicated to giving women a chance of motherhood, when there wouldn't normally have been a chance. Most people didn't know that he wasn't capable of fathering, either, and, really, the only person who knew for sure had passed on a few years ago. His mother strongly suspected, mothers always know, but he never discussed it. No, he just soldiered on keeping a record and album of his every success. The wall behind his secretary's station was covered in smiling babies and equally smiling mothers. The main difference was their teeth. Some of them were very grown up, now, and were like an extended family, you never really forget the person who was responsible for your existence, and sometimes there was no father at all. (Known, that is.) He considered it the private business of the parents, but especially the mother. If the father wasn't to be revealed, then so be it.

He knew, felt and liked the feeling of being the substitute father, a broad shoulder for tears and advice. Doctors always do, like priests. His sympathies always lay with the mother. His personal problem heightened that desire. He liked playing God, but his Catholic upbringing

He had been pioneering the service since being a young doctor in general practice and had taken some flak, over the years, finding that it helped not to talk openly about his service and tailor his opinions, in public, to the ever changing foibles of the very same. He had even had threatening letters and phone calls from 'natural conception groups' and their like, but it was like water off a very large back. "Bleeding nutters," was how he inwardly dismissed them and came to terms with the delicate, moral dilemma. Babies were his interest and life.

One of his large, soft hands held her delicate fingers whilst the other went gently around her shoulder, and, unlike other meetings, it was her lips that met his cheek, for a change. The air lost out. Dependence on a supporting figure always brings that out in a woman, though not readily admitted or realised. "Come on in Priscilla, coffee's hot, lovely to see you again." He'd noticed. He always did. Originality is a rare commodity. "Thanks, Jack." There had also been a subtle change in her address, to him. She moved to the sofa in his reception, pulled her jacket off one shoulder, undid a further button of her blouse, unselfconsciously slipped her hand under the silk and gently tugged the bottle away from her skin. The twinge of pain that went with that act, seemed appropriate. It was instinctive, but she didn't know why, nor did she care, she just wanted her charges to be in the safety of those big hands.

She felt a small emotional wrench as she passed the bottle over to Dr Jones, so much had gone into it's procurement, so much time, energy and particularly, emotion, a mixture of doubt and desire, but natural instinct had kicked in and once there, was impossible to quell. She was, after all, almost forty, and hadn't Jack warned of the lessening chance of conception, the time it could take, the possibility of having to repeat the process, it felt like she was carrying a negative time bomb, one that she ad ignored for years, yet now it was about to explode, she was frantic.

"I'll be ten minutes, or so, you'll be wanting to wait, I suppose?" It was a kindly question, posed without drawing either a breath or a pause, his Irish lilt coming out at the same time as his Irish humour, and it was followed by as much of an impish look as a man who was built like a wall, could muster, even if it was a soft wall. He didn't expect an answer.

Priscilla, relaxed into the comfort of one of the arm chairs, safe in it's luxuriance, and she had the feeling of waiting outside a ward for results of labours, and hadn't she done that a few times? She'd made the first steps and what steps they were, but there was a long way to go. She'd get there. Dalton didn't get a passing thought, but fathers didn't figure at times like these.

Dr Jones had moved through to his laboratory and got down to business. Business wasn't normally conducted at this hour in the morning, couples usually managed to time their sampling to office hours, but he was in his territory and it was a routine that he knew well, elevated to the position of alchemy by the uninitiated, and, indeed, twenty years ago, to all intents and purposes, it was. But now it was plain routine, if the beginning of life was ever routine, that is.

Gloves, glasses, white coat, everything spotless, like the gowns of a high priest in ceremony. Add the warm rinse to the sample, no shocks at this stage and gently agitate, cool under running water, this will take five minutes, whilst he checks the coolant temperature of his liquid nitrogen flask. He takes the top off and if ever there was a suggestion of alchemy, then this was it. Stainless steel had replaced sooty cast iron, but talk about hubble bubble, toil and trouble. Thick white smoke pours heavily over the lip and passing his knees before evaporating, with bubbles splashing up from the cauldron, Shakespeare would have been proud of him. So would Merlin. So might, his mother.

His long handled tweezers picked out the phial from the boiling depths and placed it in the holder on his bench. He loosely replaced the lid whilst he noted the code, then carefully poured the tiny amount of prized liquid and sealed it. Back, quickly into the allotted position, no mistakes here, and seal the lid, noting the steadying of the temperature gauge. He was through in a moment, to find Priscilla snoozing quietly where she had slumped.

"Coffee?", as he touched her arm, his enquiry being answered by a cross between a purr and a sigh.

"Do you mind if I get straight off, Jack? I am whacked."

"You just do that, Priscilla," he said, smiling, fighting off the sinking feeling in the pit of his stomach. He always felt let down, deflated, at this point, 'used', would be too strong a description.

"Now drive carefully, it's late." He showed her to the door and steadied her all the way. It had been a long day and he was sympathetic to the stress that all this could cause. "Now don't forget, drive carefully," but she was already on her way, with a faint smile, devoid of any trace of her pink frost lipstick, but the other thing that was different, and Jack had not seen it, was that her single string of pearls were now double.

Chapter Two

Priscilla, was about to leave the house, and she was wearing another of her black 'numbers', but this time a dress. It wasn't too flashy or too short, mid-calf, three quarter sleeves, black tights, this time, and patent, black shoes, with a little gold line around the low heels. She was wearing the double strand of pearls, though. Her hair was still straight, though it was drawn back slightly, not behind her ears, maybe more on one side than the other. She had a little make-up on. She wanted to fit in, without drawing attention to herself, especially male attention. She opened her clutch-bag, patent, to match her shoes, and stood in the hall, looking at the mirror, she leaned forward to inspect her eyebrows, catching sight of the cats on the stairs, again.

"No use looking at me like that," she said, in a baby voice, to the cats, behind her, whilst wetting her finger and smoothing down the hairs above each eye.

"I can see you in the mirror." The cats were unaffected.

Too long? She allowed the question to run through her head, whilst telling the cats that it didn't matter how much they looked at her, she was still going out and she would try not to be long. Maybe she should pluck them? The lip stick. Out it came and she slid the top off with hat satisfying noise that always accompanied the opening of a new stick. Quite a bit brighter than she was used too, it looked less so, in the fluorescent light of the store, still, nice. She was admiring it and closely inspecting the line when the door-bell went and she jumped, like a naughty girl caught in the act.

"Damn," she said softly, "Beatrice." She could see her silhouette in the glass door, and she knew that Beatrice could see hers. "Won't be a minute."

"Come on, Prissy, open the door, there are weirdoes out here".

She only had the comfort and thinking time of three paces before her hand was on the lock and her sister did the rest.

She was passed her in a moment, shoes and all.

"Hi, Tommy. Hi Tabs," she said to the cats, giving each one a brief stroke. Priscilla was thinking she would have the same, but her 'stroke', would be of a much more serious kind, as she followed her through to the living room, taking in the difference in her dress, bright colours, the confidence to wear flat shoes and still show her legs. Bare legs.

"I wish you wouldn't speak so loudly on the front doorstep and keep saying there are crazy people about. You were about the only crazy person, down this street, for years."

"Yes, but now there really are crazy people about, have you not heard what happened to poor Dalton? He was attacked, in the house, by a weirdo. I don't suppose you would call that crazy? Sarah Cobham was there too, the bitch."

"Oh, don't keep talking like that." She turned away, cheeks flushed. "Was he hurt", asked Priscilla, taking the smallest nip to the skin of her thumb, with her teeth, but enough to make Beatrice notice.

"Yes he was, but he called me and I've been round all this week doing my 'Florence Nightingale', poor boy."

"Did they take anything?" Priscilla forced herself to ask, still with her back turned, but glanced at Beatrice to catch her expression.

"A lousy thousand bucks and a little jewellery."

Thank God, for this high dress, thought Priscilla, she could feel each pearl on her skin, even as she spoke, and flushed a little more. Luckily, the colour was masked by the next question, though it felt and sounded like an accusation.

"You're going out, I see? Not like you." Priscilla thought the inevitable question would make her blush with embarrassment. It didn't. It made her blush with anger.

"You're not the only one who goes out, you know," she retorted, but, unabashed.

Beatrice just added, "since when?"

There was no winning this argument and Beatrice was completely unaffected by niceties. "And you're wearing lipstick."

"I always do."

"Not that colour, you don't, you always wear 'Miss Pink Frosty Face'."

"Thank you, very much for those few kind words, and where are you going, tonight?"

"Dalton's house, he's a new maid and she is cooking Mexican."

"Why Mexican?"

"Because she is Mexican, and that's all she can cook." At that point, she turned her back again, not with embarrassment, this time, but with sheer anger, but went off the boil, when the front door bell went.

"It's my cab, Beatrice, I'd better run."

"I'll stay and keep Tommy and Tabby-Boy company for a while," and she added, as she kicked her shoes off, "enjoy yourself." Sarcasm.

Priscilla was half way down the hall when Beatrice called out, "who did you say he was?"

It was under her breath, but it was a good job she wasn't heard, "I'm not going to see a he, it's a she and a call-girl, at that." How Priscilla would have liked to announce that . . . On one level. Up until last month, it would have been the most wicked thought she'd ever had, but she was in the back of the cab before those kind of thoughts could crystallise. She glanced back at the door. It wasn't locked.

"The Adelphi Hotel, if you don't mind, the Rainbow Lounge entrance, please." She made this request automatically, before she'd even straightened her dress, pulling it over the knee to avoid creases and never looked at the driver. She'd been there five times in the last week, and, in a strange way, felt comfortable with the request. The driver felt differently. He took in her smartness, her accent, the address and the destination, the number of passengers, put it all in the computer between his ears, but all it

23

came up with was, "Rainbow Lounge entrance?" Classification, 'something not right, confirmation needed . . . proceed'.

The journey, down town, took fifteen minutes, the traffic getting heavier as they progressed, and apart from checking the lipstick in her little mirror, thoughtfully provided on the inside of the gold container, more to see if it were still there than the quality of application, she was totally preoccupied. The driver made no attempt to speak to her, they were from different worlds, there was a barrier. He reinforced it, by turning up the radio. She could do with the toilet. It was her nervousness and she would have tried before she left, if it weren't for Beatrice's appearance. She knew it wouldn't have worked, she would need to go anyway. Still, straight to the powder room on arrival, check the lips and gather your thoughts. They arrived.

"Fifteen dollars, Ma'am." The notes were ready in her hand. She knew the fare and handed him two 'tens', as she stepped out into the fresh air. That unique mixture of cigarette residue, diesel and after shave, maybe a little body odour, made her sick. She claimed that it 'clung to her hair'. This was on top of the 'ocean wave', motion of the over size springs they always seemed to fit to the rear seats of taxis. She would normally always travel in her own car, but this time, she might have a couple of drinks. Drinking and driving were a no-no for her, unlike her sister. But, apart from that, on this occasion, public displays of her license plates were undesirable. No, it was taxis and anonymity for her.

Another of her three paces and she met the doorman, dressed in 'International Hotel who do you think you are kidding, livery', the sort that Priscilla liked to see. Not that she was taken in, but if she were going to spend money, she liked respect, even if was a little crass. He opened the double glass doors, with brass handles, emblazoned with gold letters, saying, 'Rainbow Lounge', on each door, and underneath, 'International Piano Bar', and, with the slightest nod of the head, and the raising of a white-gloved hand, "good evening, Ma'am."

"Why do they do that", she thought, "they always call you 'Ma'am, when you are alone." Her irritation was born of nervousness, what she had done, no, accomplished, and what she was about to do, no, achieve, she corrected, was taking it's toll. But at the same time, it made her feel alive, for the first time in her life, she was being driven by urges, not commitment and responsibility.

It was an urge of a different sort that took her straight to the 'Ladies Room', over on the right, across the deep pile carpet, that came in a particular shade of pink-purple, impossible to find, in a store, but there again, who would be trying? There were quite a few cigarette burns. It had seen better days. The atmosphere was conservative, a low hum of activity, which piano music always commands, a little smoky, but you could blame the duty-free system for that. People who smoked irregularly suddenly have a packet of two hundred under their arm, when they travel, perhaps it wasn't greed or stupidity, perhaps it was a symbol, 'I'm travelling and you're not'.

Nobody to push past, nobody looked up, there were about forty people in a room for one hundred and forty and, in fact, the average age, was forty. The main room had a scattering of people, dressed internationally and a good mixture of couples and singles, the bar seats almost exclusively, men, but there were single ladies. It was near the airport, affiliated with the airlines, so the customers were pushed in this direction. Most of them on stop-overs for long haul flights, the next morning. Loneliness and boredom made them attractive to some, targets. It wasn't what you would describe as a family atmosphere.

Her lightweight jacket was off and over one arm before she reached the door, identified by a brass silhouette of an Edwardian Lady, and she pushed straight through, to the fluorescent light and mirrored vanity units, and a line of four doors, three of them open, on the right. The music changed on entry, from the compulsory 'Lounge Live Piano', in the corner, to shopping-mall Pan-Pipes. 'Peru -en- Loo', as Beatrice called it. Once again, the music acted as a barrier, a social delineation. Quite effective it was too. Ladies could be women, here. And often were.

Immediately following the sound of flushing, from behind the solitary closed door, came a woman who definitely wasn't a lady. She looked like one, to the general public and certainly most of the men in the lounge, but she couldn't fool Priscilla. Too much sparkle. The combination of two red items, (both matching her nails), pendant earrings and stockings (no doubt), with a silver fleck, told it all. Her guess about the stockings was immediately confirmed, when she unashamedly lifted her short pleated skirt , to pull down her black blouse and straighten it under the waist-band, the effect being to emphasise her bust, her ample bust. This was a circle in which she never revolved, it was almost new to Priscilla.

"Prissy," the woman cried out as she looked up from her task, "You're late. I've turned down two deals whilst I've been waiting. Where have you been? I thought you weren't coming." By this time, Priscilla had got over the shock of seeing her appear unexpectedly from the cubicle and had gone completely off the idea of the toilet. It was the sort of experience that cured you of hiccups. She'd imagined having time to gather her thoughts. At least it saved looking for her in the bar, and at least she was here. Looking for another girl would have been an excruciating business that she could well do without, and Wendy was her third. The first two turned her down flat. "It wasn't a question of money", they'd said, "professional pride." Priscilla hadn't wasted time on analysis; it would have given her a headache. She just wanted results.

"Wendy, I'm sorry I'm late. Someone came to the door as I was leaving, and you know what that down-town traffic is like." She purposely didn't mention her sister, the least people knew the better. Secrecy was her paranoia. "Come on, lets go and sit down", she said after a single 'air-kiss', to the left cheek. Any sort of contact with a woman like this would have been unimaginable just a short time ago, but physical contact in the loo was . . . well, unimaginable. She followed Wendy out, glancing at the mirrors and thanking God that her lipstick was at least more subtle than her companion's, and that her heels were lower, not that it would have been possible for them to be anything else.

"Like them?", Wendy asked as she caught sight of Priscilla's eyes widen in the vicinity of her feet? "The men go crazy for them, never fails. It's a sort of trade mark. And they expect it. You need to be subtle, but you can't sell, unless you advertise".

"Subtle," Priscilla thought, "how about flashing neon?" But, she said, "I see what you mean. It's something that I've never thought about." And, indeed, she hadn't.

"Well it worked for you, didn't it? How else would you have known who to approach."

"Quite," thought Priscilla, as she accepted the invitation to go through the door first, but stood aside, once through, to let Wendy take the lead, admiring the woman's ability to walk straight, at that dizzy height , and managing to move her bottom in a way that was intriguing, even if it were not desirable . . . to her.

They threaded their way through the small, spaced out groups of glass-topped tables and low couches, occupied variously, between couples, groups of two and three business men. The visitors and the locals were easily distinguishable. Some of the visitors wore European, some, Eastern block, some Florida and a 'World Traveller', that practised, unshaven, unkempt, 'I've been everywhere and suffered', look. There were people who were trying to sell to customers, between flights, with hunger in their eyes, time running out, persuasive, a little too pushy. And then there were one or two single men, bored and looking round the room, their eyes resting on one group and then another, occasionally, discreetly admiring the odd, single lady and then returning to the pianist, set between artificial trees and a sunken pool of golden carp, in slightly dirty water and a dysfunctional fountain. There was one, though, who was both too busy and too polite to look around and stare, alone in the corner, 'lap-top' open, set next to the unmistakable pink of the 'Financial Times'.

Priscilla was led to a table in the centre, opposite the bar. Priscilla would have chosen a wall-side position. Wendy nodded to a couple of tables as she passed. There was already a cocktail on the table, a full one stood next to an almost empty one, and as Wendy saw it, she looked over to the next table with a group of three Asian men in very shinny suits and heavy gold bracelets and mouthed, "thank you," raising the full glass in their direction, as soon as she was seated. They proceeded to grin and congratulate the one in the party with the most weight. Priscilla was amazed that she could drink from it at all, without taking out one of her eyes and choking, or both. There seemed to be a whole fruit salad floating on the top of it, a parasol and a long plastic stirrer with a heart on the top, in fluorescent orange, going on neon, she thought to herself. The drink was split, midway down, between red and yellow. Wendy saw her looking again, and giggled.

"That is an 'Hawaiian Sunset of Love', more of an invitation card than a drink," and then, she added, "It's my third," and, as if to clarify the situation, "but I have been here half an hour," with a tone of reproach, for Priscilla being late, but Priscilla was too astounded to take the point. It was the 'three in half an hour', that had grabbed her concentration.

"Would you like one?"

"No, just a cola, with ice, please."

"They'll buy it," she offered, referring to the 'Hawaiian number', thumbing in the direction of the Asians.

"Definitely a cola, thank you," she said, firmly, and at that, the waiter was there and it was ordered.

"Now," Wendy said, as soon as the cola arrived and Priscilla had discarded the plain blue, plastic, stirrer from the three inches of expensive ice at the top of her six inch glass, "I think I've got just the deal for you tonight, you'll love it." She touched Priscilla's leg as she spoke. Priscilla considered moving away, slightly, but thought that it might offend and break the concentration. She'd seen that Wendy and her friends were prone to mood swings and she had worked hard to get to this position, gaining her confidence, most of the effort spent in overcoming her fear of wrong-doing and mixing at a level that she had never imagined existed. She was here, now, and felt a determination that she didn't recognise as her own.

"Who is it?" she asked, feeling her pulse quicken and her chest tighten slightly.

"Not so fast, Honey, relax, enjoy your drink. These things can't be rushed. Have you brought the money?"

"But who is it?"

28

"The money, Honey, first of all, the money," her tone dropping half an octave.

"Of course I have, all five hundred dollars of it."

"Good, no green stuff, no white stuff," and she threw back her head and laughed at Priscilla's face, which was funnier than the joke. Priscilla was looking a little on the white side herself, and that was before her crude remark. In fact, it took her a while to figure her meaning. She didn't even smile.

Wendy would have dearly liked to have set eyes on the cash, she'd been cheated before, and existed in a world where that was the norm, the normal terms of business in her profession, were, payment first. Every time. But could see that she wouldn't get anywhere. Dealing with Ladies was way out of her experience. Anyway, 'Boston Lady' wouldn't get what she wanted until she was paid, so there was some security in that, though the disbelief generated by her unusual request made her nervous. What the hell would she want with such a thing? She tried not to dwell on it, this was her defence mechanism, a tool of the trade. A spacious 'back of the mind' was a pre-requisite in her line of work.

"Just don't forget that I have a college education, a daughter and a heroin habit, to pay for." She laughed, at Priscilla's expression, and said, "I'm only joking, two of them are untrue," and laughed some more.

"It's the man in the corner," Wendy said, moving her hand from Priscilla's leg to her bare forearm, the bright red painted nails looking even more garish against the alabaster skin . "Over there." Priscilla, half turned, her attempt at discretion was truly pathetic, but her reflexes didn't underestimate the enormity of the situation, her head whipping round to see the man, and then back, just as quickly to stare directly at her mentor.

"Him," she said, a look of disbelief, on her face, "He must be Japanese."

" So what?"

"Well, I'm American, white, Anglo-Saxon, Boston, American."

"So what," Wendy repeated, "you're not going to have his baby, you're just going to steal from him."

Wendy thought that she had won the argument, and it did seem to take the wind out of 'Boston Lady's' sails, so she added, "anyway, he's not Japanese. He is 'Mr Rich, head of Corporation, Stock Market Whiz, Mega Two Brains'.Japanese." It was Priscilla's single brain that was working, in fact in overload. She took her eyes off Wendy and looked over at the man, still buried in the screen of his glowing lap-top. By the time her brain had thrown in, time, opportunity, he's not bad looking, successful, rich and, he's here.

She blurted out, "how do you know?" With a small smile of relief.

"Because the waiter told me."

"What? The waiter told you?" For the second time, her reflexes kicked in. Her head spun round as her eyes scanned the waiters, who seemed to be invisible, unless you were ready for a drink. She felt exposed, completely naked, the game was up, she had to leave.

"Relax, Honey," she drawled, lazily, elongating the second syllable of 'relax'. "How else would we know how to approach? Now you just tell me. They tell us who is who, who has money, or who is looking. Then they get their cut. It's their patch, we need to work with them, and they get paid. Simple." Having a working knowledge of the situation, whereas this Boston Lady didn't, gave Wendy a buzz, and if there hadn't been the risk of kissing goodbye to the five hundred bucks, she would be enjoying herself.

Any kind of knowledge, meant power, and power elevated your position. Power over her clients was what she enjoyed, she had something that they wanted. It wasn't the reason why she did the job, far from it, but it sure helped to see you through the night.

"What do you reckon", broke the minute's silence, and after another minute, Priscilla said,

"If you think it will work."

At that, she let go of Priscilla's arm, patted her hand, and said, "You're talking to the best, wait here, make yourself comfortable."

Priscilla grabbed Wendy's hand, straight after the patting, before she was out of reach, and said, in a tone that left no-one in any doubt that she meant it, "Don't forget. He must not pay you anything."

This was Wendy's territory now. She was totally confidant in her abilities. She knew the male weakness inside out and she [ ] way around it with a blindfold. She took a direct line to [ ] hesitation, but halved the size of her steps, and moved at a r[ ] Any sign of aggression or intrusion might put him off, he ne[ ] control of the situation, she was the human 'Mantris'. He shouldn't get the chance to put her off, and he didn't. By the time she'd appeared in his peripheral vision, her long legs were bending and with a half-turn ofthe stiletto, was down at his side. Japanese are polite people and have reflex behaviour and greeting postures, he immediately made to get up and half bow, but she stopped him with a handon his arm and "konbanwa", good evening, in perfectly accented Japanese.

"Konbanwa", he replied, with the last syllable very much elongated, giving himself time to take in the pleasure of her proximity, her accent and her legs, which were together, but knees in his direction.

Noting the smile and not wanting to loose momentum, "sumimasen, (excuse me), are you not Mr Kumamoto, only I was reading in the 'Times', last week, your policies on the Futures Markets?, and I think they were brilliant."

"Arigato gozaimasu, (thank you very much), and your name?"

"Wendy," and she smiled. A brief pause. She was waiting for his next move, forcing him to respond, turning him into a participant. Politeness and pleasure made him enquire what she was drinking.

He added, "what about your friend over there?"

So he had been looking. "She's OK, she's waiting for something," and without taking breath, "vodka martini. If you don't mind." The waiter was there already, a stealth bomber in a dinner jacket, didn't make a sound.

"Vodka martini, for the Lady, in fact make that two, please." When the drinks were on the table, she knew she was home. The screen saver came up on the lap-top computer, it was set for four minutes, it caught his eyes, so he said, "excuse me," came out of the program, with practised ease, closed the lid and asked her how she came to speak Japanese so well.

"I was a nanny for a lovely Japanese family after high school, to pay my way through college, they were so kind to me, I just loved the children."

The reality was, that she had shared a dingy flat with another 'Lady of the Night', for a few months, the summer before last, until she got busted for drugs and one person paying the rent was too much. She knew very little of the language, but it sounded good and flattered him, the expectation of meeting a Japanese speaker outside of his country was low. What she did know, she knew well, but overall, it was very little. That went for most things in her life.

Priscilla was sitting alone, of course, dying to know what was going on and straining to hear, but the tones were low and she picked up nothing. Wendy wouldn't have liked her to hear, either. Her techniques were her trade secret, she might not be proud of what she did, but it took skill to be successful in anything, and she was good. From that, she did derive self respect, of a sort.

Although Priscilla was the architect of this liaison, she was only interested in the outcome, not the morals or the mechanics. A few men had looked over and caught her eye, but she had looked away immediately and frozen them out. That was Priscilla's forte. She was beginning to experience the same sensations that she had had with Dalton, and she felt a mite disloyal, but hadn't Dr Jones warned her of the chances? Conception was a lottery and three to one were odds in her favour. She needed to maximise them and so she would. Jacky had been on the telephone three times this week, asking her when the next sample was arriving. He had even suggested a social call, but she had declined, she couldn't risk any close questioning. She had originally said this week, and her excuses were sounding a bit thin. She'd worked hard on this one, and her meagre savings were going. She needed a result and soon. She was beginning to wish she had worn her stockings.

Movement in the corner of her eye made her start, and over on the left, Wendy and Kumamoto were standing up. Her heart fell to her stomach, Wendy has blown it. Damn. She'd been day-dreaming and not seen what went wrong.

But far from it. Wendy was smiling, gushing, even, and he had his arm around the small of her back, steering her in the direction of the double lifts at the back of the bar. He was slightly smaller than her, but she had a four inch start. She wasn't tall, but she wasn't petite. He looked like he had won the coconut at the fair, maybe even, the goldfish too.

He hesitated at the bar and signed the tab for the drinks. It appeared like magic, without asking, already totalled, in a black leather folder, with brass corners. How do they do that? They even knew his room number. Wendy did, as well, by now.

The few moments it took to sign and put away his pen, gave Wendy the opportunity to mouth, "He's single", and send a coarse, exaggerated wink in the direction of Priscilla's table.

Priscilla was mad with herself. One of her main stipulations was that her target (an expression that she didn't like to use, but could think of no other, at the time, that would be descriptive, yet not illuminating), had to be single, not married. Wendy had realised that Priscilla had forgotten, and obviously took delight in the chance to remind her of her failing. Beatrice sprang to mind. She'd suffered that kind of put-down for years from her sister. She physically shook her head to dispel the association.

Priscilla checked the clasp of her handbag. Yes, it was definitely closed.

At that, the happy couple reached the polished aluminium doors of the lift, set in a wall of veneered cork on salmon, which simply opened, revealing a larger couple, tourists from the south.

"Is this the bar?" the fat lady drawled, speaking, without hesitation, for both parties, the cotton shorts with the flower-print threatening to burst at any moment.

"Sure is," said Wendy, loudly mimicking their accent, and stepping well aside to let them evacuate the cramped space. They'd accounted for fifty per cent of the permissible 'eight persons capacity.' Mr Kumamoto winced, and bowed slightly to the departing volume, stepping inside the lift, ahead of Wendy. He hadn't been able to believe his eyes. With no expression on his face whatsoever, he pressed the internal buttons and the door closed, without a sound, not even the ubiquitous, 'ting'.

It felt almost like a religious experience to Priscilla. It had happened so quickly, she'd prayed, in her own way, for it, and it had come to pass. Their disappearance was as total as it were sudden, followed by their ascension to another world, beyond both her experience and imaginings. Where they had gone, she could only guess; it was a tall building and a lot nearer to heaven than the hell that she would suffer during the next few minutes.

The lift doors had been closed, but half a minute, when the waiter appeared at her table with another cola and a stainless steel dish of cashew nuts. "I didn't order . . ." was hardly out of her mouth when the impassive gentleman in the dinner suit said, "It's with the compliments of Mr Kumamoto, Ma'am." The contact, however insignificant and tenuous, made her flush.

Again, she wished she were wearing her stockings. She wished she were in touch. She soon would be. The piano played Sinatra. Her fingers roamed to her ears, but dropped to the twin strands of pearls. Last time she could hear what was going on, but now she was cut off. At least there would be no violence. She had no stomach for a repeat of that risk. This might be distasteful, but at least it was voluntary.

Kenichi Kumamoto was also considering heaven. He was sure that he'd arrived. He'd opened the door and she'd followed him in, walking straight over to the bathroom. The speed of events had taken him by surprise. The answer to his question, "drink?" was answered, "Champagne," as she closed the bathroom door behind her. He walked over to the bed-side phone, sitting down. His shoes were already off, at the door. He pressed the appropriate number for reception and hit them on the second attempt, and asked for 'Bollinger'. "Sixty eight if you have it." He was well accustomed to ordering the best. Money not been a consideration in recent years. It took two minutes to appear, in ice, in the bucket wrapped in a starched cloth. It had been far too quick to have been prepared since the call, but he didn't notice, he was distracted by the bathroom door opening and Wendy appearing in view, framed by the doorway, wearing his yukata. Apart from bulges, and they were in the right places, it fitted.

His hairbrush was already secured in the plastic bag, at the bottom of her handbag, along with his comb for good luck. It had been left neatly, along with his shaving gear, on the glass shelf, in front of the mirror.

By the time that he had feasted his eyes on his own, half-opened garment, the champagne was in place and the bedroom door closed.

Wendy drifted across the room, shoes still in place, and turned the main
light out, leaving on, the bedside ones to bathe them in an subdued glow, sat on the edge of the bed and patted the covers, an offer to join her. The gown had fallen open leaving the stockings and suspenders exposing the top of her legs, white panties and low, wired cups of her brassiere. Her breasts were full and Western. He was impressed, it was obvious. It was his turn to be hot.

Her full breasts, white skin, blonde shoulder -length hair and sheer size made as big an impact as it did a contrast, to his homeland and personal experience. As he started to undress, not taking his greedy eyes off her, she lay back on the bed, at the same time, taking a small silver parcel from the right side of her bra and placing it next to the telephone with her left hand, her cheap scarlet nails in stark contrast to the expensive, cream, tasteful top-cover of the bed. He followed the action with his dark,almond eyes, and her eyes followed his. The instruction was as explicit as it were simple.

He'd undressed in a belligerent way, taking his time and feigning nonchalance, designed to signal his superiority and dominance. He needed to save face, be in control. No chance.

He lent over and picked up the packet, obediently, looking faintly ridiculous, still wearing his socks. He still looked good to Wendy. She never tired of the male form, black, white and this time, yellow, as long as it was a good one. She did try to be choosy, but a girl had a living to make, so it wasn't always possible, but there was a line drawn. It was a fuzzy one, but he was well within limits. He was fit and slim, she had never taken a man from Japan, so it had novelty value. She had shared a bed, with her friend and co-worker, Keiko, but she didn't count. They had kissed one time though.

She watched him prepare. From his point of view, it was an unwelcome break in the proceedings, but an important one. He felt a little self-conscious as he struggled with the slippy rubber, and could feel her eyes devouring him. There was amusement in her eyes, and he had to fight to keep himself in control, not to flag, but at last he mastered it and stood erect, in front of her with his hands on his hips. The male ego gave him the perception that he had been irresistible, even though he realised that payment would be required. Now he really did look ridiculous. It was all Wendy could do, not to laugh out loud, but that would have put paid to his ardour, and she had a job to do.

She held her hand out and he reciprocated, pulling him down by his short, soft, fingers, onto the bed in one firm movement, opening her legs as he struggled for his balance, awkwardly. Her split-crotch panties gaped as he was pulled toward her, to be devoured in her clutches. She moved her head to one side, skilfully avoiding his kiss. She made to gasp. It was an act, but an old one and a habit that was now a reflex. Stroking his ego was easier than stroking his cock. He almost came on entry, his pent-up excitement allowing no time for foreplay or passion.

Any thoughts of an encore were immediately dispelled, when she pushed him over onto his back. She possessed the greater strength. Resistance was both ungentlemanly and, more to the point, useless. He made a theatrical groan, in a vain attempt to regain the initiative, but it was wasted.

In one deft movement, she was on her knees, the condom off his fast deflating phallus, with the contents intact, and off to the bathroom. The small plastic bag was out of her handbag and the prize was secured within.

When the bathroom door opened this time, she was dressed. There had only been her skirt and blouse to replace, and her jacket was over her shoulder, hooked on her index finger. This time she strode across the room, his eyes following her in amazement, speechless. Stopping at the bedside table, she grabbed at the bottle of champagne and threw her head back with the dripping bottle firmly between her lips. It felt very sexual to her and very threatening to him. She gulped at it as though it were lemonade. Roughly dabbing her lips with the part of the starched napkin that hadn't been soaked by the icy water, and catching the dribbles down her chin, she looked directly at his staring eyes, burped loudly and said, referring to his satisfaction, or lack of it, "that one was on Boston."

Kenichi was still motionless on the bed when the door slammed and all that there was left was a cloud of her cheap perfume. The ice-cubes had not even begun to melt and the chinking on the side of the bucket, caused by the waves from the hastily replaced, half-empty bottle, was the only sound.

He'd been taken and he'd been had, but he never realised to what extent. In a futile bid to solve the mystery, he jumped up and checked his credit cards, but they were all there and they were intact. He wasn't sure whether he could recount this tale with his karaoke friends back home, or not. He was the one who usually did the screwing. He'd screwed most of the civilised world, via the stock markets. He was still wearing his socks, and now, he did feel ridiculous.

Priscilla had been expecting a long wait, at least a longer, wait. She had not touched her cola, not wanting to attract the attentions of anyone else wanting to replenish her drink, so she was surprised when the lift doors opened and Wendy appeared, lip-stick intact, grinning. It was Easter. Although she had disappeared into the left one, she reappeared from the right one, which, illogically surprised her all the more. She made a theatrical, arms out, one leg slightly raised and across the other, unnecessary gesture, patted her handbag twice, and disembarked, just in time, before the doors swallowed her up again.

When she arrived at the table, Priscilla jumped straight in.

"That was quick, are you sure. . . .", but was stopped by a dramatic, reproachful look and a raised eyebrow.

"It's not the sort of thing I could make a mistake over, Honey. Believe me. I know." At that, she opened her handbag and took out the two plastic bags and, a little too roughly, slapped them on the table.

"Be careful . . ." Priscilla started to say, but felt another look coming her way, and anyway, was interrupted.

"Five hundred dollars. If you please, Ma'am." The same magnolia envelope appeared from the bag, and was placed on the table, the vacant space being immediately re-filled by the plastic bags. "I'll just count that, if you don't mind." It wasn't a question. The envelope was opened and the notes flicked through, expertly, for verification.

"It's all there," Priscilla offered, but was ignored. Wendy was only interested in self confirmation.

"It was a pleasure doing business. If you ever want that kind of kick again, you know where to find me." She raised the same eyebrow again, leant forward, kissed Priscilla on the forehead, before the poor woman could retreat, got up and departed, with a laugh, leaving a pair of scarlet lips outlined on the alabaster.

One quick draught from the cola to take the taste and the dryness away, and Priscilla was on her feet, back to the ladies room. This time, she did need the toilet. She'd been crossing her legs, afraid to move. She went straight into the nearest cubicle, her arm over her handbag for safety. She flushed the toilet, but before pulling her dress back down, she took out one of the plastic bags, rolled it up and put it down her tights, pulling them back up, extra high, so that her prize wouldn't move. A further look at it, through the black nylon and she pulled the dress down, smoothing it out and replacing her handbag under her arm. As she walked out of the cubicle to the accompaniment of the 'Pan-Pipes', she hesitated in front of the mirrors to check for tell-tale outlines. Satisfied, she left, to the further accompaniment of Dean Martin. The 'lips' were still in place.

Safely in the comfort of the taxi, and having requested her destination, home, she had time to reflect. The enormity of the situation hit her when she thought that barely one hour ago, she had never even heard of the man, who would have a one in three chance of fathering her child. She smiled. Wouldn't he be surprised? A surprise was an imposition, and it was about time she left her mark. She had left the choice of partner upto another woman, but, there again, she supposed, the final selection was still hers, and she was the instigator, after all. Even so, she was travelling in the back of a taxi, with a cache of a man's sperm tucked down her tights. She shrugged. Needs must. She was focused.

Her main concern, now, was to get it back and safely installed in it's resting place. It was later, now, and the traffic was lighter on the way out of town, so she was back quite soon. As the taxi rounded the last bend, she had a sudden thought that perhaps Beatrice was still there, and, in fact, asked the driver to slow down, but the lights, apart from the security light, were out, and she breathed a sigh of relief. It was a mystery to the driver, but he was used to weird behaviour. He had clocked the lipstick on her forehead. He didn't even know the half of it.

The cats were still there where they had been left and still they made no sound, only followed her with their eyes. The special senses of cats were maybe telling them, that they were perhaps not going to be the only babies in the house for very much longer. Already, they were no longer the centre of attention. They knew that from experience.

This time, she pressed the recall button of her mobile, and asked Dr Jones if it were all right to come round now, even before she had prepared her charges. Confidence was creeping in, but it was soon dispelled, when he suggested it was rather late. Anxiety rushed back into her voice and he kindly relented. He had felt snubbed over the past couple of weeks, and he didn't like the idea of being used, rather, not getting his own way. He needed to be given his 'place'.

"Come round now, Priscilla", he consented, "I'll go down and put the light on for you". He added that he'd been doing nothing anyway. His comment was lost on Priscilla, she was pre-occupied.

She went straight to the bathroom again, and took the second bottle for preparation, warming it carefully under the tap, worrying slightly whether it was too hot or too cold and allowing the water to run on the back of her hand to test it. She wasn't happy until the bottle was taped safely in the warmth under her arm, but this time had delighted in the routine, the preparation, securing the precious liquid and it's care. Maternal instincts were kicking in, instincts that she had never experienced and thought she never would. These were her babies. Babies? She'd never considered more than one. Names, boy or girl? Her mind raced, but first the clinic. Jacky would be waiting, she'd taken longer, this time. There was one part of the routine that she had missed and she couldn't continue with out it. She re-opened her dress and pulled the bottle off her under-arm. Holding it upto the light, above her head, she brought it towards her mouth and gently kissed it. "Goodnight", she said, and re-taped it into position. She didn't even wipe off the smudge of red.

Her breasts looked quite acceptable after all, she thought, as she caught sight of them, re-buttoning her dress after wriggling her arm back in. The cats watched her go out again, without comment . . . either way.

Dr Jones took slightly longer to come to the door, than her last visit, but unless you were tuned in, you wouldn't notice. Priscilla didn't. There was still the warmth, he kissed her cheek and she handed him the little brown bottle as he ushered her to the sofa. She had retrieved it just before neatly parking the car next to the door, checking the locks and the alarm the one time.

"Just go through behind Molly's reception, now, and put the coffee on, Priscilla, I'll not be many minutes." His lilt came through all the stronger, but she was tired, drained, all of a sudden and sat where he'd left her, her head moving in the direction of the wall behind reception, casting her eyes over all the faces of those smiling babies.

Serious thought had to given to the job in hand. Dr Jones took off the lid of his 'cauldron'. It was the pet name he called it, when there was only himself and Molly, his secretary of nine years, in the building. He placed it to one side and, tweezers in hand, consulted the list of names, the owners of the various deposits, screwing up his eyes slightly to read the small print through the perspex safety glasses. A mistake here could result in an unholy mixture that was both impossible to disentangle or explain. Many of the deposits, here, were the last acts before male sterilisation. Some of the men had passed to other worlds, already. They were priceless and irreplaceable. A mistake could never be ignored. There was black and white, every racial background in this frozen world of his, and apart from that, there was now, DNA testing. There had been several mistakes in the past, not in his clinic, but others in the State. The ticking bombs of their mistakes blew up in their professional faces many years later, after routine testing through the police departments and hospitals. Quite a shock for everybody, to find that your child wasn't what you thought. Someone to blame was the next step. Blame always followed in the footsteps of shock. He shuddered at the thought. The resulting trauma would be of seismic proportions. Identifying the real parents and breaking the news would be just one painful scenario. Damages were the other. Ruination.

In this case, he found Priscilla's tube, and extracted it without fuss. Confirmation was always a relief. Still there, the contents intact and occupying around twenty percent of the space, he placed it in a small, test-tube rack, on his bench. He'd pre-cooled the fresh semen and added the saline solution, in equal proportions, giving it a gentle agitation.

It really was surprising, how, unlike any other liquid, that didn't fall into the category of dangerous, it was handled with so much respect. It was, after all, life itself. Precious.

The fresh sperm was added, unceremoniously, to the first batch, sharing, the space, yet unmixed. Twins. Not, identical twins. He replaced the tube in it's allotted place and put on the lid, cutting off the source of the boiling vapours.

He walked through to the reception, still wearing his white coat, and, against his better judgement, his protective gloves. It was the sort of stunt that many a doctor pulls. Stethoscopes were the norm. Soldiers like to be seen in their uniforms. Nothing wrong with trying to impress a lady.

He may as well not have bothered, because when he went through to the reception, his client was crying. It was a quiet, sobbing, muffled by her head buried into the back of the soft, winged chair, her dark hair covering her vulnerable face. He hurriedly pulled off the thin rubber gloves, causing them to snap back reproachingly at the back of his sensitive hands.

"What on earth is wrong, Priscilla? Dear, dear, please, come on now." He was at her side and kneeling next to the chair. She sat up, in response to his hand in hers and fell against his shoulder.

"Jack, I'm so worried. Will it be all right? Tell me it will. Please. I so need a baby, you just don't know."

"I know it will be all right, Priscilla, I know it will be all right."

"But do I have enough time, The samples seem so small. I'm almost forty, everything is too much for me. I'm useless, completely useless. I don't think that I can cope, really, I don't."

" You are not useless, you are far from useless", and he made her stand with him, holding her in his arms, stroking her hair, taking in it's scent, and wishing.

He found himself leading her into the laboratory, the door was still partially opened.

"You must be patient," he said, feeling sorry and a little foolish at his petulant antics, earlier, and hoping that she had never noticed. "Your babies are your future and they are safe with me, here. Nowadays, it is almost foolproof, standard procedure."

"Almost?" Priscilla picked up on that word.

"What I mean is, if there are enough sperms and you are ovulating, there is no problem. At all," he added, so as not to upset her further and leave any doubt in her unstable mind. "It is not a question of quantity, although the volume seems small enough, there are millions upon millions of living sperm in your two samples, all living in these flasks in suspended animation."

The sound of his hand falling on one of the flasks, and realising the proximity to her future, she stopped crying and looked up, eyes smudged and running with black mascara.

"Is this really it?" Her eyes were wide and alert again, now that she was close to the results of all her effort, she felt whole, again. "They seem rather large containers for something so small." Jacky laughed, as kindly and reassuringly as he could muster. It was as much an effort to calm and normalise the atmosphere as anything else.

"Priscilla, there are over four thousand samples in this one container, alone." At that, he picked up the record book, made of loose leaves from the computer, flicked to the back page and said, "actually, four thousand and twenty one. You are four thousand and ten." He thought that would impress her. And it did. He'd planted a seed. "Each one is numbered and in it's own little resting place, waiting, to be woken up. Ten minutes to rub it's little eyes and then, ready for action."

"I'm sorry for being such a big silly, Jacky," she pushed gently away, but holding both his hands and looking into his greying eyes, "I'm just feeling the emotions of motherhood, for the first time. It might be a little premature, but it's a fact. I'm new to this."

"You just get off home and have a good night's rest, you'll feel better, honestly." One more look, from Priscilla, as they reached the door and without another word, left and got straight into her car.

Dr Jones was still in the same place long after she had disappeared from view. He was reluctant to go back inside, although it was late, and cold. A layer of moisture glistened with the reflection of the street lights, on his car, but he gave no thought to whether it was the result of a light shower, or dew . He was more concerned with the moisture at the corners of both eyes.

Chapter Three

Priscilla wasn't sure whether it was the cats moving on the bed as a result of the ringing, or the ringing itself, that had brought her from one of the deepest sleeps of her life. It was certainly one of the longest. Ten in the morning was late for Priscilla, verging on decadence. The ringing was followed up by the sound of someone calling out 'Prissy'. Even with the sound being distorted by the letter box, the stairs, the almost closed bedroom door and the duvet over her ears, she could tell that it was Beatrice. That deep, rasping voice, the softness ripped out of it by the twenty cigarettes a day, could never be mistaken. She considered ignoring it. It would have been difficult, but a glance at the glowing, green numerals of her bed-side clock, screaming ten-o-clock at her, demolished all resistance.

The cats flew in two, opposite directions as the covers came back, rather too quickly for their liking. They weren't used to it. There was a flash of Royal Blue pyjama, as she went for the door and shouted, "I'm coming, hang on," and added, under her breath, "damn you." She reached out for her white dressing gown behind the door, as the bell went yet again, annoying her.

Jumping up to Beatrice's every brash command had been a habit, one that was difficult to overcome, but this time, she stopped, her weight on one leg, and turned to the cats at her heels.

"Sorry, Darlings," she said, stroking Tommy's head and running her hand along his back and the full length of his tail, which rose up automatically to take the full pleasure. "Sorry, Tabs," and scratched under his white chin with her three middle fingers. By this time, the bell had gone again.

"I've never known you to be in bed so late, Priscilla, It must have been a late night."

"And good morning to you, dear sister," said Priscilla, brushing aside the question.

"Good, morning," without feeling. "I was here until midnight, waiting for either you to return or Dalton to phone. Neither happened." Beatrice was already passed her, through to the kitchen and reaching for the cafetiere. "Come on, who were you out with last night, tell me." It was a poor display, an attempt to make the questions fun, but jealousy had it's foot in the door.

"No", said Priscilla. There was more conviction in her voice than there had ever been. Just that slight tonal difference, an imperceptible change in timing , made all the difference. Beatrice wouldn't repeat the question.

She chose something simpler. "Coffee?" and switched on the grinder, the noise making the protest for her, and drowning Priscilla's reply in the affirmative. If she wasn't going to hear what she wanted, then she would hear nothing.

When the coffee was ready, Beatrice brought it to the conservatory, where her sister was sitting on the sun-lounger, staring out of the window.

"You really ought to get a move on with your life, you know, Prissy. Mother hasn't been with us for ages, now. A man and a baby is what you need," and she added, with a snigger, "in that order."

"For your information, it has not been four months, yet. You wouldn't be missing her quite as much as I do, because you were never here. At least, you were never here for her, only if you wanted something. For yourself. Always yourself."

Priscilla's directness surprised her, but she surprised herself more than anyone.

"Your not getting any younger, yourself, you might be thinking of a family."

"Not me, at least not yet. I'm not ready, when I'm good and ready, then I will."

Priscilla was fuming, Beatrice was so cocky, what an attitude. She thought she could stand no more when Beatrice added the last straw.

"I had an abortion last month."

Priscilla's head was reeling, she couldn't believe her ears. After all she had gone through, herself, the anguish, and here was her sister, her own flesh and blood, throwing life away, life that she was so desperate for.

"You bloody, spoilt, selfish, bitch," she screamed, and instinctively kicked the wicker coffee table to the other side of the room, the cafetiere flying along with it and smashing into a thousand pieces, leaving the brass frame to bounce off the glass of the patio doors.

Beatrice jumped back. She had never heard anything remotely like it come from Priscilla. Her initial shock drained the colour from her face. She turned and fled. The last thing that Priscilla could have heard, was the front door slamming, followed by the car, leaving with a squeal from the tyres.

Priscilla heard nothing. She was banging one of the wicker chairs up and down on the quarry tiled floor, until she could bang it down no more. She collapsed to her knees, sobbing and then slumped on the floor breathing deeply and moaning.

The cats could take no more, either. They ran upstairs and shot straight under the bed.

The mobile phone was in her line of vision when she finally opened her eyes. It was their turn to be red, now. She instinctively picked it up stared at it for a moment, taking a deep, deep, breath and pressed redial.

As soon as sensed the phone was being lifted at the other end, she started. "Jack, please, I must come round . . .", but she was interrupted.

"Dr Jones is not available at the moment, he's out on a . . ." It was Molly, his secretary, but now it was her turn to be interrupted.

"It's Priscilla, Priscilla Glover, I must see him this morning." Molly had far more experience in the interruption business, and she wasn't about to be upstaged.

"I'm afraid, Miss Glover, that Dr Jones will not be back until lunch time and will not be taking calls or visitors until the early afternoon."

"I must, see him, I'll come over and wait." His secretary was about to protest further, but she realised the phone was dead.

Priscilla dragged herself upstairs and turned on the shower. Was it all worth it, she asked herself. Everything felt so futile. "I'll come clean and tell Jacky everything, it's the only way, clear my mind. He'll understand." But she knew she was kidding herself. No one could hear her. No-one could understand. She would have to go through with it, but she had set her mind on three men. She couldn't face a repeat of the last encounter, and she simply didn't know any really eligible men, other than Dalton. Although he had socially rejected her, he was ideal.

The thought of teaching him a lesson, and beating Beatrice all in the one fell swoop brightened her up and she let the dressing gown fall from her shoulders and onto the floor. It must have been the first time that it was not hung up before showering, but she was in that sort of mood and the steam was beckoning.

This time, she caught sight of herself in the full length mirror in the bathroom, and although it was a little steamy, she could see her form, plainly. She held her hair up at the back, with both hands and made a half turn, first to the left and then to the right, keeping her eyes forward. She didn't feel plain, she never had, she said to herself as she continued to turn this way and that, the rhythmic splashing of the water, music to her ears, lulling her, singing her a natural melody. There was colour returning to her cheeks. She could never remember a time where she had looked at herself, really looked at herself, before. She had always taken herself, and particularly, her body, for granted. And then she realised what the difference was. There was a spark coming from within. The lure of motherhood had ignited something inside and it wasn't about to die. She couldn't allow it, even if she wanted to.

She let her hair drop back to her shoulders and sprang into the shower with enthusiasm. The water was hot. It felt good. She was revived, reborn. A third man would come her way, she knew it. She would make it happen, like she had done on the previous occasions. No-one had helped her. A mother's strength was kicking in, she could feel it, and she liked it. She had always taken strength from her own mother, but now it was upto her.

She felt so much more alive after the shower, and wanted to see her new-found self in the mirror again, but it was frosted over, with condensation. Instead, she took a fresh bath towel, wrapped herself like a baby and rolled, still wet, on the bed, pulling the towel tighter and tighter, her legs and bottom, pink from the hot water, smooth, like a baby. At last, on her back, she flung the towel open, revelling in her nakedness, and vowed to carry on. "When you come back to that clinic, Dr Jones, I'll be there".

Chapter Four

This time, when she pulled up, and neatly parked her car, she was, wearing her stockings. They were complemented by a red skirt, navy blue suede shoes, white blouse and blazer with three brass buttons. They shone when they caught the sun. One, two, three.

She was early, it was just after noon, and she knew that Dr Jones wouldn't be back just yet, and even then, not be taking patients until early afternoon, presumably, until after his lunch. She might get lucky and he would come back early. What she didn't want to admit to herself, was that, apart from really just wanting to see him, and he made her feel safe, she wanted to put Miss Molly in her place. She was taking no more from any other jumped up woman, and that was final. When women wanted to push her, they'd better watch out. She smiled at the very thought. "Who said that? It can't have been me." She gave the car door a slightly heavier slam than usual. She didn't press and point the central locking devise on her key-ring, she fired it. Once.

She had no sooner walked into the reception, with what she considered to be a real determination to be pleasant, firm, but pleasant, just to sit in the proximity of her future, feel close, when she was met by a secretarial onslaught.

"Miss Glover," with a slight over emphasis on the 'Miss', part of the exclamation, especially, considering that Molly's position was the same as her own, "as I told you on the telephone, the Doctor was not expected back yet, nor has he, indeed, arrived."

"I don't mind waiting, really." She was apologising already, she knew it and she hated herself for it, but her resolve was like crystal and could shatter at any moment. She was on the edge.

"That's not the point," Molly persisted. "Even when he does arrive, he will not," and this time the emphasis was definitely on, 'not', "be seeing anyone until after his lunch." There was a full two second break whilst Molly assessed whether she had said enough. Obviously not. "He has had a very busy schedule, today, and he will need to rest." Pathetic. Molly knew it and so did the usurper.

"You over protective bitch," Priscilla thought to herself, not the sort of thing that normally even passed through her head. "I'll wait anyway," she said, surprised at the strength of her assertion, and added, matching the two second pause of her adversary, "If you don't mind." Molly realised it was a rhetorical question.

"I'll have to lock the door behind me, you understand,, Molly said, putting as much threat into the sentence as she could muster. It was the last 'say', she was determined to gain that point, at least. Priscilla realised it of course, but it was a small concession, after getting her own way, and anyway, she was pleased to get this woman out of her face, and at the other side of a locked door. Isolation was fine by her.

Molly was just the sort of woman she despised. White hair, neat, prim, self-satisfied and single at sixty. She felt pained when she realised she had almost described her own mother, with the exception of single. Even then, her mother might as well have been, she was alone for most of her life, since before the birth of Beatrice. Perhaps it was because of Beatrice. She actually shook her head to rid herself of that line of thought, at the same time, realising she missed her mother not one iota. With the shaking, her hair fell from behind her ears and shielded her face. No. She brushed it back.

Her mother had controlled Priscilla all her life, and although the shackles were off, the marks and the scars remained. Perhaps the damage was permanent. It was shortly after her Father left that her nervous disposition was noticed and her habits crept in. Her Mother didn't try to help, but fed on them and used them to entrap her, strengthening her fears. It was abuse, mild, but abuse all the same, little by little over most of her life. In total, it was enormous, a comfortable monster that was impossible to control.

She also realised that there was a shade of her own future in Molly. Determination was growing, and feeding it, made it grow all the faster.

Anyway, she sat herself down on one of the chairs and let her eyes wander over the magazines that were all well out of date and unanimously dealt with the subject of home and garden improvement.

Molly was busy preparing herself for her departure, switching on the answer phone and studiously ignoring Priscilla. Pulling out all the plugs and switching off all the sockets. She picked up her bag and keys, rattling the latter with a flourish, to underline her point, and, with the faintest of false smiles, and not one word, swept through the outer glass door and locked it behind her.

With Molly out of sight, she would go to the bathroom and freshen up. She hadn't wanted to do that whilst she was there. It was a slight sign of weakness, she felt, that she didn't want to reveal, and anyway, she wanted to see her leave the premises and feel alone, again, next to her future, some private time.

She hadn't wanted the toilet, when she entered the ladies room, she would just pass a brush through her hair and check her lips. Jacky was bound to be here soon, and did want to look her best. When she opened the bag, balancing it precariously on the edge of the wash-hand basin, she smiled to herself when, the first thing that she saw, was an empty brown bottle, ready for another sample, she ran her finger over the smooth glass and her pulse quickened. She squeezed it tightly and passed some energy over from the palm of her hands until it became body temperature and checked it against her cheek. As she replaced it, her eyes then went to the electric stunner. It was just as shiny and looked so innocent, until you focused onto the two lethal looking probes at the end. Something so small, yet so powerful, innocent, yet deadly. She never gave her only victim a passing thought, but picked it out and squeezed it in her hand. Power. She liked the feeling.

Her attention shifted to the corners of her mouth, in the mirror. The lipstick was slightly smudged, so she took out a tissue, tidied it up and re-applied a coat of the red wax. Standing back slightly, she brushed her hair, one side at a time, behind her ears, with her fingers and straightened the double row of pearls. There was a red smudge on one of her teeth, her tongue dealt with the problem as she turned away.

Satisfied, she went out of the loo and strolled over to the reception desk. Boredom breeds nosiness. Behind it, were all the photos of the children and mothers. Not one picture of a father out of, . . . maybe, two hundred. The photos all overlapped and each one contained at least one smile. To get a closer look, she invaded Molly's space, behind the desk. There were messages written on many of them. The messages were similar, congratulatory, good luck, thanks Jacky, 'life complete', and the like. Dr Jones was a special man to many women. Priscilla allowed these thoughts to vibrate softly around her head, she didn't try to focus on any one of them in particular. She needed to feel special at this time. Her recent actions wouldn't stand up to close scrutiny, personal or otherwise. It was the end product that was Priscilla's focal point.

Bored with other people's babies, her attention wandered to the laboratory door. Just behind that magical door, was her future. This was invading Jacky's space, but she was drawn toward it, and the pull was far too strong to resist. She didn't resist.

Her heart raced slightly as she tried the handle, which , of course, moved, but would the door open? It could be locked. It should be locked. She didn't yank on it, she had too much respect for what was behind it, for that, and that was almost the end of the story, because it was a heavy fire-door with a self-closing spring, but just as she was about to give up, telling herself to come to her senses, it must be locked . . . it gave. Had there been ten thousand screaming banshees behind the door, waiting to pounce, she would have opened it with the same degree of caution. It was opened an inch or two at a time as she lent against the frame, surveying the interior, carefully, a cold draft blowing through the gap and bouncing her hair back and forth, where it had fallen from behind one ear.

The room was plain, tiled in white, with a laboratory work-bench across the wall on the right. There were double inset, stainless steel sinks. To the left was a broad window, venetian blinds a quarter way open, allowing stripes of glare to bounce around the room. Two stainless steel cylinders dominated the vista, placed in the centre of the room, with umbilical cords running down to them from the white ceiling. Both had a little screen, upright, on the lid, displaying the temperatures within, in red LEDs. The temperatures were identical, but for the two figures after the decimal place, which kept rising and falling, one or two points, but always within a narrow band. They reminded Priscilla of old-fashioned milk churns, but fatter and shinier. There was a handle on either side of the lids.

At last the door was finally open and she gingerly slipped inside, her whole appearance, in such a clinical environment made her feel alien. Her red skirt was offensive and her pearls, simple though they were normally, and understated, became frivolous decadence.

Which cylinder were her babies to come from? God, this was exciting. Scary. It was this innocent curiosity that drove her on. Admittedly, Jacky had shown her which one, even patted it, but was he just saying it was that one, and which one was it anyway? She couldn't quite remember. Her view of the situation had been a tearful blur, and her concentration, far from accurate. Recall was unreliable.

The record book was in view. It was the only book there. It was on the shelf under the bench and it wasn't as if she were opening a drawer, or anything. She knew from the number that he had said, that her name must be near the end. The names were listed chronologically, and not alphabetically. In columns. First, the date, then the name. She found it immediately, straight off the computer, Priscilla Glover, second visit, with the first visit dated alongside. Father undisclosed. Following that, there was a code. A capital 'B', small, 'd', next to the word, 'level', and then, 0802.

Priscilla walked over to the cylinders. The letter 'B' was clearly stencilled on the nearest. She touched it, gingerly, at first, expecting it to be cold, but it was warm to the touch, not too warm, but warm enough to remind her of flesh, smooth flesh. Baby's flesh. It was standing on a frame, bolted firmly to the ground, and she found herself leaning on it, with one arm loosely around the 'neck'. She felt relaxed. At ease. Next to the stencilled letter 'B', was a plaque, screwed in position, four inches square. WARNING, NEVER REMOVE LID WITHOUT PROTECTIVE GLASSES AND GLOVES. The next word was in red. DANGER. PARTS OF THE BODY SHOULD NOT GO BELOW RIM. EXTREME LOW TEMPERATURES. USE INSTRUMENTS FOR ENTRY ONLY. The message was repeated on the other container in the same position, next to the stencilled letter, 'A'. Also stencilled, in a continuous line around the container, were the words, LIQUID NITROGEN. LIQUID NITROGEN. LIQUID NITROGEN.

She had left her handbag next to the book, open at the page containing her name. She wandered back, over, with every intention of leaving there and then, and even had her hand on the bag. Her eye caught sight of her name and rested there for a moment. Her line of vision took in three or four names at the same time, though, and she was surprised to see the names of men. It wasn't to find out who the men were, that she looked further, it was just that she had somehow assumed that all the names would be ladies, because they would be the ones who were wanting the treatment. It didn't exactly say 'Mr', or anything, but the Christian names were quite clear, George, Frank etc. It looked like almost fifty per cent of them were men. It was a natural next step to flick through several pages to confirm the percentage that she had guessed. Some of the names had hand-written notes beside them, obviously as an aide-memoir, perhaps there were several people of the same name and it was a way of distinguishing between them. Richmond, Keith, (Competitor Services). Elvira, Martel, (Travel International). Then there were other notes next to the names, a couple that made her flinch, Carney, Brian, (Deceased). There was one more category, that had a much greater effect on her. Castence, Irene, (Terminated) and the date, written in a neat hand and tidily crossed out with a ruled line. It was the cold, meticulous hand of

Molly. Priscilla needed no confirmation. Neither did she seek it.

Termination. It had caused Priscilla to feel faint and not a little angry. She didn't know the circumstances, of course, but never considered them. Even so, her mind recognised, or at least, identified the culprit. Molly was the messenger.

She felt that she shouldn't be looking through the book at all and guilt flowed through her, because there were one or two names that she recognised. Hadn't this always been her sister's style? Priscilla couldn't stop. Being alone, she allowed herself to continue, free from the hypocrosy of public convention and social behaviour. Put simply, it was interesting.

It became even more interesting when her eyes came to rest, no, fixated, on the next name. Van De Clouet, Maurice. There was only one Van De Clouet, called Maurice, and the additional word, 'Democrat', was totally superfluous. The neat hand, again, only revealed the opposing political views of Molly. She was a well known 'Republican', serving the party faithfully over the last twenty years. Organising and fund-raising had been her life, her husband and lover. The pencil had been used with a harshness reserved for this man, and only this man. The impression was sharp and deep.

The book was closed and Priscilla left the room, quicker than she had entered, re-taking her seat in reception. The room was boring, in comparison, the pastel green of the paper and the white ceiling offering nothing to focus on, nothing to anchor her mind, keep it away from thoughts of Maurice Van De Clouet, Leader of the party in this State, tipped as next Governor, rich and hellishly handsome. Catalogue handsome. His power made her cross her legs. She folded her arms over her breasts, tighter than usual. Nothing happened in this State without the approval of this man, at least nothing of consequence. Even if he didn't originate it, he got the credit. He rarely got blame.

She tried to put him out of her mind, but she was a fatalist, it was more than a sign, it was divine. It was viral, once there, it stayed. No cure.

She had no idea why she went back into the laboratory, there was certainly no specific plan in her head. She wandered over to the book again. She opened it at her page, then to the page containing the details of Van De Clouet. Although they were five pages apart, they were in the same position on the page. Exactly the same position. She counted them. They were both fifth line up, in the second column, on the right-hand page. She counted them again. She decided to write down the reference numbers and opened the hand-bag to extract her diary.

Her hand bag was full, and she had to get past her purse, large bunch of house and car keys, make-up bag . . . and stunner. She placed them all out on the bench and extracted the slim, black diary and opened it at the day. The little pencil was tucked along the spine of the book, but now she held it in her left hand. It's slim shaft complemented her fingers.

First of all, she wrote down, Bd802, her own number, and then, Bd 0208, below it. There was a symmetry, that she registered immediately. They were both in the same container, both on the same level.

She closed the book, leaving it exactly where she had found it and pushed the slim, black pencil, with it's brass tip back down the spine.

The last two samples she had secured, had cost her quite a lot of money and effort. Her resources were far from endless and, after all, she would soon have a family to pay for. At least in the short term. A cheaper, quicker and more immediate solution sprang to mind. Maurice Van Der Clouet, being the father of her child would have been beyond her wildest dreams. Would it be possible? Could she do it? What did she know? And, what if she were caught?

Gloves, protective glasses and the long instruments of extraction were just lying there. What about just opening the flask and looking? If it was too difficult, or looked impossible, she said to herself, she could just replace the lid.

This Pandora's Box would not be so easy to close.

A glance at her watch told her she had at least forty minutes.

She tried on the gloves. They were far too big, and felt unwieldy, the insulation was thick and cumbersome. The glasses would have been too big, but the thickness of her hair made up the difference in the size between herself and Dr Jones. Her heart was pounding as she made the single step toward the flask. There was an arrow on the top indicating the direction to turn for opening and a red line to mark the alignment for sealing. She was to find that leaving it partially open would be impossible, for when she turned it slightly, thick, white vapour streamed from the gap.

Her lessons in chemistry at school told her that nitrogen was inert. It was also heavy and flowed down the side of the flask like a heavenly waterfall. Even so, lack of experience made her very apprehensive, and the numbers on the temperature panel flashed at her in red, winding up, steadily in hundredths of a degree, the difference between her flask and the one on her left becoming greater by the second.

With an almost inaudible 'plop', the lid detached and she moved it to one side. The rush of vapours as the liquid boiled off, made it impossible to see inside and she almost replaced the lid there and then. As the temperature rose by degrees, blurring the last two decimal place digits on the control, into a fuzzy, dark pink, the rush of thick vapour diminished. She could see inside, now, as long as the air above the clear liquid was not disturbed. There were racks full of small test-tubes, tiny, with even smaller glass stoppers in the tops. Each one had a number on it. Level 'd', was the top one, basically the most recent, and, she assumed, as there were four levels, then 'a', would be at the bottom.

There they were. Hers was nearest, on the outer circle, plain as can be, marked, 0802. 0208 was 90 degrees from hers on the next circle inwards.

She hadn't considered the practicalities of adding one to the other or even extracting them from their resting places, but the tweezers, hanging on the side of each container had a small, semi-circular notch in them, the same diameter as the tubes, so she lifted out 0208, with her trembling hands gripping the tweezers, turned and placed it in the rack on the bench. As soon as it was out, it stopped producing vapour, although there was a little steam, falling from it, caused by the condensation of the humid air in the laboratory, on the super-cooled glass. She felt confidant enough , now, to take out her own. The experiment had been done on somebody else, hers was not to be the first. She repeated the performance until they were both sitting side by side in the same rack, steaming together. She loosely replaced the lid on the flask to arrest the rise in temperature and give her time to think. It was the luckiest thing she could have done. The flasks were only four degrees from setting off the temperature alarm, and without the code, she would never have stopped it. The 'game', would have been up . . . in a big way.

It would have been impossible to have taken the stoppers out, with the gloves on, but she noticed that beads of condensation had formed on the glass of the tube. The glass had quickly warmed. She carefully touched the stopper with her finger, putting both gloves to one side. Her hands were hot and there was perspiration running down her temples, the wispy, fine hairs, in front of her ears, were sticking to her skin, and she wiped them away with her forearm, one side after another. Her whole world was concentrated into what was before her eyes on the bench.

Glass on glass was, necessarily, a tight fit, but it came out with a tug and she looked inside the open tube from the top. Of course, the view was the same as through the glass, and she estimated, in comparison to her own bottle, that there was similar amounts, maybe two visits. She tipped the bottle, rather too enthusiastically, not expecting anything to happen. But it did. One half of the contents began to slide out, and she instinctively held out her hand to catch it. It bounced into her palm and stuck, bonded by the frozen sweat. She yelped like a puppy with pain. The contents were hard, the same size as a broad bean, covered in frost, but had been a better insulator than the glass and was still very cold, indeed. She shook her hand violently and it detached, landing on the bench, a piece of her skin attached. This sort of bonding was not what she had had in mind. It stung like hell and she squeezed the wrist of her injured hand, cursing the lack of care.

She forced herself to continue, and took out the stopper of her own bottle. With a piece of paper, a sheet from her diary, she scooped it up and slide it down her own tube. It didn't fill it, and could only hope that it wouldn't be noticed.

A glance at her watch made her panic slightly. She moved toward the container and took off the top. She still had the glasses on, but no gloves.

She picked up both tubes and moved toward the harmless looking clear water. A bubble of vapour popped to the surface, just in time, and she jumped back. The thought of what could have happened, without the gloves, made the pit of her stomach churn. Her stinging hand was an unwelcome reminder. Replacing the tubes in the rack, she donned the gloves, picked them up by the tweezers and, one by one replaced them in the shallow liquid. The warmer tubes made the liquid nitrogen boil throwing up a plume of vapour, and it reminded her of putting potato chips into boiling oil, at home.

If Priscilla's heart had been beating faster, this time, it nearly stopped. The sound of keys in the door nearly killed her. The lab door was only open an inch but she could see Molly's arm fiddling with the lock. It could have only been worse, had it been Dr Jones, but only just. Priscilla jumped back across the room and roughly replaced the lid. It was all she had time for. As she snatched her handbag from the bench, the outer door opened and she managed to step back, behind the door, using that noise as her cover. Discovery was only a matter of 'when', not 'if'.

Molly, far from stupid, knew something was wrong, immediately. Priscilla wasn't in view, although that, in itself wasn't a crime. She could easily have been in the loo. She felt that there was something amiss, but to give her the benefit of the doubt, she stood still, and listened, her right hand still on the large, vertical door handle. She held her breath, so as not to make a sound. They were both holding their breath. Molly's pulse was quickening, degrading her ability to refrain from breathing very much longer. Priscilla's chest was bursting and her legs were shaking. One arm was through the straps of her open hand-bag and she held it tighter, not wanting to make the slightest sound. It was only putting off the inevitable. She was under no illusion.

Molly's eyes were already focused on the laboratory door, ajar. Priscilla heard her footsteps on the cord carpet approach, her mind racing.

The door was pushed back, by a thin leg, wearing 'American Tan', supermarket, tights. "And just what do you think you are oing in there, Miss Glover." She knew she was there, behind the door, but hadn't yet actually set eyes on her, but she knew, all right.

No response.

At that point, Molly caught sight of movement, heavy vapour running, like a divine waterfall, down the sides of 'flask B'. "Good God," she gasped, when she realised the lifeblood of the clinic had been tampered with. Ten years of product had been banked here. "You stupid Bitch," she shouted, and fairly sprinted to the leaking cask, letting the heavy door close on it's springs behind her.

Priscilla was revealed in her full glory, now, the red and black of her clothing, screaming her presence against the white tiles.

Molly had snatched up the insulated gloves and turned to Priscilla, as she hurriedly pulled them on.

"You tart. You bloody tart. What the hell do you think you were doing?" As she turned her back, she added, "you will pay for this, Madam." In her rage and nervousness, she messed up the first attempt to refit the lid and cross-threaded it. It was a mistake she would regret bitterly, if only for a very short time.

Priscilla's hand had closed round the stunner, and the switch for activating the discharge, was moved forward, by her thumb, even as she moved forward herself.

As the last quarter turn of the lid was completed, Molly caught a glimpse of two stainless steel prongs approaching her. The tips, reflecting on the stainless steel of the flask, was again a form of symmetry, but any poetry, was lost on the pair. Had the reflection been clearer, evading action might have been taken, but it wasn't and neither was her mind, a millisecond later, as they connected, simultaneously, with the nape of her neck. They didn't jab, they touched They would leave no mark.

She was an old women, not having the constitution of the hapless Ian. She never even made a sound, just collapsed from the legs up, like a rag-doll on the tiled floor. She never felt the pain of striking the floor, because she was dead on arrival, and anyway, she crumpled, rather than fell.

Priscilla, meanwhile, was far from dead. She was hyperventilating. There were two causes, holding her breath for so long and tangible fear.

Molly's stillness was a welcome relief, and at the same time, an anti-climax. Shocked, as Priscilla was, she could tell that she was dead, even before she had checked her pulse. It was the way she had hit the ground. Lifeless was the only way to describe it, trite though it may sound. She had the very same appearance that her mother had. The likeness was even more startling. There was sorrow in neither case.

What could she do now? Her car had been outside for over an hour, Jacky was about to return and Molly might have told anyone of Priscilla's presence, during her lunch break. She gathered her handbag from behind the door, and hesitated. Molly just lay there. The clinic wasn't overlooked, so nobody would have registered occupants, or otherwise, in the car. She closed the lab door after her and walked back through the reception. Survival instincts had kicked in and the adrenaline had almost worn off. Her legs had stopped shaking and she was back in control. She looked round, and out through the front window. Jacky appearing at this moment would be disaster.

There was one more risk that she had to take. She had to see if Molly, the ever efficient secretary, had left notes. Rekindling her nervousness, she stepped behind reception and searched the shelf, which was lower than the front counter. She knew enough, not to touch anything with her fingers, but there was only a note-pad and today's entry was blank. Satisfied, she was about to straighten up, but was startled by a vehicle pulling up, outside.

It was to the right of the window, so she couldn't tell who it was. It must surely be Dr Jones. The only course of action, now, was to keep behind reception. Her plans and life went no further than that decision. The cover was pathetic. It was her only option. The second biggest dose of adrenaline in her lifetime hit her heart. Twice in one hour. It beat like a steam hammer, loud enough, seemingly, for everyone to hear. The handle was tried, followed by a shake, the vibrations conveying the intruders annoyance. Whoever it was, was expecting the door, at this time, to be open. It must be the Doctor, without his keys. "Damn." The door-bell rang. It rang twice. It was lucky for Priscilla that the door had not been kept unlocked, because, in her haste, Molly, deceased, had left the snib up when she closed it behind her and the lock remained deployed.

There was a metallic noise, a pushing, and a small metallic clink. "It was the postman. Thank God," she said to herself.

When she heard him reverse and then pull away, she was out like a shot. She was not going to risk being caught a second time.

With the door pulled closed, behind her, she reached her car, looking round as much as she dare. Her mind was racing, but crystal clear. Sharp. She was in danger, but alive, very much alive, more than she had ever been, unlike her victim. Molly was not Priscilla's victim, though, she was her vanquished enemy. She had stood between a mother and her baby.

She must walk. Someone, the postman, had seen the empty car. She must walk, clear the rushing blood in her legs, refresh the thoughts in her mind, and certainly not be there when the discovery was made. She opened the trunk of the car, threw her handbag in, slammed it shut, and set off at a pace.

Chapter Five

Priscilla had walked further and for longer than she had anticipated. The park was only one block away. It was spacious, ordered, yet, at the same time, it had a certain sort of wildness. On a scale of one to ten, it wouldn't have registered, in this capacity, to a country boy, but to her, a 'townie', it possessed free spirit. There was a natural lake in the middle, and she had cut, off the path, directly toward it. The leaves were still full on the trees, although there were now a scattering on the grass. She sat, motionless, her mind drifting over the different facets of her life, especially the recent ones. The ducks were still directing their young, although they were well on the way to their grown up feathers, losing their down and changing from khaki, to white. Everywhere she looked there was family activity, these days. Mother and child. Mother and baby.

Crows, circling and screeching at each other brought her to her senses. It was time to go back, face the consequences, or hopefully, not face the consequences. Her feet were heavy, she was tired. The events of the day had drained her and it took at least twice as long to retrace her steps.

When she got back, the only difference was that Jacky's car was parked next to hers. She had expected drama, questions, flashing lights. But nothing. It was with trepidation that she approached the door, she felt as though she were walking into a silent trap. It was laying in wait for her. Each step brought her nearer to the moment when something awful would leap out and devour her. But nothing.

Opening the door was the second, great, anti-climax of the day. Little did she know it, but there was to be a third, the biggest one of her life. Still nothing happened.

"Hello. Hello," she called out, fairly softly, and as casually as she could muster. Each step was now gradually refilling her with a quiet confidence. She had decided that she could live with guilt, but not discovery. The more that she went through for her babies, the greater the cost, then the greater the value. They were already priceless.

"Priscilla." The voice startled her, and she spun round. It was Dr Jones, or at least what was left of Dr Jones. He looked awful.

"Where have you been, Priscilla? I have been worried about you."

She was wondering how to start her explanation, but she was saved by his eagerness to continue.

"Something terrible has happened. My poor Molly has passed away. A heart attack, it looks like. If only I had been here," and he broke down into tears, those large, soft shoulders heaving, one hand over his eyes. Big men don't cry, or so they say. Well this one, was.

"I was in the Park, I was waiting . . . Oh sit down Jacky." Her instincts had kicked in again. With one hand on his arm and the other as far up his shoulders as she could reach, she led him to one of the chairs, sitting herself on one of the broad arms, next to him.

"I came back and found her on the floor, in the lab. I knew it could happen at any time. The medication . . ." and he tailed off, sobbing. "She loved this place. She lived for the work."

"And you," Priscilla said before she thought it through.

"She lived for it".

"I'll make tea, you stay there."

"No, Priscilla, not from reception. I couldn't stand it. I'm not seeing anyone else today. Could I offer you refreshment in my apartment. This feels like the end. The end of the bloody world."

Priscilla reached over the desk and took some tissues from the box. She placed them on the arm of his chair and, momentarily placed her hand on his, before crossing the reception and letting the lock click into place. Jacky was already up on his feet and drying the tears on his soft, slightly sagging cheeks. The fullness of his features partially masked his age. If he were to loose a stone in weight, it would add ten years. His thick hair, although white, was an even colour. It added, rather than detracted, from his age. He could have easily claimed to be in his early sixties, rather than two years short of seventy, but he always chose a smile, by way of an answer. He was far from in a smiling mood now, though, and, until he had his tea, he would look his age, every day of it.

t was a door marked 'PRIVATE', at the far side of reception, that led to his private stair, and onto his apartment. Priscilla had never even noticed it, it could easily have been a broom cupboard. Had he not been in this line of work, all those smiling women wouldn't have noticed him, either. His work had brought him adoration.

It made her feel uneasy, even going through the door. It was at the exact moment that she passed the doorway, that she realised how lonely this man really was. He had his work and he had, had Molly. He had never been married and never had children, not of his own, that is. In many ways, he was surrogate to hundreds, maybe thousands, but he was always on the periphery. An outsider. It left a bad taste, an awful feeling, Priscilla had tasted it. There was a parallel, a kinship.

It made her feel very bad. Of course she was to blame, which made her feel worse, a lot worse. Survival was a strong instinct. Here was the man she was relying on, learning to rely on more by the day, and he was crying, the first time she had seen a man show any where near this amount of emotion. She followed him up the stairs, her right hand in the small of his back, as he dragged his feet, heavy with disappointment verging on despair.

The apartment was one large room, rafters remaining exposed, chimney breast and large open fire, hardly any evidence of usage, at one end, bed at the other. It was double, not king size. He was a big man for the bed, but not prone to athletics. It was functional , dedicated to sleeping, only. The whole room was functional, and . . . well . . . male. Bachelor male. Professional, architect, well read, interior designed, it was everything but warm. It was functional, stylish, but not a home. The busiest area was the desk, piled high with papers, files, the desk-lamp left on, always on, with coffee mugs strategically placed amongst the paraphernalia. There were clean clothes hanging over the end of the bed, immaculately pressed, but they were from the cleaners. There was a pizza box, open, but empty, next to the bed, and a half finished, half bottle of whisky, Irish Whisky.

He threw himself, face-down on the bed, she sat on the edge, beside him.

"I just can't believe that that is the end of poor old Molly. Here one minute and gone the next."

"But there will be an inquest or something, to go through?", Priscilla asked, thankful that he couldn't see her face.

"No. She had a weak heart and was on strong medication. It was only a matter of time. I was her doctor, always had been since the first days of my private practice. I signed the death certificate, myself."

Priscilla, leaned forward and squeezed him. It was real pleasure, mixed with relief, a kaleidoscope of emotions, that were impossible to separate.

"The tea," she said, pushing herself up from the bed, and walking over to the kitchen area. It had everything, but was obviously unused. He shuffled around and sat up, leaning against the plain white pillows. It wasn't just to get a better look at her, he needed to direct her around the kitchen. But she did look good.

"There is milk in the fridge, it should be all right."

"I'll make it in mugs," Priscilla said, selecting two, which were decorated by the signs of the zodiac.

"Make mine Virgo. No sugar."

She did, and selected Aries, for herself.

"Aries and Virgo, are they compatible?"

"Coffee and cream," he twinkled. The light in his eyes was back on. Dimly, but back on, all the same. He'd lied about the zodiac, he knew nothing about the subject. Astrology and Catholicism were 'oil and water'.

"Blarney," Priscilla retorted. She suspected that he knew nothing but appreciated the sentiment.

Tea made, she carefully carried them over to the bed, automatically walking to the opposite side to Jacky, and sitting on the edge again, but he patted the position next to himself, offering her more comfort, leaning against the pillows. She accepted.

Kicking her shoes off, gently, she straightened her legs, on the bed, and in the silence that followed, whilst the tea cooled enough to take the first sip, admired her own legs. They weren't a bad pair, she thought, good shape, slim, smooth. They looked good in black stockings.

Jacky was thinking the same thing, with the addition of admiring her neat ankles. He'd always admired a neat ankle, he thought to himself.

"Molly used to have nice legs, you know". It wasn't intentional, and was said absent mindly, but by inference, he compared and admired Priscilla's legs. It was indirect enough to be inoffensive, but enough to be noticed. She wasn't used to complements. She had always surrounded herself with armour, which discouraged those sorts of comments, but this had penetrated a chink in her defences. It was insecurity that caused her to act like that, but this wasn't how she had felt in Jack's company.

Her defence system was made of very brittle stuff, it didn't crack, it shattered, destructed. A thousand pieces. Super strong though it might have been, intact, it was now reduced to zero. The forces within her had been building up pressure over all these years, suppressing her femininity. Suppressing her desires. The events of the last few months, including the death of her mother, and now, today's scene, were quickly becoming an irresistible force. When his arm slipped around her shoulders, she didn't freeze, she melted. The result of that thaw, were tears, lots of them. She cried like a baby. It was her turn.

She half-rolled, onto his chest, her hair draping over his heavily pressed, cotton shirt. It had that clean, washing powder smell, but strong as it was, his pheromones were stronger. She'd never been this close to masculinity, he was a big man, and his arms felt strong, it was a strong heart that she could hear beating. She reeled under the onslaught of 'firsts'. She was a virgin in many more ways than one. However, it's a fact that not many killers are virgins, it's almost unknown. Another 'first'.

Wham! The vacuum created by the loss of Molly was filled. Not replaced, but filled. The softness of her hair, her light perfume, her youth and the sheer woman in her, overwhelmed him. He had his own void, the passion filled it, and, overflowed, some.

"Priscilla, Priscilla. Don't cry."

"I'm sorry, Jacky, I just can't help it. If only you knew what I was going through." She hesitated. "I so want my baby." The sobbing gave way to several heavy breaths. "I've made such an awful mess of your shirt with my silly tears."

She pulled herself up, closer, with his help, and looked into his greying eyes. Their eyes were locked. He kissed her salty, wet, cheeks, gently. The tears flowed freely, but she had stopped crying, she was comfortable. Her tears of anguish gave way to tears of pleasure . . . and relief.

They didn't speak another word, nor did they even kiss. Priscilla rolled onto her back. It would be ludicrous to suggest that she pulled him onto her, she was so light, in comparison, but she led him and he responded to the command. She had that feeling again, but this time, instead of squeezing her legs together, she opened them.

It was a moment that he had longed for, for years, but, at the same time, dreaded. His inability had haunted him, a spectre that drove away any thoughts of a relationship, but now, it never even crossed his mind. How they undressed, neither would remember, they came together more of necessity than urgency, business that was long overdue, business that was fulfilled, to their mutual benefit and satisfaction. Any initial discomfort was nothing compared to what Priscilla had suffered, a rite of passage that was welcome. Both had lived with demons, but the exorcism was complete, Priscilla's race to motherhood had started, now, in earnest, and it would be impossible to wait any longer, Jacky was reborn. It was a climax of emotion, rather than passion, and emotion was satisfied. As they lay side by side, in silence, both lost in their own thoughts, without a thought, Priscilla said, "Jacky, I'd like you to make a start on my treatment tomorrow." Dr Jones just held her tightly, he understood and was happy. Of course he would oblige, he would do anything for her.

"Tomorrow's just fine, by me, Prissy." It was the one time that she didn't mind the title, she just fell asleep where she lay, in his arms, a woman.

Chapter Six

When Priscilla awoke, it was to an unfamiliar world. It wasn't the smell of a different bed, subtle yet obvious, nor the feeling of starched linen, a sort of hospital, professional, obsessional cleanliness. Nor was it the light coming from a different direction, to her room at home, which she could see through her eyelids, loosely closed, but closed all the same. It wasn't even the fact that her legs were extra warm, because she still had her stockings on, and the rubber hold up section at the tops was irritating her slightly. It wasn't even the slightly scratchy lace of the black bra she was wearing. She understood all those differences and the reasons behind them. She hadn't forgotten the love making, nor did she regret it. That hadn't been the reason, only the catalyst. For the first time in her life, she had woken up as a whole woman, fulfilled and complete, her self-denial, ended.

She had lain awake for, perhaps, fifteen minutes, her eyes still closed, listening. Dr Jones had been moving around quietly, as considerate as ever, cupboard doors opening and closing, crockery moving around, water running and general breakfast preparation. She could smell fresh coffee. He was even humming to himself. She didn't know the title, but imagined it contained the word, 'Tipperary'.

Her signal for contact, was to move one arm from under the duvet and roll onto her back. He immediately stopped in mid tune.

"Good morning, Miss, what a sleepy-head you are, do you know the time?"

"No, what time is it?" She felt totally relaxed and natural, no embarrassment or shame.

"It's ten o'clock, you must have needed it, though."

"Good God," she said, sitting up and leaning on one elbow, "what about your clinic?"

"I'm not opening today, I've made one or two calls and put off the patients until tomorrow. You are my only patient, today, I promised you last night and besides, my priorities have changed. This is the new Dr Jones, Jackie to yourself, now." He didn't elaborate, but she took it as a positive alteration, for the better, and anyway, he was approaching with a tray full of breakfast. This was a first indeed.

"I've assumed it was coffee, grapefruit and toast, how's that?" He smiled at her, and added, "I have this every morning, same every day, only difference being that I'm alone." It wasn't a word she wanted to dwell on, so she tried to ignore it.

"No wonder you are such a fine figure of a man, Jack Jones," in a very poor Irish accent.

"The Irish have always had a good breakfast, so they have," in a great, exaggerated Irish accent. "My great Uncle Patrick used to say that a breakfast without bacon and soda-bread wasn't a proper Irish breakfast. And fried potatoes. He'd be ashamed of me, so he would."

"It's not what I'm used to, Jack, believe me". She smiled, wonder on her features, innocent wonder, that masked the recent events. "And where does he live?" Jacky looked at her. "Your Uncle."

"He died of coronary heart disease."

They finished breakfast, without speaking, happy to remain silent, and enjoying the unaccustomed company. When they had finished, Jacky took the tray.

"Thanks Jacky, that was marvellous, thank you very much." He put his hand on hers.

"That was my pleasure, believe me, Priscilla," and stood up, turning to the kitchen, subdued by his stupid mention of death. "I'll leave those for later," he said, "we have work to do."

71

He padded, like a bear, across the room. " There's the shower to the right, clean towel on the rail. Help yourself. I'll be downstairs when you're ready". As he put down the tray, he turned, one last time, and his voice changed to 'Doctor'. It was quite distinct.

"When did you finish your last period?" He noticed her wince. "Don't worry, it's for your treatment, nothing to do with my abilities, or otherwise. I can't father children, it's one of life's ironies and my cross, it can be a cruel old world."

Priscilla felt bad for him and bad that her reaction had shown, and she tried to make up for it by speaking as softly and sympathetically as possible.

"About ten days ago. This is about the strangest consultation I've ever imagined, is it not Dr Jones?"

"Don't even joke about that, Priscilla, or I'll have to leave by the window.' He made a mock grimace as he left, but she imagined that he meant it. He did mean it, he knew many a Doctor who had been forced into that sort of decision. An occupational hazard.

She felt like a new girl at school, when she stepped in the shower. She virtually never stayed out at night, and here she was, in a man's flat, naked and showering. One of her main worries, and it was illogical and out of all proportion, was having to put the same clothes on to go home in. It was something she never did, clothes were always changed. When she had noticed Beatrice wearing the same clothes, she had despised her, and said so, especially having stayed with one of her men. She still did. She'd never change.

This particular anxiety was postponed, at least for a while, when Dr Jones called out,

"I've left a new toothbrush on the basin for you, and a dressing gown for you." She noticed them both. "I'm afraid I've no slippers to fit, you'll have to wear your shoes. See you downstairs. We need an examination."

"Thanks, OK."

Her washing took on a new urgency, this was it. The hot water stung the open, red sore on the palm of her hand, a sharp reminder of yesterday, although it could have been a lifetime away. The wound had religious overtones that didn't sit well with her conscience. She forced them out of view. She held her head back, as the warm soapy water caressed her back, washing away the heat of the night and the smell of the Doctor, real or imagined. It was real to her. Everyone would smell it. She remained there for a full twenty minutes, her whole world concentrated in that cubicle, the mesmerising jets of water playing on her tense shoulders, relieving her, that tortured spring within, gradually unwinding. She would have dearly liked to scrub her hands, she felt the need, but the pain of the wound was too intense, accusing. She was undecided whether or not to scrub between her legs. She didn't feel the same need.

Meanwhile, the Doctor was in his laboratory. He'd extracted the sample number, after checking in the registry, Bd 802, and with the stopper still home, let icy cold water play over the tube. He knew the procedure, he didn't have to think about it. He'd invented the procedure . . . almost. It was Priscilla's good fortune that he didn't check the contents before the thaw, because at that point, there were three distinct frozen globs, not two. After ten minutes, when he was sure that it had all melted, her shook it gently to mix it thoroughly. The evidence had all but disappeared.

"No cold spots, there," he said to himself, and increased the temperature by way of the mixer tap, to luke warm. "Don't worry, my beauties, you'll get no shocks from me," he said to the tube, addressing the inhabitants as though they understood. "Some people talked to plants",
 he'd said, defensively, to some people in the past, but he knew himself, that he'd meant Molly, she was the only one that he'd ever been open about his work, with.

He heard a movement outside the door. "Just go in, Priscilla, I'll be with you."

Priscilla entered the door, marked 'Consulting Room', she was certainly going no-where near the lab. The room was warm, there was a plain desk, black couch along one wall and a seat, both behind and in front of the desks, in fact there were two, in front, presumably for consultations with couples. It said 'Dr J. Jones', on a sign, facing her, on the desk top. She pulled her dressing gown tighter as she heard him approach.

He thought to himself that she looked radiant, when he saw her, her cheeks were still flushed from the hot water, but he kept his thoughts to himself. When he was downstairs, he really was a 'Doctor of Medicine'.

He took his seat behind the desk and put on his glasses, as much for effect as anything, he just looked over the top of them. Habits.

"Now," he said, picking up her case notes, "you are ten days past your period, we need a sample of your blood and a smear. Just hop onto the couch, could you?" She felt herself flush, no woman liked to be subjected to this, but it was the end result that always won the day. Firstly, he pricked her thumb with a device that clicked once and gave one sharp sensation. She thought of the night before. He squeezed a tiny amount of blood from the wound, only two drops, into a tiny tube and put it onto the desk. She was thankful that it was her right hand, the left one felt sore and was quite raw. She had wasted her time. He'd already seen it.

"Now the smear, knees up and heels pressed down, please." It was as ignominious a position as one could imagine, and she turned her head to the wall, not knowing what was to come, but she never felt a thing.

"It's just a mucous test, it reveals you're hormone level, and tells us whether you're ovulating. Sit back down, we've finished, and make yourself comfortable it'll take me two minutes. Help yourself to the coffee, it's fresh."

At that, he left the room, with his samples, but she didn't help herself to coffee, it was too close to her breakfast experience. These activities needed to be kept separate, in their own compartments.

She'd always despised it, but she couldn't help putting her fingers to her mouth, not that she bit her nails, but nibbled at her skin. It was a recent habit. When she realised what she was doing, she scolded herself and actually sat on her hands in an attempt to stop. Before she knew it, she was rocking back and forth, nervously, like a crazy, caged animal. And when she stopped herself doing that, she started running her fingers through her hair at the back of her neck. The only solution, and it wasn't long in coming, was the return of Dr Jones.

He burst through the door, softly, in an Irish sort of a way, beaming in anticipation of her own smiles.

"We're on, Priscilla, it's positive." It had become his crusade as well as her own".

"What about the samples?"

"Sample. Singular. They are both thawed and mixed, now. They are already prepared, I took the opportunity whilst you were getting ready. Now we're ready to go." He looked at her face, which was showing a little apprehension.

She looked at his. Did he emphasise the word 'both', or did she imagine it? Did he realise that there were three pieces? She felt nauseous. Bit early for 'morning sickness'.

"As long as you're not sore, or anything?" he asked, a little shame faced. It wouldn't have mattered whether she was or not, she would have lied. She'd waited too long, and brushed off the question by wrinkling her nose and shaking her head.

"Back to the couch, then, Priscilla, I'll be back in a mo'."
Priscilla settled down in the same position, her head reeling and thoughts flying in every direction.

"This was it, there was little chance of turning back," she muttered to herself, being strong and invoking as much resolution as she could muster. "What happens if it doesn't work first time, do I have to go through the sample routine again?" she called out in the direction of the lab. It was something that she hadn't thought about until now, and realised the impossible situation she would be in, if that were the case. She'd thought of a lot of things, but asking the questions also revealed her motives, so most of them remained unanswered or imagined. She was a prisoner of that imagination. There was no parole.

"Not at all," he said, when he re-entered the room, bringing in the Irish brogue, to relax her as best he could. "This is a watered down sample, well sort of watered, in a manner of speaking, diluted, actually. There is plenty left, but it is introduced as near to it's goal as possible and it should take first time. It's the way I do it," he quipped, bringing out the accent again

75

and placing his hands on his hips in a comedy pose. "It arrives much closer than natural methods, which really are quite hit and miss. Eighty five per cent of my cases take first time, don't worry."

Ten inches of minute filament tube were eased into position at the end of a syringe, and with the tiniest of tweaks later, it was all over. She was relieved to cover herself.

"Don't play basketball for a few days, and no sky-diving," he said, looking over the top of his glasses, sternly.

She leant across, after swinging her legs back over the edge of the couch and straightening her gown, and kissed him on the cheek.

"Do you mind Madam, I'm your Doctor." She wrinkled her nose in his direction and just smiled. The smile had a dimension to it. One he was not familiar with. It could mean eternal bliss and a long, long friendship, but such a plane was unknown territory, it had it's dangers. There was always danger in uncharted territories.

He smiled and wrinkled back.

He had his own dimensions, but suspected that they were simpler. Priscilla wasn't to know that, though.

Chapter Seven

It had been three weeks since the introduction of the sample. The weeks had passed quickly, in one sense. She'd not done very much, but there again, had little to do. Beatrice had not been to see her, nor had she phoned. She was obviously still reeling from the shock of the last meeting, and Priscilla had no inclination to make a move. Dr Jones had, made his moves, he had phoned five times, under the pretext of asking how she was. In fact he was concerned, and curious on this point, but it was more than that. They both knew it. It was unspoken, but understood. The previous Wednesday, she had missed her period. This was far from normal, as she had never, before, done anything that might have given it the slightest excuse to be irregular, and it had always returned the complement by being obligingly on time. Priscilla had never made demands upon it, and it had reciprocated. There was, of course, the night spent at the surgery, that raised enough doubt to give it the benefit of the same doubt, by one week. But now it was Wednesday again.

Dr Jones had won the bet with himself. He didn't predict the call to the day, but he had managed it within the three day period that he had set as his parameters.

"Hello, Priscilla, how are you?" He resisted adding, that he thought it would be her.

"I'm fine Jacky, just fine, I'm just a little worried by something, though," she hesitated. "I've missed my period, and it is a week over due."

"Worried, I thought that was the whole object of the exercise?"

"Well, yes, I suppose it is." It had just been the thought of coming straight out with it, and the fear that he would think she was silly imagining a pregnancy, it was still very much unreal to her, alien. She had needed a link, a mental link, between action and pregnancy, a cause. The time with Jacky had been a substitute for that link but it was a weak one and it could break at any moment. Her three weeks had been a nightmare of fear and self doubt. She was snapped back into reality. During that time, her obsessions had become greater, checking the locks, the cats, cleaning, she couldn't stop. It helped pass the time.

Now for the mechanics of the procedure.

"You need to drop around to the surgery and we'll take a urine sample. I'll tell you straight away."

"OK. This afternoon?"

"Around two, if it suits, Priscilla, I don't have a consultation until three."

"What time is it now?" she asked, but the question was rhetorical and she answered it herself. "Eleven . . . I'll get ready and see you there." There was a slight pause at his end of the phone, so she said "goodbye," and hung up, but the softness in her voice and the timing conveyed her feelings well.

Priscilla knew that Dr Jones had not found a replacement for Molly. She had heard that there had been a funeral, and this had been one of the reasons that she had remained at home. She had not crossed the doorstep once. If she didn't go out, then she couldn't get caught out. That was the logic. It was a variety of things that had kept her in; the funeral; not wanting to be confronted by Jacky's presence, not that she was embarrassed or felt awkward, it was just that she wanted to feel closeted, pure, too late for 'virginal'.

There was one other reason though. Dr Jones had said not to do anything strenuous and she had taken his warning very much to heart. It had become her other obsession and had taken the place of many things, her security checks being one.

She had spent many hours in bed, reading, daydreaming, looking for a sign, physical or spiritual . . . every time she caught sight of her stomach, she held it and wondered. She even prayed and that was a thing that she hadn't even done at her mother's funeral.

She'd picked up a poem and read it, by chance. It had become her mantra. She knew she shouldn't read it but it was how she felt. She was on the edge of the abyss.

I'm much too far out and I realise it now.

"We'll witness a drowning," is what somebody said.

I'm out of my depth, can't get back, don't know how.

An acute lack of air is affecting my head.

She never read it all out at once, she had to pause, but pausing led to reflection and her fear was mirrored in the lines.

I was warned of the risks, but the risks were all mine.

There were strong undercurrents and it's true, I can't swim.

"Should we help," someone said, "should we throw out a line?"

"I don't know. It's so dangerous. And it is only him."

Now it's time. I've no options. I'll just have to wave.

I've been irresponsible, now I'm out on a limb.

They're discussing, debating. I'm too far to save.

I'm drowning, I'm sure. I repeat . . . I can't SWIM.

Priscilla was that person, but she had been thrown a line. Three weeks of drifting and the line was within her grasp, but was she strong enough, for the long haul? She had come to the conclusion that she wasn't, but now there was the focus, it was back in her eyes and her mind.

For the first time in nineteen days, she closed the book and stretched, a large, spine twisting, bent arm stretch, followed by a long yawn. She didn't even put her hand over her mouth. She could feel the skin over her breasts tighten and the right-hand side one point upward. Cupping them both in her hands, she walked to the shower and turned it to full heat and stared into the mirror, looking into her eyes, deeply, not making a single move, until the condensation on the glass obscured her own image. Her destiny was mapped out, of that she was sure and her future lay within her. She needed no test.

Chapter Eight

Serene would be the word which would describe the way that Priscilla felt, now. At least that would be Jacky's description, but he was biased. Someone who didn't know her would say, 'spaced out'. Dr Jones had been surprised by her. He was used to the changes in a woman, after she had been told that she was expecting a baby, but Priscilla was in a slightly different state. He couldn't quite put his finger on it, but it was there on her arrival and long before his confirmation. When he told her the date to expect, she wasn't phased, the smile was already fixed and all that was added was her characteristic wrinkle of the nose.

She'd refused a coffee and was uncharitably thinking that she just wanted to get home, into her own space.

"I suppose you will be thinking about names, Priscilla? Although it will be a while before the sex can be determined."

"Not yet," she lied. She'd be thinking of names, all right. There were three to choose from. She'd be thinking of names, but the names of the father. That would come first.

Chapter Nine

The cats were back in favour, at least in the short term. The stockings were out of favour. She was sitting on the old wicker chair amongst the cat hairs, in a long dressing gown that was well past it's best, pulling it over her legs, that were folded under her and trying to cover her ankles, from view. Not that there was anybody to see them, she hadn't had any visitors. Any attempts, from the people that she knew, at socialising, had been rebuffed with the expertise of the receptionist whom she had despatched. She had moved both of the cats from the cushion, which was still warm from their bodies, when she had sat down. They had both jumped straight back up onto her lap. They were certainly not interested in warming a second location. Settling into their place, with free heating and a tickle under the chin to boot, they both purred.

"We'll soon have a new baby in the house to play with," she said in a mother-baby voice, with the mandatory pout. They weren't impressed and never bothered to open their eyes. They just purred all the louder.

The cats had enjoyed the new-found interest. Food had improved and was always on time and on demand. Their mistress was at home and a feeling of peace and tranquillity was in the air. Priscilla was eking out her living from her savings. She had no investments, at least not in the normal sense. Her investment was inside her and it was growing at a rate that would have astounded the financial markets. From day one, there was growth, of over one hundred per cent. Daily at first, with the smooth curve of the graph levelling steadily, but pointing directly at a dividend date of nine months.

Two months had already passed and an ultrasound scan had been taken. The minuscule vibrations, administered by the new nurse/receptionist at the clinic of 'Fertility and Motherhood', had coursed through the jelly on the sensor, on through her abdomen and bounced back from the womb. The grainy image was revealed on the screen and the features pointed out. The head size, pulsating heart . . . genitals. It was a boy.

Dimensions verified his date of arrival and the mother was given a hard copy, four inches square, which was secreted in her patent leather bag.

Now she really had something to focus on. Her preoccupation with her image in the mirror of the shower room, was now trained on her stomach. Could she detect a change? She went through the ritual several times a day, but the change was a stealthy, subtle transformation. Her discovery, like many discoveries, was a sudden one, even though she was expecting it. Expectation took on a whole new meaning for Priscilla.

She was getting ready to go to the supermarket in the mall, for a little half-hearted, baby-product browsing, when she found that the trousers of her charcoal-grey suit wouldn't fit. At first, she breathed in. Then she tried to force the waistband to join together, but at last, she realised. Just when her mind was off the subject, she realised, and it came as a surprise. The first real tangible sign. Eureka, sprang to mind.

She flung open her blouse, pulling it from her shoulders and dropping it to the floor whilst racing across the bedroom to the open door of the bathroom. Down came the side zipper, and there it was. Compared to her bottom in the neat fitting trousers, it was enormous, almost hanging over the elastic of her panties, a mountain.

"How could I not have seen that?" she asked herself loudly and whooping for joy. The cats made a hasty departure from their cushion. Three disturbances were quite enough for cats who were intent on serious resting. It was, in reality, only a slight swelling, but it was there all thesame, the interpretation of the size was in equal proportion to the desire, but there was nothing slight about it, for Priscilla. It was pure, unadulterated, joy.

Chapter Ten

It was the endoscope that Pat Ensell was using. He had his best eye glued to it and the other one screwed up. It was less comfortable than the video monitor and he still had to wear the headphones, to hear anything other than muffled sound, but it felt real. He was closer to the action, not physically, but in essence. The monitor reminded him of a cheap 'B' movie, a black and white one, at that. He felt remote from what was going on, therefore less interested and therefore less able to concentrate for the long period that surveillance demanded. The whirr of the video recorder, the old, cheap, utilitarian, manual video was like a lullaby to a baby. The department expected miracles on a diet of under investment and lack of personnel, against massive wealth and awesome power. "Bunch of fucking amateurs playing in a professional game," was what he often spat. "No wonder we're at the bottom of the league."

Tom, Tom Scott, never responded. His eyes were glued to the monitor and wide open. He liked black and white movies and a comfortable chair to view them from. He'd have a beer as well, if it hadn't been Pat who he was on the shift with. Having his feet up on the desk was as hard as he dared push. It felt like a weekend at home. For him, this job was a walk in the park, a holiday, even the film content was familiar.

Tom was clean cut.

"A little too clean cut," was how Pat described him, at his own home. "And blotchy." But he kept his thoughts to himself and his lady. Pat was senior in service only, but that counted for everything. In Pat's estimation,

Tom was the equivalent of the video, better than nothing, sort of useful, but something insubstantial and unreliable about him. The product of under funding and a bad attitude from the city. It had percolated down.

Pat was far from clean cut. Even at his wedding he had looked awful. When he turned up for the ceremony, the doorman had blocked his path with his arm over the doorway.

"Sorry, Pal, you can't come in, there's a wedding here today."

"Not without me there ain't. I'm the groom," was all he replied, well, 'growled'. He didn't need to say more. The conviction and control in his voice and demeanour cleared his path, like a scythe, even if he left a shaking head and a look of disbelief in his wake. Pat had been in deep cover for almost five years and he wasn't about to let a wedding break that, even if it was his own, no, especially, if it were his own.

When his bespectacled wife to be, greeted him with "Hi, ya bum." He took it as a complement. They'd both arrived separately for the ceremony, as convention demanded, but they had left home together, by motorcycle. Pat was packing 1339cc, and, although it ran on unleaded, it emitted testosterone.

"You go down Ocean Boulevard, I'll take East 34, and see you there." It wasn't so much a race, but was a matter of honour, being first. They both understood that. There would be a lifetime to suffer second place.

"Where should I turn for East'?" Helen had asked, innocently. He should have known better than to point with his left hand. It was the sort of mistake that would have got him killed, at work, but he was about to marry the blasted women, so who was on guard? Come on. It had meant letting go of the clutch and before he could do that, he had to be in neutral. As he pointed, she let go of her own clutch. But she was in 'first' and she left him breathing rubber and monoxide fumes. He was fuming, himself.

"Bastard," he shouted after his bride, "I'll have you for that." She never heard, but imagined that to be the case, anyway, it was her wedding night, after all.

It wasn't the church organ that announced their arrival to the congregation of six, but the resonant tune played on the two double set of pipes, complements of Mr Harley and Mr Davidson. Helen wore white, but to be honest, white underwear was the extent of it. The rest, was denim.

"Don't want to get you a bad reputation in the department, now. Do we Patsy?" If anyone else had called him that, they would be eating sidewalk, but with Helen, he was putty. When they entered the chapel, it wasn't to a hushed silence, it was to a cheer.

Pat's mind wasn't on that happy day. He'd been forced into it, but it had still been his happiest, though he had never admitted it. Today wasn't the happiest day, that was for sure. He'd described today's activities as 'rummaging through the trash can with your bare hands and rubbing your face in the contents'. The main constituent was right in front of him. Neither of the men wanted anyone to commit a crime, but they were here and needed a climax. One more than the other.

It had been four days, now, three hours out of each afternoon. There had been hints, but nothing positive. The office was only occupied for an hour each day but then there was the setting up time. The department only had one camera and their time allocation was nearly up. It was wanted for a drugs stake' and 'E' division were pressing. The build up for this case had been difficult, not too long, but there had been a wall of disinterest and outright hostility. If the shit were to hit the fan, the commander wasn't sure which direction it would fly. It might hit them all, but whatever, the smell wouldn't be nice.

Tom Scott was the only officer willing to enthuse.

All that had happened, upto now, was the subject had come in, taken a few calls, read some papers and left after the hour. They hadn't got a wire tap on his line, the commander had broken wind when the request went in.

"You've got no fucking proof, and it is against my better judgement to allow the investigation in the first place," was what he had added, when the air had cleared. It was the fear of refusing a request to Officer Ensell, that had sanctioned the operation. He knew that giving them a week was a face saving exercise, one that he would have to forget as soon as he had said it.

Pat knew that he would have to come up with the goods. He had a feeling about it, but loosing face was something to be avoided by most people, and "give me a week", meant a week, to Pat.

Pat wasn't that preoccupied with saving anyone's face, really. If the subject was upto what he suspected, then he really did want a result. His favourite informant never let him down. He would have to be good for Pat to pay him out of his own salary when he needed to go out on a limb. His salary wasn't that great to start with, but a word or two, a pointer, could save weeks of work, dead ends and sometimes, dead men. This lead had started, as usual, with, "I suppose that you might be interested to know . . . ?" He was interested. He had no children of his own, he'd been married to the department for too long, but that didn't mean that he didn't care about other people's.

The information, when shared in certain quarters, down at the station, had been met with sneers and scepticism. This he could take. The ribald comments, he couldn't, not on this subject, at least. Scott hadn't been privy at the time, he was suggested by the officer know to everyone as 'Dibble'. He'd been called that, so long, everyone had forgotten his real name.

" 'Scotty' will be perfect for the job," he'd said before the snigger. Now Scott was here and was about to break Pat's concentration and line of thought.

"You realise that instrument has been up someone's arse, don't you?"

"It might not be the last time, if you don't keep quiet."

"Prefer the video myself, you know where it's been."

Neither of them looked at each other. They were engrossed in their own itineraries.

"For God's sake, keep quiet, Scott, these walls are not that thick." Pat had never uttered his first name. It had been noted. 'Close' was not an adjective one would associate with Pat Ensell. 'Closed', yes, but not 'close'.

The wall he was referring to was between adjoining offices. They had rented the one next door and tried to be cute about it, but the agent knew it was the cops and suggested tripling the price for the week, "taking into consideration the risk to the good name of the block and the danger to the other tenants and any damage."

"The only danger you are in, is me coming round to your office and doing an immigration check, Pal. Got that?" The agent agreed at once to the normal rate and shook Pat's hand to conclude the bargain.

"No damage, eh? amigo."

"No damage," agreed Pat. Of course there was damage. The first job was to drill through the wall, before the neighbour came to work, but he did it behind a picture. The stain told him that it hadn't been moved for years.

"Now you know why they made you a detective," quipped Tom, but he was ignored.

The wall was made of single cinder block and below the hole, at the other side, was a spot of grey dust on the skirting. Only the occupant would know how much, but only a 'rookie' would let it worry him. The public saw shit all. Blind.

The senior detective had a positive feeling. Three minutes into today's stake, the subject had accepted a call and agreed to a third party visit, on the hour. At last, another face, but there was something on the existing face that told a story. He looked far too pleased with himself, even before he rubbed his hands together in obvious glee. The subject had shuffled the papers and placed them back in his bag. The office was spacious, with the desk backing up to their position. He couldn't quite read what the papers said, but he could see that his ears needed a de-wax. The subject went to the bathroom, off the office to the right and washed, combing his hair and taking some little time over the routine. He was a good looking guy, described by Tom as a 'pretty smart bloke', a 'looker'. He'd taken off his jacket and shirt, replacing them with a casual top, that buttoned up from the waist, all the way to the neck, but the top three buttons were left open. It was mustard colour, verging on gold. He took out a chain bracelet, that was gold, from his briefcase, a heavy, gold chain, and fastened it around his right wrist. There was a heavy gold watch on his left.

There was a knock on the door, muffled, but distinct. Pat flashed Tom an angry glance, hiseyes reminded Tom that it was possible to hear things in both directions. The game wouldhave been up, if they had been heard, because floor six was unoccupied, had been for two years. A pin dropping would have been enough. Pat was now agitated, pissed off, in fact. He knew that the public were stupid, but this man was well above average, yet stupid in other ways. Very stupid.

"Come right in," was called out, with confidence, from the target behind the desk. Another dark glance in the direction of Tom.

Now Tom was pissed off.

A man in his mid twenties, wearing a baseball cap back to front , and a heavy tan, made the first entrance, followed by a boy in his early teens, no more than fourteen, with a youthful, pale complexion. The boy looked nervous, unlike the older male who strode across the room in his tight jeans, and wiggling his bum in an exaggerated way.

"Mo, how goes?" said the 'cap'. He'd walked straight upto the target and gave him a fairly prolonged embrace. There could even have been a kiss to the cheek, but it was the cheek furthest away from them, so Pat couldn't be sure. Tom was sure. It was a kiss all right.

"Nice, very nice," said the target, theatrically keeping hold of one of the newcomer's hands, whilst looking the boy up and down. The boy didn't resist or pull away, but looked awkward.

"Tell Mo your name, boy, don't go shy on me now, remember what I told you."

"John."

"John who?" said the target. "Come on over." The boy didn't answer, but walked to the side of the desk. The target ran his fingers up the back of the boy's neck, like you would do to a cat, and pulled his head onto his shoulder giving him a single kiss to the temple. The boy didn't flinch.

"I've got things to do and people to see," said the baseball cap. "Pick you up a four, right?" looking directly at the youth and then pointing his finger right between the boy's eyes. "You behave now." He changed the pointed finger into the shape of a pistol.

"POW." he laughed. "See you later, Mo. Enjoy," and left.

Pat looked over at Tom Scott, expecting the movement to attract his attention and share a self-congratulatory moment. Tom's eyes never left the screen.

The target was back at his seat, leaning back, looking both smug and lascivious. He patted the desk next to him, whilst throwing his legs onto the desk, like Tom.

" Put your cute little self here, John, and don't be nervous." The boy was nervous. He attempted a smile. John might not have been able to read or write, but he knew when to smile, even when he was nervous. He was expecting more of what he received at the children's home. Smiling was his defence, but this time he would be paid for what was usually taken. That fact alone, made him smile and added a little realism to the gesture.

The was no sound out of the detectives. Pat was coiled, like a spring, anger welling in his stomach, his breathing was laboured, his eye glued to the 'scope. His mind jumped to the tape, hoping there was enough on it without having to change at the crucial time. It would be just his bleeding luck, he was thinking, when a movement caught his bad eye, just as he blinked it open to relieve the strain of holding it closed.

The target was moving his hand up the boy's leg, as he turned his head and looked at his partner in disbelief. He had his hand in his trousers and he certainly wasn't just re-arranging his 'Ys'.

"You fucking bastard," Pat screamed. Tom, confidant that his partner had been pre-occupied, nearly died of shock, and that was before he hit the ground. The light garden chair, supplied by the department, 'for surveillance in the field', shot from under him, leaving an impression that the occupant was paralysed and levitating both at the same time. The paralysis between his legs disappeared in a flash. Pat was on him even as he reached mother earth. Because his legs had been up on the desk, his head hit the bare boards first, leaving him dazed for the second time in a millisecond. He had no time to draw the breath that had been forced out of him before his windpipe had been closed by hands that were used to gripping the handlebars of a big machine for hours at a time. The aluminium frame of the chair had ricocheted off two walls making one dreadful row. As the grip was released, Tom let out a garbled scream, only to be instantly silenced by two blows to the mouth, in quick succession.

If the target had thought that the sixth floor had been unoccupied, he now believed that not to be the case. The boy was pushed roughly to one side as he leapt to his feet, grabbing the evidence of his presence, namely his coat and briefcase. He was across the room in a trice. John was still on the ground, the occupation level of office space had not interested him one iota and the significance of the sounds had not registered. He still might not have been able to read or write, but needed no extra coaching to realise there was something amiss. He followed the target like a hound after a rabbit.

Pat was red in the face. Tom was the same colour, except brighter. Both examples of coloration were caused by blood, but in Tom's case, it was more serious. Much more serious. His coloration was external.

For the second time, in less than a minute, Pat's peripheral vision detected an unwelcome movement. This time, it was in the glare of the hated monitor. Both sets of headphones had gone flying, but he heard the exit door of the office bang open, against the cinder block wall, and the fleeing inhabitants of the neighbouring office were just disappearing from view. It was the sight of the soles of their shoes that he would remember vividly. Pat's one saving grace, had been to pick the office on the side of the stairwell. They had to pass his door to get out and there was no lift available. The electricity to it was switched off, because the building was unoccupied above the ground floor. The hapless and panicked pair had twenty yards to cover, compared to Pat's couple of yards. It was no contest, even taking into account the fact that he was on his knees at the time. Of course, the boy really had no reason to run, it was partly habit, but panic was infectious and he'd been hit with a large dose. The front runner had every reason to flee.

When the door along corridor flew open, they were two paces from it. The sight of a filthy bearded maniac with a blood splattered face, leaping out in front of them stopped them both dead. The boy was behind the target. He was young, small and used to dodging maniacs. He took the risk, read the situation fluently and realised that waiting would not help his case. He shot forward and past Pat. He was like a whippet, extra baggage was never acquired at the sort of place John called home. He wasn't followed, even by the maniac's eyes, John was a victim, not a suspect. Pat's brown eyes were primeval in their intensity, fixed firmly on the target. There was a stand-off which lasted upwards of a minute, the only sound was the feet of the boy scampering down twelve half flights of stairs, the echoes becoming more pronounced as the descent continued and culminating in the double doors at the bottom smashing open. Tom staggered into view, framed by the doorway and his face a pulp.

That was quite enough for the target, he tried to emulate the ease with which the hound had made his escape, but here was one unlucky bunny. He was jerked back by the collar, and brought to heel to an accompanying roar. It was the roar of a mammoth, a hairy one, at that. His flailing arms were pushed up his back in one fluid movement. He acquired another pair of bracelets. This time they were not gold, they were cold steel.

"Maurice Van De Clouet, I arrest you on suspicion of child molestation and anything you say, may well be used in evidence."

It was Tom Scott's turn to spit, but his effort contained two teeth.

The target required the toilet.

Chapter Eleven

"Priscilla, It's Beatrice." Priscilla didn't have to be told. "I would like to come round and see you, this evening," she hesitated, "if that is all right?" There was still silence. Priscilla was six month's pregnant, now, and she was looking enormous. She had given Beatrice no thought at all, such was her pre-occupation with the oncoming birth, but now she was forced to focus.

"When?" was all she could think of saying, her outburst was in the past and in fact, she'd almost forgotten the reason.

"Late this afternoon, I'll not be alone, I have news for you."

"What is it?"

"Let's leave it as a surprise, should we? Four it is, then. Bye Prissy." The phone was squealing for it's return, before she replaced the handset. She was in a dilemma. She had successfully avoided everyone she knew and told no-one about her condition. In fact, her social situation had unexpectedly improved. She had met new people through being pregnant. She went for her regular check ups and relaxation classes had started. She had something in common with people, female people. It would be unkind to liken it to wartime spirit, but it was, sort of, what she felt like. She felt she had to be guarded, to avoid attack. Everyone was in the same boat, their problems were along the same lines and it was a pleasure to help one another. Hers was not the position of the young, happy, married mother to be, no there were problems now, that she couldn't share, and many more ahead. Storm clouds.

She was realistic enough to realise that she would have to face Beatrice sooner or later, but until the baby was born, she wouldn't know the father and that caused a great logistical problem. Of course, there could be problems with the birth and the baby. She shuddered at the thought and filed it as far out of reach as possible. She had become very much more fatalistic than she had ever been, and now there was an arrangement, to meet Beatrice, she welcomed the push. It was much easier than jumping.

As the afternoon drew on, far from becoming nervous, she felt more serene, she had a sense of floating, almost out of control. But, she reasoned, the position she was in, was of her own creation, the product of effort and desire. She was going through this equation of balance for the hundredth time when the door bell took her by surprise. No more preparation, this was it. She felt prepared. She wasn't. Far from it.

The first surprise was that there were two figures behind the glass, and the nearest one was her sister, her mop of blond hair was unmistakable. Judging by the size of the second figure, it was a man, but the frosted glass made identification impossible. She absorbed the physical information without mental comment. As soon as the door was open, Beatrice pushed forward and took her in her arms, giving her a tight hug, and in any other circumstance she would have accused her of doing it for effect. It was just a tiny bit too long to be natural. She was about to go down that very path. Her eyes had closed automatically as the kiss to her cheek was placed, and the mop of golden hair obscured her forward view. It was a universal reflex action, and she returned both the kiss and the squeeze in the spirit it was meant. It was quite another matter when she opened her eyes. They had been closed for but a moment. It wasn't the blue sky that was in her line of sight, it was the blue eyes and smiling face of Dalton.

"Dalton," cried out Priscilla, pushing her sister away from her but clinging onto her shoulders, using her as a shield.

"Of course, you know each other, already," said Beatrice.

"We certainly do," said Dalton, smoothly, in the nicest sense of the word. Like cream. "A year ago last October, when we had that evening at Concert Hall." Beatrice looked at his face. "Great night, wasn't it, Priscilla?" His smile revealed those perfect white teeth and the tip of his tongue, she felt passion and guilt in equal proportions, his eyes as warm and open as his demeanour. The proximity of Beatrice prevented contact. She was sure that she would have had a hug, but equally sure that he would have had a shock.

Although Priscilla was taken by surprise, she had just main-lined a litre of adrenaline and although her flushed face was out of control, her mind wasn't. He had just dug the first spade-full of his grave, he'd publicly admitted a relationship, no matter how tenuous. It wouldn't be forgotten.

"That truly was a great night, Dalton, but that wasn't the last time we met, surely?" The minute hesitation before her last word was almost imperceptible, but it might just as well have lasted an hour. It was as obvious as the timing of the hug. It had the effect, subconsciously, perhaps, of making Beatrice take Dalton's hand to lead him through. Territorial body language, for those who were fluent. It was when she tried to push past, Priscilla stepping to one side, that Beatrice's hips, in the tight camel coloured jodhpurs connected with something firm. Her brain focused her eyes on the attitude of her sister's shoulders and discounted the possibility of having connected with a hip bone. Further information could only be gathered by looking down.

"God Almighty," said Beatrice, her hands automatically reaching for her sister's stomach. Her eyes shot back up to meet a blank expression, not totally blank, but one containing more than a small amount of resignation. There was no point in claiming that, that was where she'd decided to keep all the spare household linen or saying that it was awful what ten pints of beer a day does to a women, so she just said,

"Never seen a pregnant lady before, Beatrice?" and pushed the front door closed.

Of course, Dalton wasn't privy to everything that went on in the family, and in truth, didn't know Priscilla very well. He had accompanied her to the concert, on the one occasion, but it was innocence itself. The night out had been far from a safe one, in the long term. It was what had set off the ideas in Priscilla's mind, made him one of the targets. He knew that there had been some sort of a family dispute and that this meeting was important to Beatrice, it should mend the rift. His immediate feeling now, was that everything was going wobbly.

Beatrice had held Dalton's hand long enough, the point had been made and the crisis had passed, well not passed entirely, as it happened, but certainly been over shadowed. She took Priscilla's hand instead, but Priscilla had never been comfortable with physical contact and withdrew it, using coffee as the excuse.

"Coffee, both of you? I have decaff', Dalton." She turned to the kitchen surface with it's slightly passé pine doors and took out the two jars, whilst avoiding any looks that the couple might be giving each other. It was an old conjuring trick, throwing in a comment based on information that she had picked up casually over a long period of time, as though she had come across it directly. It meant nothing to either of them at this moment. But it was logged and recorded. It would do eventually. Exhibit 'x'.

"Coffee is the last thing on my mind, Priscilla, how long have you gone already and what is more to the point, why didn't you tell us?" Beatrice was staring at the bulging abdomen of her sister, such a potent symbol of motherhood. There was something alien in it's very existence, but it was there, for all to see. She would view her sister in a different light from now on. A completely different light. It would become blinding. It was as though she had been haring along for years only to find out, at the last minute, that the tortoise was past the post. She forced down that welling feeling in her own stomach before she could have taken the next question.

"I thought you weren't interested in babies, Beatrice," said Priscilla, not being able to disguise a sneer in her voice. It didn't go unnoticed. She had carried on with the coffee preparation anyway, but cast her sister a long look over her shoulder. It was an obvious reference to her abortion and it hit home.

"That's not fair, Prissy, the circumstances were just not right."

"Well mine are."

"Who is the father?" There was a silence. Dalton had already walked to the conservatory, leaving them to it. Priscilla wondered if it was the last comment that had hastened his departure. Maybe, he hadn't known. Maybe the aborted baby had been his, but it was a scenario that would have to be thought through at a later date. The thought made her shudder.

"Well, who is the father?" she repeated. Priscilla stopped the preparation of the coffee now and turned to her sister looking her straight in the face.

"You never told me the name of the father when you were pregnant. So don't ask me now." It had just come to her, attack was the best form of defence at this point. "Still take sugar, Dalton?" she called out.

"I never take sugar, Priscilla, just a little cream," he called back. Priscilla didn't want to 'over egg the pudding', and thought it wise to throw in a diversionary error. It was better not to appear to know everything. She didn't anyway, in fact she was beginning to realise that she knew very little. The engagement was just one thing. She carried all three beakers through to the conservatory on a tray. She really didn't know who the father was yet, and had to be careful. So the irony was, that she couldn't have answered, even if she wanted. More than one smile would disappear, if she could. It didn't stop her wondering, though. When she saw his face, she realised that his last comment and his tone was an attempt to distance himself from any suspicion of intimacy, for the benefit of Beatrice. So, the game had begun.

"I believe you were going to tell me some exciting news, Beatrice. Sit down by the window, come on cats, off that seat, let Aunt Beatrice get in." The cats reluctantly moved, but only with a helping push from the back. They had known they would have to move, but they'd kept their eyes closed anyway, hoping not to rush the process. They accepted defeat and walked off stiffly, in line, toward the kitchen, Tommy giving a little jump as he went, just to show that he still had it in him, and a single flick of the tail, indicating his disapproval. Sleeping is a serious business for cats.

Dalton had put the television on to get the update on the baseball. He loved to watch sport, but preferred to participate. Winning was important, but better when it was him who was doing the winning. The volume was quite loud, as much to give the girls an illusion of not being overheard, but now they were all together, he pressed the 'mute' button, leaving just the picture and the lightest of sounds. He would still like to know the results. Beatrice had not taken the offer of the now vacant seat by the window, but had sat next to Dalton and had re-taken possession of his hand. Dalton was laid back, in every sense, not a care, he looked great, sharp, and oozed confidence, coffee in one hand and one leg crossed over the other, the navy blue deck shoes with the white leather laces and soles, contrasting with the soft yellow socks. He was relaxed. The girls were tense, but Priscilla tensed a lot more, because a split second before Priscilla spoke, she realised what she was about to announce, but it was out before the brain could override the auto-response system controlling her facial expressions.

"Dalton and I were engaged last night and we are to marry in the spring, January the 15th, to be precise."

One would have imagined her face to have gone white, but it didn't, it reddened, over laid with contortions. She thought her head would explode and was hit by a wave of nausea.

"Engaged?" It was barely audible.

"Yes, engaged, and that gives us precisely five months, on Saturday, to prepare."

"Congratulations," Priscilla whispered, hoping the tears just behind her eyes would stay where they were, but she turned away and looked out of the window, just in case. "I didn't know . . ." but she tailed off, her thoughts were racing around her head, bouncing around and crashing into each other, like a nuclear reaction about to go critical, her hand resting on her stomach automatically.

"Well we have been thinking about it for some time, and we, well Dalton, came to a decision and asked me and that was that, really."

"Some of us aren't getting any younger," he interjected, trying to brighten the proceedings, "and we'd both like children. We don't want to leave it too late, miss the boat."

"Looks like quite a family then, doesn't it?" said Priscilla in attempt to close the subject, and keep the lid on her emotions.

"We are all not getting any younger," said Beatrice. "We love each other and we both want a family." Priscilla was gripping to the arms of her chair and trying to keep a simultaneous grip on consciousness.

Through her barely focused eyes, she saw that Dalton, although smiling, was not gushing, unlike Beatrice. "So the bitch got her claws in," was what she found herself repeating under her breath. "The bitch has got her claws in."

"Looks like you've beaten us to it though, sister. I didn't know you had it in you."

Priscilla was staring past them both, her eyes transfixed, like a zombie. There was a small neat sparkle entering her peripheral vision, but she refused to focus on Beatrice's left hand.

"Well she certainly has now," Dalton said, rather crudely. The look on her face made him throw in the desperate bid to brighten up the proceedings. And then, "I think that we have been rather rude, Beatrice, it's an important time for Priscilla, never mind our plans. We need something to celebrate her good news. That's the main thing, right now," he said, leaning forward and touching her hand, as much to get her attention as to show affection. Priscilla's eyes were still fixed and she was certainly pale, there was no doubting it this time. Deathly pale.

It was Dalton who looked around, following her line of sight. Although Priscilla's eyes were vacant, they were focused on something. It was the television. There was a news break in progress, and although there was no sound, the gist of what was going on was plain to see. There was a man. Everybody would recognise him, even with unusually ruffled hair and open-necked shirt. He was plainly handcuffed, with his arms behind him, flanked and pinioned by two uniformed police officers, being helped into the back of a wagon. Fifty per cent of the words, 'Correctional Institute', were visible on the one door that was closed. The second half of the puzzle was easy to guess. He was certainly not being arrested for a traffic offence. He turned around before the one, remaining, door was slammed behind him, his tanned face looking sickly in contrast to his pearl-white, capped teeth, set between thin stark lips, frozen in a grimace where there would normally be a permanent smile. Governor Van de Clouet.

Three pairs of eyes were on the screen, but one pair was wavering, misting. The crashing sound, of cups, teaspoons and the luckless cafetiere hitting the floor, alerted the remaining pairs, to the fact that all was not well. As their heads swung around, Priscilla was hitting the floor face first, only the glancing blow of the wicker coffee table breaking her fall. Sugar, coffee and cream were her companions on the tiles, a rolling saucer playing the finale. She was well and truly out for the count and was, before she left the vertical.

Chapter Twelve

Her first conscious memory was the feeling in one hand. She was back in her childhood, the big gentle hands of her father, holding hers, while she gripped his enormous thumb. Priscilla had only ever known massive hands, she hadn't had her father long enough to catch up with his proportions. She squeezed it even now. It moved and as her brain fought to sort dreams from reality, she half opened her eyes. The problem with coming back to reality is that you engage all feelings and sensations, not just the selection of your desires, and that might include a throbbing head and blinding light. It did in this case.

The light was approaching her in horizontal waves. She'd seen it before. It was only when she rolled her head a few degrees to one side, rather than risk the muscles in her eyes, that she realised where. Those big hands were Irish and so were the eyes that were so famous for smiling. They were smiling now.

"Jacky . . . where am I?" She knew perfectly well where she was by now, but her brain still hadn't engaged logic mode, and Jacky told her so.

"You know where you are, my girl, so you do, so don't you try and say otherwise, now." The words may have been harsh but the tone was as soft as the rolling hills of Tipperary, and his smile was like the cream of that very same county. He was close to her face, she could smell it, it was familiar and she was thankful for that. She would have dearly welcomed a kiss, the kiss of a father on the forehead of innocence. Women are innocents, innocents abroad, there may be fallen angels, but they are angels, all the same.

"But how did I . . . ?" she whispered.

"Questions, questions, questions, that's all I ever get from you women. You just relax. You need a good cup of English tea. The English might know next to nothing, but they certainly know their tea, without their tea they would never have done it." If she had felt anything like normal she would have asked what, but she didn't, she didn't question anything more, just drifted to the retreating lullaby of Jacky's steps and enjoyed the sun on her face through the half opened venetian blinds at the side of that great double bed.

It could have been a minute or an hour when she sensed his presence again. He wasn't touching her hand, just sitting at the side of the bed. It was the dip in the mattress and the tightened sheet that pointed him out.

"Your tea is just right for drinking now, Priscilla. Milk and sugar?" She stirred, bringing herself to a sitting position, and screwing up her eyes against the sun-light.

"My head," she said, putting her hand to her forehead. "I don't take sugar." It wasn't a statement, it was a plea.

"You do in this case. There is something there for you to take with your tea, come on," and he passed her the mug. It was Aries, Virgo was in his hands, along with her destiny. She picked up the two tablets at the side of the bed, where the mug had stood and with her head back on the soft pillows, let them rest on her open palm whilst she gathered her strength, tea in her left hand. Raising her head to the vertical, again, she tried to focus on the two pills, but there were three shapes where there should be two. One of them was dark red. She realised what the third one was, and quickly threw the two white ones into her mouth, followed by a gulp of the sweet, milky, tea. She closed her hand to blot out that physical reminder of what had gone before. She was too slow.

"Snap," Jacky said.

"Snap what?"

He unfolded her right hand which was already back on the duvet. It was both stupid and useless to resist, an insult not to comply, and he placed his open palm next to hers. She felt like she had been caught with her sticky fingers in the sweety-jar. They were certainly sticky now, they were sweating. Her eyes were half closed, to avoid his, but she had no option other than to look down. There, in the centre of both palms, were matching scars, Priscilla's being the newest and reddest. It was both unmistakable and undeniable. He re-closed her fist with those delicate and vulnerable fingers, unpainted nails, and looked straight into her eyes.

"You are the light of my life, Priscilla Glover." And his eyes searched her face, framed by that dark shiny hair obscuring her ears, her pale bare lips. "The light of my life," he repeated.

She replied with a squeeze to his injured hand. It was enough, there was understanding.

Jacky's eyes were wet. He turned away.

"I'll leave you to get some rest, Priscilla," he was half standing, "you need it." And he meant it.

"No, wait," her voice was raised and the tone was one of anxiety. He stopped and turned back to face her. Priscilla's hands had gone under the sheets, everything felt unreal and she wanted to male sure that the baby was still there, that she hadn't dreamt the whole thing. "Is everything all right, Jacky? How did I even get here?"

"Yes everything is all right, don't worry. Your blood pressure was very high last night, probably caused by general stress. You were out for the count, that's for certain."

Priscilla was looking at her most serene, he was thinking. She was thinking that she looked all washed up. There is a vast difference between what one person thinks they ought to look like and what the partner is happy with. Of course, Jacky wasn't her partner, and she'd noticed the other side of the bed was still tidy. The tension had gone from her, she was cocooned, safe, someone had taken charge, that is what she craved at the moment, perhaps that was what she had always craved. She was back in her cradle. We are not capable of recognising and admitting our true needs, and observers usually have an agenda.

"Dalton Feinnes called me from your house and got me to call around

103

for you and bring you back here. He's quite a man." He looked the look of a puppy, searching her face.

"He just got engaged to my sister." It was what he wanted to hear.

"Anyway, I brought you here when they left. You could have taken the overnight patient room, but I took it myself. It's the first time I've slept in it, having subjected lots of others to the experience. I must say, it's given me another perspective. You don't know a room until you have slept in it. A hotel owner once told me that, but I never understood. I felt like I'd been 'committed'. There needs to be some improvements, a women's touch, perhaps. It's the nearest thing that an old Doctor like me, has to a guest room." He looked over to the blind, There were stripes of light and dark across his face. The light ones made him squint. "I hope you didn't mind?" With his eyes screwed up, she couldn't see them, but she knew where he was coming from.

"As it happens, I do mind." His eyes froze. And widened. "Have you seen the state of this nightwear? Hardly 'haute couture', now, is it?" and for the first time she smiled, weakly, but Jacky just beat her to it. He grinned. Then he exhaled.

"What time is it, anyway? I've lost all track."

"It's ten thirty and I have a patient to see any minute, the new receptionist is only a young thing and she doesn't know the first thing about impatient patients." It was as near to a quip that he could bring himself to utter, considering the subject, but it was enough of a distraction, for them both to get past the hurdle.

"Could I watch the television for a while, before I get up?"

"Of course, as long as you don't mock it". He pushed the television across the room. "One comment and I'm taking it away." It was on an old trolley from the lab. "It might not be stylish but it is practical." He laughed to himself. "Bit of an Irish arrangement. Here is the remote." He handed her the remote control and went off down the stairs. She could here him chuckling until the 'private' door, closed behind him.

Priscilla had slept well and really did feel the better for it, she'd not even dreamt. The nightmare had been before she slept. She searched the channels for the local news station, fumbling with the unfamiliar button pattern. When she found the right one, it took her by surprise. She heard the word 'Governor', looked up and Van De Clouet's drawn face filled the screen. She needn't have bothered looking for the local station. He was on every single one. She couldn't call him Maurice, even in her head, it was too personal, she didn't even know him. Now, she didn't want to. Her hands went involuntarily to her abdomen, it was swelling by the day and today had been the longest break between inspections. She was sure that she could feel the difference. It made her feel both uncomfortable and unclean, even desperate. She knew that whatever happened today, she couldn't leave here, she couldn't go home, not yet. This was another world, an institution. She needed to be away from reality, and it provided that barrier.

The phone rang. She started. It rang some more. She felt nervous. There is something in the ring of a telephone, that tells people that it is a good or a bad call. This was one of those occasions. She knew there was a receptionist on downstairs, so it must be for herself. The receptionist must have put the call through. It was at the side of the bed, so she picked it up with her left hand.

"There's a call for you," said a nice voice on the other end, with real 'trying to please', tone.

"Who is it?"

"It's a lady. She says that she is your sister, Ma'am, Beatrice."

"I'm asleep, thanks. I won't take the call, if you don't mind." It was a major lesson for reception. The phone rang again.

"I told her you were asleep, that you were fine and that you would be given the message, later."

"Lovely, thank you very much." She was a fast learner, Priscilla noted. Her thoughts went back to the television and she reinstated the volume. Her head swam, as the known details of the case were described. It included the video of the boy. There was a scruffy undercover agent, Officer Edsell, describing the events, the black and white images of the candid recording seeming to emphasise the sordidness of the whole episode. It was an 'open-shut' case, he'd been caught red-handed, confessed to many other such offences. He'd already resigned from office. The officer had no look of pleasure, just resignation. Priscilla was revolted. It is funny, that after an event, after something is pointed out, it becomes obvious. He was just too smooth, just too handsome, verging on pretty. What a fool she had been not to see it, she must have been blind, but prophesy and hindsight often go unnoticed. The rest of the State was thinking the same but as they had invested their past in this creature, she had invested her future.

There was a resignation developing within her. She was down a road where there was no turning back, it was too late for that. If he was the father, then she would have to keep the secret of it to herself. The lustre was wearing off a future that was just beginning to shine.

She tried to be positive. She shook her head. Get a grip. Then her mind drifted back to fate. Perhaps the fates were with her after all. Something had made her pick three men, perhaps, just perhaps, the fates were being kind to her and the eventualities were covered by that decision. It wouldn't be him. Then she thought of Molly. God, was this retribution? It wasn't a blasphemous use of the title, it was a direct question. She sank lower into the bed, pulling the covers up and blotting out all but the smallest of light, retreating into the security of the warmth, her own smell, her own feeling. Her fingers moved to the palm of her right hand and played over the hardening scar tissue. It could be a cigarette burn to most people, but not all, not anyone who mattered. Not to Jacky. It felt like she'd had a nail driven through her hand. Her religious upbringing had left a superstitious mantle that was hard to discard. She closed her eyes. Tightly.

"Good bye, Mrs McLachlan, now don't forget, take it easy, relax and don't worry. I'll see you next Wednesday, same time." Jacky was soft-voicing one of his clients, caressing her with his lilt. If he'd added, 'top of the morning', it wouldn't have sounded out of place. She was hanging on his every word. It was as though they, the clients, taped the conversation. His word was their law, they took in every syllable and if they ever had to repeat it, they could recite the whole lot. He had to be well on his toes, it could and often did, come right back at him. "Did you give Mrs McLachlan an appointment card?" he added, in the direction of reception, further allaying any fears or doubts in the mind of his patient. Neurosis was often part of the baggage that came with his client base, it bred in this fertile ground and was never far beneath the surface.

"Of course, Dr Jones," said the receptionist, accentuating her full glossy lips and closing her eyes for part of the sentence to reassure him. She didn't realise. She lacked the experience to know that he knew perfectly well that she had, he was just checking publicly for dramatic effect and for the benefit of Mrs McLachlan and her nerves.

He had walked her to the door, and as he arrived back at the reception desk, he was reminded of Priscilla.

"Miss Glover had a call." A pause. The receptionist was old enough and experienced enough to be interested in his reaction to the name of the woman, who was claiming to be 'still' asleep, was there when she arrived this morning, was on his patient list, because she had checked, and must be in his bed, because there was only one bed upstairs. That much she did know. The pause was as long as she dare leave it. No reaction. She looked back down at her desk. "It was her sister, Beatrice. She'll call back later. Miss Glover didn't want to take the call." She also realised that no reaction was as revealing as any reaction, but harder to pull off

Jacky knew what her game was, playing the game was inevitable, every working woman he knew participated. You couldn't stop it, any attempt would only make it worse. No, one could only hope that they tired of it. He went through the lab door and closed it firmly behind him. It wasn't slammed just closed firmly. Dee, the receptionist, knew what was meant and knew the reason, she shouldn't be nosy, she knew, but she couldn't help herself. She wouldn't change. Couldn't. Her black face covered any embarrassment, but the same skin emphasised the whiteness of her teeth as she broke into a wide grin, licked her fore-finger and marked up one point on her imaginary slate, in the air, just in front of her. A girl just had to have her pleasures.

To Jacky, it was an old story, not worth dwelling on. He had skin on his mind, but not black skin. He walked over to the fridge-freezer. It wasn't a brisk step, there was a reluctance to make the journey, short as it was. His feet were heavy. So was his heart. On the top shelf of the freezer compartment, which was almost empty, except for two containers, one, contrary to all regulations, was a half litre of ice-cream, pistachio flavour and a smaller one. It was the smaller one that he reached for, the larger one was only ever shared, but now he couldn't bring himself to throw it out, the memories were too painful.

The small one was covered in frost, but it wasn't the frost of his flasks, approaching absolute zero, it was the frost of the winter, a paltry minus three degrees centigrade, the sensation in his fingers was almost welcome after the heat of the consulting room, it nipped, but was refreshing.

He had a high chair, like a bar stool, at the bench. He dragged it over to the vicinity of the light with the bendy neck, the metal legs protesting noisily at being dragged over the tiles of the floor and flopping his bulk down onto it, heavily. He turned the opaque plastic box over in his fingers a few times, in front of the light. Putting it down, he prised off the lid, stiff and brittle, with the cold, and put it to one side. He removed the cotton pad and also placed it to one side. He rested.

It wasn't a physical rest he needed, though tiredness was what he felt. He had to think. With habitual care and slowness, born of professionalism, rather than sloth, he lifted out a pair of glass slides, held tightly together, using both thumbs and both forefingers. He lifted them higher, with the light shining from behind, and, releasing his grip with his right hand, he wiped his forefinger across the top, dislodging a thick coating of frost. He held both the slide and his right hand upto the light. There was a small, round piece of skin, perfectly preserved, between the slides. It carried none of the patterning known to the 'prints' department, at the precinct. It was certainly not from a finger. There was a solitary line crossing it. It was a mirror image of the shape of the scar on his own palm. He certainly knew where it was from, but how it got there was something he dreaded to think about.

Chapter Thirteen

It was only the strength of the wind that had both persuaded Mr Morris and allowed Mr Morris to attend work, today. It was strong, very strong, and gusty. Having arrived at work, it was against his better judgement to leave the hanger doors open. It hadn't been his decision. Luckily, it wasn't blowing straight in. It was blowing across the cavernous opening, but the tin sheets were rattling and the doors were banging, there was an awful lot of windage on doors measuring fifty feet or more in height and half as much again in width. They had sheltered a lot of aeroplanes in their time, but today, they were sheltering police officers. There was always play on the wheels that supported this type of door, but more so when they were war-time vintage, they'd stood a lot of wind, but they'd seen a lot of wind, too.

So had Mr Morris. He'd also seen a lot of air, hot air. The day before, it had been blowing in his direction. Security had brought over a scruffy son of a bitch, who he normally wouldn't have allowed in his workplace. "An untidy hanger was a dangerous hanger," was what he often stated. "That goes for the workers, too." He'd seen air accidents before, but he sure as hell wasn't going to sign his name to one. He was in charge and what licensed air mechanics said, went. And they knew it, but it was for good reasons. Aircraft were accidents waiting to happen and any deviance from professional, measured, behaviour, usually spelt trouble. Like many in this line of work, he didn't fly, himself, and that meant never. He left nothing to chance, it was his nature, that was why he was in this job. That was why he was alive and that was why he didn't fly.

He'd been asked nicely, but when he hesitated for too long, the option was withdrawn, the niceties finished. Twenty seconds was a long time for some people. The four police officers would be coming along the next day, like it or not. Alone. They wanted nobody there.

"Don't speak to anybody about this, bar none. Understand?" was what the officer had said.

"So let me get this right," he'd answered, hands in his overall pockets, "just for clarification." There was a half smirk, the expression of a man who was used to people telling him what to do, until they found out that he had the last say. "You want me to give my three men, who have a living to make and families to keep, the day off without telling them the reason?"

"Yes."

"Sounds rather difficult to me. And who will be paying?"

"The police department, will pay all the expenses."

"And I can have that in writing, in advance, can I?" said Mr Morris.

"Yes, if you don't trust your own police department."

Morris had seen too many planes take off with a promise of payment later, off into the blue yonder, never to be seen again. The boys in blue, were not going to get the chance. It was a big police department out there. One big blue was like another big blue. "I'll have to be here, of course, otherwise you won't even know how to open those big doors. Then there is the Cessna 410," he said, thumbing over his shoulder in the direction of the twin engined aeroplane behind him.

"What of it." The detective's eyes followed the direction of the thumb.

"Well, it has to be ready, after it's check tomorrow. I'm the only one who can sign it off and it's going to Denver on charter, tomorrow night. Have you any idea of the cost involved in cancelling a baby like that?" this time adding a jab to the thumbing motion. "I'll list them if you want. It'll bankrupt me and your department."

The police officer looked thoughtful, snookered. He was imagining how many video recorders that they could buy for those sort of losses.

"Anyway, if you are waiting for that old Cessna 172 to come in, your wasting your time." Morris stuck his hands even deeper into his pockets. He thumbed a couple of sockets and a spanner. The policeman wasn't sure what he was doing down there, with his fingers, but tried not to let it distract him.

"What made you think we were waiting for that plane?" The officer growled.

" 'Cos I heard that it was supposed to come back tomorrow and anyway," he paused for dramatic effect, "it is the only one out."

"Why do you say he won't be back?"

" 'Cos he's a private pilot, not commercial and there's a fucking great gale due across the whole region, that's why. He'd have to be desperate to attempt it."

"In that case," the policeman said, piercing the chief mechanic with his eyes, and pausing himself, sensing that he was back on the high ground, "he'll be back. Tell your blokes they have the day off and we'll see you nine am., sharp." He turned on his heals, in the direction of the security block, but looked over his shoulder. "The name is Edsell, Detective Pat Edsell, I'll bring your letter with me in the morning." Mr Morris had thought that that was the end of it, but he'd turned again. "Thanks."

So here they all were. There were four of them, dressed in company overalls, hanging around and drinking tea. Mr Morris, (he insisted on being called that to the point where nobody even new of, let alone thought of, his Christian name) chuckled to himself, in that airforce-lower-echelon, getting one over the officer way, that had given the ranks years of pleasure. It was a habit that he had brought to civvy street with him. The business was low on work and he was happy to lay the men off for the day. He actually thought that it would turn into two days, because of the weather. It was far too dangerous to land a light plane in these gusts and he knew Michael Stevenson well, he flew safely, for pleasure, not to break his neck or the aircraft. He also knew that he was at a small farm strip and had been, for two nights, that he had gone alone and was staying with friends. Interest by the police department was beyond him. Mike was as law abiding as he was unassuming. It would give the old git a fright though, and he chuckled at the thought of it. The wind wasn't as bad there, it was one hundred nautical miles away and he'd checked the direction, it was straight down the runway. He could easily have called the owner of the strip, he knew him well, but he had been warned not too. He had to partially satisfy himself with listening in on the airband radio, tower frequency. This in itself was not unusual, but the volume was, it was on high. Background was the norm. He didn't want to miss anything when he had his head buried in the fuselage of the '410.

Of course, you wouldn't have known the radio was on, and the officers, who were totally bored, didn't. It hadn't made a peep, because there was no traffic, nobody was flying. Apart from odd charter stuff, everything was private, for pleasure, and today's weather didn't fall anywhere near that category. The tower knew virtually nothing, except that they were required to clear the Cessna 172 directly to the hanger and nowhere else.

Pat Edsell, was the only one showing interest. He kept going to the open doors and looking up at the sky. Morris could see that they were well armed, and he'd been told to leave the hanger by the side door, and retreat to the security block, if the plane was spotted. They kept having little meetings and running over strategy, speaking in low voices, but it was all in vain, hangers have acoustics all of their own. It's difficult to keep secrets in this environment.

They had been studying photographs of two men. One of them was Michael, Morris had verified it and they had marked this photo with a fluorescent pen. "Don't forget, this man is not a target, get that into your thick heads," was what Edsell kept repeating. A study in management style. It was like being back in the forces for Morris, he'd heard this tone before. Oh yeah, just a few times. "Scott, you take the left side with Big Jim, Steve you stay here with me."

Tom Scott was still simmering since the attack on him. It didn't go unnoticed that Pat Edsell only called him by his last name. There was no love lost in either direction. The only piece of luck had been that Pat had kept the incident to himself. His colleagues thought that his facial injuries had been received in the line of duty. It had in a way, but only in the course of duty. Subtle difference. Ironically, his reluctance to talk about the issue had worked to his credit, the Force thought that he was just being modest, and thought the more of him for it.

Tom Scott was feeling nervous. He had good reason. Pat had picked up on it, because he was tuned in to that sort of thing, but that was what made him so good, a natural. That was what kept him alive.

It was two in the afternoon, patches of sun, blobs of cloud, wind gusty, averaging forty five knots, when the radio screamed into life.

"Good afternoon, Approach, this is November two double four, inbound to you from Kent's Farm. I'd like to join downwind for runway zero nine." It had made everybody jump, including Mr Morris.

"Quick Morris, out. Get to your positions everyone and apart from Stevie, keep out of sight."

"He might sound like he's almost up your butt, Officer, but he is still twenty miles away, he'll be five minutes yet, ten before he's taxied." It was that measured drawl that made the 'boys in blue', feel a little silly.

"Right," was all that Pat could think of saying.

"November Two Double Four, cleared to join downwind. Call short finals for zero nine. Be warned that the wind is gusting forty six knots, at two seven zero." There was a pause from the radio. The policemen looked at Mr Morris. He'd been wrong about their arrival, and this was his environment, so he certainly wasn't going to commit himself to the luxury of a facial expression and a possible double fault.

"It's marginal, but straight down the runway. Will call finals," replied the pilot. " If you could give me the local gusts on the way down, I would appreciate it."

"Roger." The hanger could here both sides of the conversation.

Steve was standing around at the back of the hanger, trying to look busy. There had to be some sign of a worker there. Morris had reluctantly left. His parting statement had been a warning of the expensive nature of the hardware and bullet holes came in millions of dollars. The ignition of Avgas came in single 'booms'.

Big Jim was hiding behind the hanger door, opposite side to Pat. Tom

Scott was out of the side door, behind oil drums, covering the route to the car. It had been his idea.

They had heard the aircraft call finals, the wings were bouncing and it hung in the air, like a vulture, fighting against the gusty onslaught. Groundspeed was minimal, but airspeed was high, to cover gusts and wind-shear.

In the aircraft, Mike Stevenson was hot. It was anxiety, not solar activity. He'd flown back, against his better judgement. Getting home at all cost was a disease, often fatal once contracted. There was a better forecast for late evening and if not, certainly in the morning. He'd accepted a cash payment for the flight, which was illegal, but he had taken it anyway, aeroplanes were expensive toys. The money had clouded his judgement and he'd persuaded himself that he could manage, and anyway, his passenger was a powerful man, in every sense. It was difficult to say no. The passenger had not threatened him, but he didn't want to give him cause. He was wishing that he hadn't got involved.

Everything had gone not too badly, it was bumpy, admittedly, his mind had been on the flying, but his passenger was hanging on and looking increasingly nervous. It wasn't a massive runway, concrete, but plenty of room against this wind. He didn't put down the flaps, they were going slow enough, in fact he kept on a little power as they sank to the ground, coupled with added speed, insurance against a rogue gust. Wind sheer was an invisible killer, but they landed, main wheels first, with a tiny squeak from the tyres. Far from needing to use the brakes, he needed power to taxi forward against the howling elements.

"November Two Double Four, you have landed at two thirty-five, cleared taxi directly to the hanger," said the Tower. Both occupants of the plane heard it clearly through the headphones.

"Negative, Tower, I would like to taxi for fuel." Mike was conscientious and always left the aircraft topped up with fuel, avoiding condensation in the tanks, and in preparation for the next flight.

"Negative. Two double Four. Fuel not available, at this time. Please proceed to hanger."

"Shit," Mike said and gunned the engine for the other end of the runway, before turning off to the left and the hanger, the nose dipping slightly as the accelerated prop dug the blustery air. The passenger had suffered in silence. He was agitated, he didn't like anything that he felt was not normal. Too much was at stake. Three kilos of heroin attached to his body, and his freedom were but two of them.

They turned off the main runway, the wings rocking as they moved across the wind, reminding them both that they were not home yet. It was only thirty yards and Mike started to turn the aircraft, with a burst of power, and a poke at the brakes, into wind, for safe parking. A mechanic was working at the bench. Mike saw him and had just begun to say that he had never seen the guy before, when the passenger noticed movement outside. Another mechanic at the side door.

"It's fucking Tom, fucking Scott," he shouted down the microphone, nearly taking out the pilots eardrums. The aircraft was still rolling, in a turn. Stevenson had never even heard of Tom Scott, but the tone and the volume told him all he needed. "Fucking get out of here, move it. Move it," he screamed. Mike instinctively fire-walled the throttle, and carried on the turn, locking the starboard wheel and leaving a black smudge of rubber. "Back to the runway. Now." More screaming.

Pat couldn't believe his eyes, or his ears. The aircraft was fuel injected, with a variable pitch prop. It made a lot of noise. It wasn't the sort of thing to approach without caution, being fitted with the equivalent of the biggest mincer he'd ever been near.

It was as the machine burst into life, that he caught sight of Tom Scott, in the reflection of the perspex canopy, standing around the corner in full view, both arms raised. Pat was raging. Murderous. His screaming outburst of profanity was blood curdling as he ran forward, but it was to no avail. It was accelerating away. He couldn't fire his weapon, the occupants were too close together. He turned and ran back towards the car, Jim and Stevie in hot pursuit. Scott had caught Pat's eye in the reflection and knew that the game was up. He didn't follow. His face still ached. His balls made up the duo.

When November Two Double Four reached the runway, all was confusion, aboard. Mike was deeply regretting his involvement. From where he was sitting, the money was beginning to loose it's appeal. Fuel wasn't that expensive after all. The tower was protesting. Loudly.

"Take off. Go. Get this fucker moving," the passenger was shouting.

"I need to go to the other end of the runway, we can't take off down-wind," protested the pilot.

"Fuck the rules, there's no time."

Mike turned to look at his crazed passenger, but found that he was looking down the barrel of a colt 45. This time it was registered to the man in possession.

"Go, or I'll blow you away." Mike knew that he meant it. Now it was far, far from his better judgement. Take-off was never down wind, let alone down-gale. It was a lot more than just rules of the aerodrome, they were rules of physics. Aeroplanes need airspeed for take-off, not ground speed, but ground speed was what they had in plenty. They quickly accelerated and were racing along before the airspeed indicator left the stops.

They were doing almost a hundred miles an hour and they were still on the ground. The undercarriage was not happy. Neither was the pilot. Only the undercaraige had the courage to protest. The end of the runway was looming, the Tower could see that, Morris could see that, even the non flying passenger could see it.

"Pull up, get us in the fucking air," screamed the passenger. They were eating concrete, gobbling up the runway at a sickening rate. It couldn't continue. It was Mike's only option, now. They'd passed the stripes at the end. The hedge and the landing lights were careering toward them. He yanked at the yoke. It was an act of desperation and futility. It was dual controls, the passenger did likewise, all the way back. The nose wheel lifted, the stall warning sounded like the horn from hell and slam. Straight into the hedge. The propeller bit wood and crunched aluminium. One blade parted, scything viciously through the air. Perspex turned to shrapnel. The undercarriage remained on the airfield and the aeroplane cartwheeled, losing one wing on the second bounce. They stopped in the direction that they had come from, but inverted, hanging in their straps. Somebody's blood was all over the screen, the smell of the red liquid quickly being over-powered by the stink of fuel. They were both alive. The silent aftermath of an aeroplane crash is deafening. The pilot was groaning but not moving. The passenger undid his belt and dropped to the ceiling, kicking wildly at the side window. It gave. He scrambled out to the area where there should have been a wing. Screams of pain were suppressed by shock and fear. He bounced off the crumpled wing-strut, pushing bone into muscle and sprinted away from the wreck, like a drunken man, his right arm broken and hanging uselessly, unintentionally waving a last farewell to the hapless pilot, as he covered the distance to relative safety.

Pat also had two terrified passengers at the end of the runway, heading for the same hedge, similar speed, but they knew better than to make a sound. 'Ninety miles an hour, girl, is the speed I drive', Jimi Hendrix, went through his mind. It was ridiculous. Their teeth were clenched tightly together and their vision blurred, as his car ploughed through what was left of the arrangement, bouncing the occupants around violently, but when they left the car, it was upright and in one piece. He rolled out of the car. It was still moving. A tackle to the legs stopped the fugitive in his tracks at the exact same time as the promised 'boom'. They were thirty yards from the plane as it erupted. They were singed, but not fried. Stevenson had no chance. He was toast. The other two detectives arrived, panting, a mixture of fear and exhaustion, as Pat shouted, at the screaming mince meat beneath him. "You're nicked, you bastard."

By the time the ambulance and fire-crew arrived, the heroin, twenty thousand dollars and a very expensive Rolex were taken as evidence.

"You really fucked up there, Ian," Pat said. "So did Scotty."

Chapter Fourteen

Dr Jones was beginning to think that he was becoming too reliant on Priscilla. Priscilla was becoming too reliant on him. Admittedly, they hadn't had sex since the first time, but Priscilla discounted that event, anyway. Jacky was no stranger to celibacy. It had been her first time. She was forty and it should have been momentous, but it wasn't. That was the funny thing. There is always so much gossip, speculation, dreaming about the subject, that results in the anticipation overshadowing the event. By the time you have reached forty, there are plenty of dreams behind you. The event itself is spoiled by anxiety and inexperience, sex is an art, an art that needs to be practised. Natural ability is but a small part.

The psychological impact is usually the greater, but in Priscilla's case, this was again overshadowed, overshadowed by the decision to have a baby. The sex had begun with the procurement and ended with the deposit. The planning had been the foreplay and the insemination was the climax. She had always been a cold woman. No, she'd already had sex. Jacky had been her fourth time.

It was in the emotional arena that she had been virginal. Until that evening, with Jacky, she'd never let herself go, never opened, the pressure had been building, but now it was out. Opening her heart had been more difficult than opening her legs. She had imagined the two to be connected, but they weren't. She was in a difficult situation and so was Jacky. She knew that in two weeks, she was due to give birth to a child and that child was a boy. What she didn't know, was the identity of the father. There had been several times when her enthusiasm had wavered. She could choose not to reveal the identity of the father and live the life of a single mother. It was no longer socially unacceptable and she could live with that. There was a financial crisis looming, though, and the resolution of that, had always been part of the plan, though it's importance was now waning.

What was still important to her, and it burnt within, was the way that she despised Beatrice. Far from her sister mellowing, concentrating on her own future and being supportive to Priscilla, she was getting worse. There had, apparently, been many attempts to conceive, with Dalton, but it hadn't come to pass. Priscilla had preferred to 'pass', on the details. They were engaged, but plans to be married were far from secure. The only concern came from the direction of Dalton, himself.

There had never been as many flowers in the house. Dalton never visited without them, but never visited without Beatrice, either. The question about the father was never raised but she could feel that it was just below the surface. It was this very question that kept Jacky at bay. Jacky never visited the house and never would, his imagination was too fertile for that. He was of Irish descent and jealousy came with that baggage. Priscilla's capacity to put things to the back of her mind was her saving grace. That awful business with the ex-Governor, Van De Clouet was ever present. The television just wouldn't let up and the trial was not far away. Legal machinations were slowing the process, but this man was slippery and had friends in high places, friends who might not want their own social preferences scrutinised too closely.

What turn would her life take if the father was Kenichi Kumamoto, two brains and two fortunes? Her dreams often took her to the East.

What about Dalton? The fan would be hit squarely, and that's for sure. She did like him very much, but Beatrice knew that. It was instinctive. She tried to distance herself, the opposite to her historical conduct, but he was not deterred. Perhaps, in the past she had looked too desperate, now she was trying to remain aloof, and she could feel the change in the attitudes towards her, now she had done something and she was interesting, a lady of mystery.

Jacky had just been on the phone, asking her how she was. It gave him a good excuse to call, but his concern was genuine and she welcomed the calls, she'd had to cut him short, though, on this occasion, because her sister and Dalton were due at any minute.

The hand-set was no sooner down than the door bell sounded. The phone she was using, was in the hall, so she only had to turn and the door was in view. There was only one person there. It was Dalton, she could tell. The broad shoulders were his signature. It was more difficult to move quickly, now that she was such a size. Her front was round, the loose dress hanging vertically from her bust, which was swollen in proportion, stark reminders of her femininity. Even Beatrice couldn't ignore them, now, those engorged nipples pointed accusingly at her, an ever-present reminder of her failure to conceive and the guilt of her abortion.

"Hello, Dalton, where's Beatrice?" was the immediate question. It was the first time that she had been alone with Dalton in almost a year.

"She'll be along in a while. She had to go down to the studio, a photo shoot went belly-up." The reference hadn't been intended and he rolled his eyes when he realised what he had said. Priscilla had both hands cupping her swollen abdomen, elbows out at right angles. She couldn't decide whether the comment had been intentional or not, it had probably erupted spontaneously from his sub-conscious. He kissed her on the cheek, flowers appearing from behind at the same moment.

God, he was smooth, adorable.

"Thanks, Dalton." Suppressing a beam was impossible. "Coffee?"

"Yes, please, but it's not something that you should be drinking, he'll kick you to death with all that caffeine." He emphasised the word 'you', his eyes on her midriff. He touched her distended form, something that he had never done before. She was also touched, by his concern.

"I'm having fruit juice, he's been kicking all night."

God, she felt relaxed in his company.

She followed him through to the conservatory. She wanted to be the observer, she'd always liked the view of him from behind. Her own bottom felt enormous. His was tight. She revelled in the wake of his pheromones.

She rattled away at the coffee preparation, whilst he read the newspaper. It always impressed him, the way she had the Financial Times and the Wall Street Journal, at hand. They were always well-thumbed. He noticed details like that. Beatrice never read. Period. He had both papers himself, but for very different reasons. Kenichi Kumamoto meant very little to Dalton.

"They caught the guy who broke into my house and assaulted me and that girl, Sarah." His eyes were running down the page. The Japanese were buying another studio, perhaps his would be next, he thought, and he could retire to the pleasures of life. There was silence from the kitchen. "I even got my wristwatch back," he called out. Still silence. He walked through towards the kitchen, to show her.

"Look," and held it out. She was still holding her stomach, but bent over. "Priscilla, are you all right?" he asked, but she was obviously not. There was no sound from her. Her eyes were closed. He helped her to the conservatory and the sofa. She dropped back, stiffly. It was the first time that he'd touched her legs, but he hoisted them up, a cushion under her knees.

Her eyes were still closed, one hand rubbing her forehead. "Are you OK?" She shook her head, and took deep breaths, her head back, face contorted.

He was used to making decisions at work, dealing with everything from broken equipment to broken hearts, but this was different.

"Where's the number for the hospital, Priscilla? I'm going to call them." There was still no answer. His voice wasn't raised by an octave, but certainly a couple of tones. He'd no idea where to look, who was looking after her or which hospital. Nine-one-one. His finger jabbed out the number on the phone keys and wiped a bead of perspiration from one temple.

It seemed like an hour before the ambulance arrived, although it was less than ten minutes. Priscilla never said a word, her fingers were gripped tightly around his own and her eyes were screwed. She looked so vulnerable which was exactly how he felt. It never entered his head to call Beatrice. Now he was sweating.

When the ambulance arrived he let the two men in. They took one look and made a call. The bed was booked. 'Birth imminent', sounded a little dramatic. Dalton was surprised to find himself bundled into the back of the ambulance. The speed at which they set off put the drama in perspective. She still refused to speak, or at least, refused to acknowledge questions, nor did she open her eyes. He could tell that they were assuming that he was the father, and fired questions at him in search of her details. He felt that it was politic not to say anything about the father.

Priscilla might not be speaking, but she was surely hearing, and when the subject was raised, any mention of the word 'father', the pressure increased on her grip of his hand. Substantially.

By the time they had reached hospital, her waters had broken and she was on a weak mixture of oxygen. It had developed into some kind of nightmare, with spasms of pain making her cry out. Dalton was as hot as she was, there was perspiration running down the pair of them. Dalton's shirt was sticking to his back. Both occupants were white as ghosts. The medic looked like he was on a his weekly shopping run, he didn't exactly stifle a yawn, but Dalton wouldn't have been surprised if he had done. Priscilla didn't notice. This was one part of the operation that she had never considered. The birth had been something well into the future, it was an abstract concept, even the swelling had not alerted her to the inevitable realities of what goes in, must come out. She'd had two weeks more to lodge it in the back of her mind, but now it had come tumbling forward. Like it or not, and she didn't, she was pushing. Divine retribution revolved around her head again, punishment and guilt intertwining like a serpent from hell, and wrenching at her guts.

Having a siren, scream just above their heads didn't add to the calm, the only useful purpose seemed to be that when it stopped, they knew they had arrived. The back flew open and she was lifted out. His hand was in a clamp. He was obliged to follow, and raced along the corridor like some sort of cheap television drama. It was the nurse who prised her fingers from his, and suggested that he step behind the screens for a moment whilst the doctor checked the baby's position. He did more than that, he stepped out of the room for some air. The shock, the warm air and that horrible antiseptic smell was making his head spin in the opposite direction to his stomach. Even out here with the heavy door closed behind him, he could hear the commotion, and he was thankful for the plastic cup of tea that was thrust into his hand, from God knew where, and by God knows who.

He was breathing deeply and doing it in the direction of his tea, partly to cool the same and partly to re-oxygenate his brain cells, when the nurse re-appeared and told him that he had better come back in. It was more of a command than a request, and he obeyed. Hospitals have that effect.

"Leave the tea outside, if you don't mind, Sir," was all the consideration he got. It was still an order. He chose to swig it down, cooled or not. It was a token protest, but all that he could manage. His throat was screaming it's objection to the savage assault when he followed the nurse back in, who was impatiently holding the door ajar. Protest registered by the nurse, protest registered by the throat.

He was met by more screaming. It was disbelief that knocked him. The screams were high pitched and feeble, yet earnest. They came from a half-finished bundle at the side of the bed, with a red face and closed eyes, red gums and the tiniest tongue that he had ever seen. The nurse was completing the job and her grin was one of real pleasure, no boredom here, it was labour of love. Priscilla's wasn't as pronounced, but every bit as sincere. Everyone in the room, and even those who popped into the room, were at it. He joined them. Evidently, grinning was infectious at times like this. Ninety per cent of parent bonding takes place in the first few minutes, and the man of the world, committed bachelor, lover, simply could not hold back the first tears since his childhood. It's the men that cry at a time like this, but it was spotted by Priscilla who held out both hands and they were taken. At last, she was not alone. That would never be the case. Never.

The bundle was finished, as tight as tight can be, squeaky clean hospital cotton holding the arms, drawing comfort from his new womb. The baby's head turning and searching, it was a new world and he was eager to discover. The whereabouts of warm milk would have been his first choice.

"Would you like to take the baby now, Mrs Glover?" the midwife said. 'Mrs', was a term they always used, rightly or wrongly, correctly or incorrectly. There was an obsession with forced bonding and bonding with a title was part of that system. It was what they passionately believed in. It was their religion and they were the disciples, missionaries, and their mission was to convert. There was no place for a 'Miss', in their Kingdom.

Priscilla struggled to get up onto her elbows, grimacing slightly at her discomfort. Ian flashed through her mind. She almost fell back. She needed a hand. The infant was thrust into Dalton's hands. He was taken by surprise, was awkward, it was overwhelming and he could feel the warmth from the baby's back coming through the soft blanket. The boy's head was twisting this way and that. He was also surprised by the strength and determination of the mite.

The door opened behind him.

"Priscilla." Priscilla's eyes went to the door, out of Dalton's line of vision. He couldn't turn quickly, he'd been charged with the care of something most fragile and precious.

"How are you? I came as soon as I heard, from the studio." Beatrice was going to push past Dalton and rush to the bed. She'd taken three of the five paces necessary to reach her goal before the realisation struck her. There was a white bundle that Dalton was holding. For a moment, she hesitated, then recovered.

"Priscilla. You've only been out of the house an hour. I never imagined. Nobody told me." Beatrice was caught by the infection. It might have been weaker, but she smiled anyway.

"Isn't he just the greatest," said Dalton. His grin reached both ears and his face was as red as the charge in his arms. Beatrice was recovering quickly.

Chapter Fifteen

Kenichi Kumamoto was known to his immediate colleagues as the 'Motor'. He'd liked the title at first. It set him apart. But standing out was not the natural way. He was Japanese and that meant group action, not personal idolatry. The international market of futures and derivatives demanded decisiveness, quick reaction, individual thoughts, yet retaining the group effort. Herein lay the paradox. It also demanded, within that elite band, something to aspire to. The pack needed to believe that there was a way through the wilderness, someone to follow, a star. Kumamoto was that unlikely person, or, at least that's what he had become.

Amongst the ranks of accountants and number-crunchers, the people who worked the trends, he stood head and shoulders above the braying mob, for that is what they were.

He was good looking, slightly taller than normal and quite young. His most impressive attribute though, and this was where it counted, were his results. He bucked the trends and bucking the trends was the only way. It was a crowded path they trod, but well trodden it was. New routes were hard to find and dangerous. Extremely dangerous.

He rarely joined the others, after hours, in the Kareoke bars and restaurants, drinking sake and singing loudly until the early hours. He worked on. He stayed, whilst the others were out playing. They were the ones who were bonding, swapping stories of triumph and failure. Failure wasn't something that he was associated with. The word never passed his lips, and the longer it didn't reach the ears of everyone on the floor, the more unassailable his position became. At the same time, though, failure was a thing to be feared and he felt that a fall would have been fatal. He was much too high for that.

There were failures, of course, but only he knew of them. They certainly weren't acknowledged. His inscrutability, in the face of disaster, was the stuff of Eastern legends. He recognised the pathetic futility of sharing problems in the hope of sympathy, sympathy which might somehow bring forgiveness. This was an unforgiving environment. Totally. He was approaching the status of deity.

Gods don't sweat. This particular afternoon, he was hot. Very hot. He was also sweating, not perspiring. He could feel it running across the olive-tan skin of his lower back, where the white, summer vest failed to make contact. It was Friday and there were twenty minutes to go before the floor closed.

Tokyo was sweltering in the summer heat, that approached ninety per cent humidity. A casual visitor to the Exchange would not have noticed it, the air conditioning would have seen to that. But everybody here was hot. Kumamoto was the hottest. He had no idea how he had reached Friday, let alone the afternoon. Nineteen minutes to go. A feeling of fatalism was creeping over him. That, and panic. He must hold on. He could feel the eyes of everyone else glancing over at him, stripping him, raping him, he was being abused big time by that male hoard. It was his own fault. It was a set-up. Success, in this business, was at the expense of others. He had been massively successful.

There were managers in the back offices of every company registered on the exchange demanding to know why their men were not able to compete at the same level. They all demanded, but not one of them analysed the reason. They looked only at the results. Even his parent company didn't. They were fat cats getting fatter. Cats don't concern themselves with the origin of the cream. Their sights were focused on the man who delivered it.

The markets had been steadily rising for almost the last ten years, since the last levelling. It was only the dealers who refereed to it as levelling. The investors didn't. Levelling meant a clean slate, to dealers, whereas levelling represented losses to investors, that would include many who would lose everything. In Japan, that could include your life.

There were those in the back office that were sceptical, and, to be fair, did ask questions, but those who were above the back office, linked only by a fibre optic, did not want the 'Motor' to slow down, let alone, stop. The opinions of the sceptics were frozen out and ignored. The 'Motor' was dictating the market and dictators have never been good people to argue with.

Dictating the market had indeed been what Kumamoto had been doing. That he was very bright and gifted was undeniable. He had proved it over the last ten years. He was gifted with around the same proportion of honesty as the next man. He was also secretive, which in itself, wasn't a bad thing, but add in a pinch of slyness and manipulation and a dangerous situation was developing. He was not the instigator of the predicament, but nor was he the master. No, it fed on him. It was a predator. Darkness was closing in. Judgement was giving way to fortune and gambling is indeed a dark monster.

All the world markets are inter-related and it is impossible for one man or one institution to affect them very much. Market manipulation is the Holy Grail. Kumamoto's big gains were built on solid foundation, following the previous fall, or levelling, a decade ago. He had been clever and analytical, patient . . . lucky. This success elevated him, he was the hero of the day. He liked it. Face was important to him and what had started as basically an accountant's job, had now become glamorous. He was the toast of the floor. When the markets levelled again, last year, his star should have faded, but he missed the bright lights. He went out on a limb, buying more than he should. It was on impulse.

He had spent all weekend, carrying over his purchases, vomiting several times in his single roomed flat on the outskirts of Tokyo, whilst he waited for the market to open on the Monday. His abdominal muscles pushed on an empty stomach that craved no food. A sudden surge of the Dow-Jones in New York made the difference, and he couldn't wait to get back in before the bubble popped. His only luxury, apart from his futon, was his computer console in the Spartan room. Sitting cross-legged on the 'tatami', in front of it, he prayed that it wouldn't change and stayed on-line for the duration.

Behind him, was the ochre and black altar-box of his father and his father before him. Incense didn't burn this weekend. Photos of them both stood beneath the Samurai sword that they had both carried into their separate battles. The battles had been in different arenas, but for the same cause, the Emperor. Both had died with it in their possession. The ten thousand-ply steel blade with it's hard edge and softer shank, were hidden behind a sheath of bamboo and ivory. It's exact position on the wall being far from accidental. It had been the subject of long and serious deliberation. His father's side-arm was secreted in the drawer below, pushed to the back. It had been invaluable in the field, but could never be a substitute. His back was turned. Prayer was not in this direction. This weekend, his alter was his console.

The receipts to the transactions were in another drawer, the drawer at the Exchange. His lucky drawer. The company rules were that everything had to be accounted at the end of the day's trading. A big party was on. His floor manager had been waiting to get away to that party. He had a drink problem.

"Give me the fuckers on Monday . . ." or the Japanese equivalent, was how it was left, when they weren't forthcoming, ". . . Mr Kumamoto." It was a curious mix of abuse and politeness, that the West would never fathom. He bowed when he left.

When Monday arrived, he went straight in with a small purchase, to cover his tracks then he sold with a massive gain. It was the biggest gain in one day, the company had ever had. He worked the market for the rest of the day, buying and selling in a declining market that was finding it's own level after the surge. Because he had bought before the weekend, and, consequently, before the surge, he was the only one on the crest. He'd caught the seventh wave. When the receipts were added, he felt nervous. They were checked. He knew about the gain but was more worried that he would be found out about his weekend dalliance. 'Holding over', was strictly against the rules of the company and the rules of the House. This was his first and fatal lesson. Had he been caught now, a reprimand would have blocked his path, but only a reprimand. They were blinded by the success. They looked only at the results. He was now the golden goose. The mother of all parties followed. He was exhausted by the ordeal, and his reticence was mistaken for modesty, he didn't join the celebrations, but returned to his desk. The company, and his bosses liked that. He'd risen without overshadowing, a difficult thing to achieve. Face was secured all round. From that day, whatever he said was accepted, and whatever he did was followed. It was a great and awful position to be in. He knew that it was wrong. He began to believe in his own myth.

He began to hide his receipts again, just pushing them to the back of his drawer. Discovery was a matter of how many inches the drawer was withdrawn. As simple as that. He opened a ghost account to hide his losses. Computers reveal everything, but you do need to look. A flock is always the easiest place to hide. Kenichi revealed only his gains. He was way past the point of no return, now.

One bunch of stock had been ignored by everybody on the floor. He started to buy. It was a desperate throw of the dice. He stood up and bought everything he could at speed. It started a wave of panic, others following where he had gone, desperate not to miss out. The screen flickered up the price. It was nudged higher and higher. Then he started to sell. Wham. He sold several blocks, but his high profile in buying on the way up, hindered him on the way down. He was competing in a mass of waving arms and screaming voices. It bottomed lower than when he had started. The market closed. It had been noticed by the top office.

The floor manager had been recently sent from Osaka. He'd arrived when the 'Motor' was running at full speed. He was already a legend. The new boy, who was out of his depth anyway, was unable to keep up. Even if he had the hours in the day and the understanding to unravel a mass of complicated transactions bought and sold around the globe he would have found it difficult. He just looked at the results. Ironically, the 'end' was the easiest point at which to start, it was clearer, it was the 'bottom line'. The 'Motor' would have stalled there and then, but he extracted his losses and just showed the gains. Even a cursory check would have revealed the truth, but the bottom line always shines brightest. His drawer was never fully opened.

His losses, in the secret account were now colossal, and trading out was making matters worse. He was attempting the old gamblers trick of 'doubling up', hoping for a break, but it was running away from him.

Interest on the account was running at millions of Yen per day. This was someone else with a large cavity at the back of his mind, but it was filling up fast. When he was forced to smile, it was thinly. His undeclared receipts were so numerous that he even threw some away. His drawer was bursting with them. There was no way that the position would ever come good, he knew that. It was just a matter of time. It was as though he wished to be caught. Even cleaners knew that pink receipts weren't supposed to be in the bin.

There were some things that the new manager from Osaka didn't understand. The discrepancy in funds drawn and funds returned was enormous. Millions of Yen couldn't be a mistake, he obviously didn't understand the system here, and that worried him. If he couldn't understand the simplest of concepts, then what else would he not know at the balance at the end of the month. His future was on the line. Fifteen minutes to go before the end of trading. He needed very deep breaths before he could pick up the phone and disturb Mr Kumamoto. The question would reveal his own lack of competence, but it had to be done. He was in possession of the dilemma of his life. He could see Kenichi at his desk, down below, in the pit. He was engaged on two telephones at the same time, alternating between sitting and standing, shouting and listening. Syoko trembled, he imagined every call to be worth hundreds of thousands of Yen and his call would cost the company in the region of those amounts, perhaps as much as his year's salary. The 'Motor' was never disturbed. In reality, his call would be saving the company that money, not costing it.

He dialled the number. Two seven two. He was in the queuing system. The red light on his desk was flashing, to indicate the incoming call and Kenichi glanced at it. It was Mr Ryu's turn to sweat. His arm was shaking as he held the phone to his ear, waiting.

"Yes." It wasn't even a question.

"Moshi moshi," was the greeting for a phone conversation. "It's Mr Ryu." There was a pause. "Syoko Ryu." That didn't help, the pause continued, the 'Motor' had never heard of such a lowly worker, so adding his first name was a complete waste. Stupid.

Kenichi Kumamoto knew at that instant the game was up. He looked up from the pit and their eyes met. Both pairs contained fear, but the polarity was different. The 'new-boy' had to say something, admit his lack of understanding.

"I don't understand the balance system between company accounts and this account, nine eight nine". The light was flashing for more incoming calls. It made Mr Ryu very uncomfortable. His stupid question could be costing the company millions of Yen when there was only fifteen minutes to go before the Floor closed. It could also be saving billions.

"We'll talk on Monday, before the Market opens. I'll explain then".

It would have been very impolite to argue and anyway, the line was dead. He'd been dismissed. But he had, after all, spoken to God. The 'Motor', had already turned away and had accepted further calls. His actions had been seamless. Mr Ryu was in the firing line, now. His questions had better be good ones. He would work on, tonight. He wasn't in the mood for singing. He had all weekend to understand . . and worry.

When the bell rang for the close of business, Kenichi Kumamoto congratulated himself. He'd not been sick on his console. His stomach might be screaming but at least it was still intact. He left his jacket over the chair and walked straight out. There was no point in playing out the last act. Making up the day's balance was just one fucking waste of time. He went straight back to his flat. Now, time was going quickly. The subway ride was over in an instant. It was full but he noticed no-one. The pretty secretaries with their sleepy eyes and shiny, black hair, were invisible, at best a blur.

Even before he could get the key in the lock, he could hear the telephone ringing. Aggravated by the sound as he was, he still took off his shoes before entering, untying them and placing them neatly in the direction of the outer door in readiness for his departure. He realised the futility of the act. It wasn't habit, it was more than that. It was the way of things. The natural order. He changed into his kimono, which used to belong to his father, ignoring the persistence of the phone. The firmness of the tatami floor with it's tightly woven strands of reed, the smell of the Old World, the Old Order rising from it, made him think of his ancestral past.

Flight, a prison in Germany, incarceration and family shame wasn't his way. With great deliberation he took the sword from the wall. He rested it across his knees, whilst he adjusted the position of the photos, his Grandfather and his Father looking out impassively, but sternly. Resolve, unbending resolve, when the Emperor call, you replied.

Unsheathing this object was not to be taken lightly. The hard edge, tinged with blue, was as sharp as the day it was blessed. He raised it above his head, gripping it tightly with both hands. It was the first and last time he would use it in earnest.

Slash. He brought it down, through the air to the left side of his terminal. The umbilical cord attaching it to the outside world offered no resistance. The screen died.

Slash. He brought it down again, to the right side. The ringing stopped. Communication was terminated. Silence. He was back in the 'Old- World'.

With the same amount of care, he knelt and replaced it on the top of the alter-box. He bowed, this time in the direction of the two photos, his fore-head touching the shiny reed of his beloved 'tatami', the lingering smell of the country filling his nostrils.

He opened the other secret drawer in his life and gripped the cold steel of the army-issue, butt. He was standing completely erect, now, his expression was as inscrutable as ever, as he put the barrel to his temple and simultaneously pulled the trigger. Hesitation would always have been costly and this time was no exception. How this life ended was the foundation for the next and an honourable exit was imperative. His brains matched the colour of the paper screens on which they were scattered, like the rays of the fading light. Darkness came to both.

Chapter Sixteen

"I think we ought to wait a little while, that's all I said."

"I knew you were going to say this. You've been building up to it, Dalton. I know. I knew it, I knew it, I knew it."

"You know nothing of the sort, Beatrice. It's just that with your sister back in hospital and all, and the baby . . ."

"There. It's the blasted baby. Your obsessed with it. You think I won't be able to have one." She looked at him, tried to fix his eyes with her own. Hers were blazing. "I wish that we hadn't even tried until after the fucking wedding." The last two words came out a full octave higher than the rest. That included the decibel count. It was followed by a stamp of the foot.

"I think the term for that is 'entrapment'." As soon as he had said it, he wished he hadn't. Beatrice was going ballistic. The wedding hadn't been mentioned, and there certainly hadn't been any plans made. Dalton had been busy at the studios. There were three films coming through and the contracts alone were driving him to the brink. Those bastards were always desperate to be in the rotten film, but once they were picked, they demanded the earth. Buckstoppers were there for a reason, but a punchbag would do just as nicely. Being in charge was an unpleasant illusion.

The fall in the stock market had put pressure on the Dollar and made it more expensive for foreign investment. Money from the Far East had all but dried up, so he was struggling to fund the three films that were under contract and in the pipe-line. Hongkong and Japan had always been keen. Now they wouldn't answer the phone. Luckily, one was small-time, for television. Another was low-budget, but the third would blow the minds of the bank if they knew the extent of exposure. It had been attributed to that yellow shit, in Tokyo. The colour referred to his conduct rather than his skin.

"His sun has already set. He's out of it. Let's hope the same doesn't happen to my studio", was what he had said many times over the last two weeks. Wedding bells were the last thing on his mind. He already had the sound of bells in his head. Alarm bells.

Then there had been the trouble with Priscilla. About the same time, she had been taken back into hospital with high blood pressure and anaemia. To the lay-man, and Dalton was one of them, it sounded a contradiction of terms. Maybe they were just guessing. He was all for a second opinion, but Dr Jones was calling the shots. It niggled him. He hadn't explored the reason.

What had pushed Beatrice over the edge, was Dalton's agreement, to have the baby at his house. Beatrice was convinced it was Dalton's suggestion, although he denied it. The baby, still unnamed, was disturbing Priscilla to the extent that she wasn't getting any rest and therefore, not getting better. Dalton had staff at the house, so he could manage more than anyone. Priscilla's sister was also there most of the time, so it would work nicely.

"The baby is your nephew, after all, Beatrice."

"Maybe so, but we still don't know the father. I wonder where he is hiding."

"Maybe she doesn't know who he is," Dalton offered. It was a silly remark to make but was in jest. Many a true word spoken'.

"Oh for fucks' sake, Dalton."

When Dalton had asked his Mexican maid, who came from the sort of large families that South America can ill-afford, she had almost lactated on the spot. She caught the grinning disease big-time. Her hands moved instinctively to her chest, and it was with some relief that Dalton saw her make the sign of the cross. However, she wouldn't let go of Dalton's arm for a full two minutes. He thought she was going to kiss him and he had to

135

take a precautionary step back. Her teeth were not the sort of thing with which he needed a close encounter.

"Bastards," Beatrice screamed up into the air, turned on her high heels and slammed the door behind her. It was only by great fortune that the glass remained in one piece. The thought that she could have been meaning the baby never occurred to him, he just assumed that it was him.

Historically, that had always been the case when women didn't get their own way. He failed to notice that it had been used in the plural form. Rosario, Rose for short, had entered the room with a tray of fruit juice at the very same moment, and had, in fact, heard everything. She was heartened by the departure and the look that followed Beatrice would have done a voodoo priest proud, she had all on, to resist a flick of the head in the customary style, South of the Border. Dalton looked at her with the sort of resignation that only a young boy with a flea in his ear, could manage.

"I think you had better accompany me to the hospital, Rose." He screwed up one corner of his mouth, raised his eyebrows and shrugged his shoulders simultaneously. It was the sort of innocent expression that had endeared him to countless women. She took no second asking. Of course, if he'd have asked her to jump over a cliff, she would, but this request, well, she would have included a triple somersault. The quiet speech and the balance of his manner contrasted sharply with that of the harridan.

When they both arrived in the ward, Priscilla was dressed. The pale blue dress was loose fitting and was complemented by a string of double pearls. She looked pale, but there again, she always did. Dr Jones was sitting next to her looking out of the window. He was close, but not too close. Respectful. She had been moved to the mother and baby rooms. Dr Jones had influence here and a few strings had felt his influence on this occasion. The rooms were private, with patio doors out onto the gardens. It reminded Dalton of his own garden. It was ate afternoon and the sunlight was fading with an orange glow that made you thankful it was spring. The days were lengthening quickly.

"Hello Dalton. Hello Rosario." Priscilla never shortened names. It wasn't polite, even when it was requested. The gesture itself was always appreciated but gesture it was. She never took up the option.

Baby was sleeping. Dalton had brought Rose to see Priscilla, before. He knew that the baby could never be cared for by a stranger. They were happy with each other and Jacky had urged the agreement. It came in the form of a medical command. Priscilla would move into Jacky's clinic for a few days to gain strength. Priscilla seemed to be in a daze, she was being carried along with the tide. The discovery of the death and the circumstances of the death, of the Japanese financier had knocked her for six. Everything seemed to be collapsing around her ears. She couldn't even confide in anyone, that was one of the hardest parts, she'd never had a real girlfriend, someone to talk to. Her Mother had always taught her to keep her own council and that was what she had done. It was for her Mother's benefit though, she had been trapped by the closeness.

She had gained a son, the friendship of Jacky and a closer relationship with Dalton, but Dalton had been so kind, how could she go through with the plan. She was far too close. Was there any way she could distance herself? Was there any point? No, she was already decided on the course of action. She would not take the test. An unmarried mother, and a poor one, at that, looked likely to be her future. The prospect of a simple, normal life and a full dose of post-natal depression looked more like a tea party, by the minute, from where she was standing. She was in the middle of a full-blown nightmare. Of course, the whole point of the test was to establish the father. She didn't want it to be Van de Clouet, Kumamoto was dead and . . and then there was Dalton, good, kind, considerate Dalton. What had she done? What the hell had she done?

Jacky took her by the arm. Her legs felt like jelly. She had turned into Mrs Pathetic-Person, she knew that. She reminded herself that she was not entitled to the first part of that title, she was still 'Miss', but the second part fitted like a glove.

The baby things were gathered and Rose swept up the baby. She looked so natural. Some women are like that and she was one of them. It was a gift, a gift that set Priscilla's mind at rest. Baby didn't even make a murmur.

They know when they are in good hands, it's not a discovery that they make, it's an instinct.

Chapter Seventeen

It had been five days now, that Priscilla had been at Jacky's place. She had been at the house, or to be more precise, the apartment, not the clinic. When she had arrived, flowers were in the guest room downstairs and Jacky had carried her bag through to the very same room. There were new curtains. It was more human. Dee had enjoyed the challenge. Priscilla smiled in recognition of Jacky's effort.

"If it's all right by you, Jacky," she'd said, "I'll stay upstairs."

"And put me out of my bed, young girl?" he'd replied, looking over the top of his glasses at her.

"No." She faltered, not sure of herself anymore. "I'd like it if we were together." Her eyes were not far from crying and she glanced at him for reassurance. "I need to feel close." A jig would have been natural at this point but he restricted himself to a dead-pan expression, with a hint of concern. He regretted using the word 'young'.

"What about your family? Won't they be visiting?" Jacky had included the possibility of the father of her son in that loose description, but it was not a subject that he dare allude to. This was the real concern.

"Nobody will be visiting. Anyway I'm a grown woman, Dr Jones. A mother. I think I'm old enough to do what I want. Don't you?" It was a valiant attempt at bravery and she threw in a lilt to lighten up.

"If that is the best Irish accent you can muster, Miss, then it's pathetic. Anyway, you'll always be a young girl to me Prissy," he retorted, assuming his own, pronounced, Irish accent in a further attempt to lighten the proceedings. "Come on then," and carried the bag through the fateful door marked 'private'. It was a hurdle that they'd both had to clear.

Dee shuffled her papers in a nonchalant way and studiously ignored the events.

Priscilla had telephoned every morning and every evening. Rosario had that super balance of a professional help, exuding confidence without intrusion, and a mother, but one who would set the mind of the real mother at rest. Sympathetic discretion was her hallmark. Her appearance belied her true ability. Faithful evaluation of other cultures is always so difficult.

Dalton had not been around. Priscilla had spoken to him a couple of times but didn't encourage a visit. She certainly didn't want to expose her circumstances and relationship at this stage. Her cards were better played close to her chest.

Her chest was actually throbbing, at least her breasts were, because she hadn't been using the milk, but it was in short supply and her period in hospital had not encouraged it's use. She felt sad that she really wouldn't be able to go back to feeding, but she secretly resolved to try. The baby, sucking, gave her great comfort. She must return to the baby the next day. Her strength was surely on the increase. Dark thoughts and anxiety in the night, are what had really been at the bottom of the breakdown. She had a lot behind her, but a lot more in front.

Beatrice had been back to see Dalton and visit the child, herself, but she hadn't stayed the night, and was out of town for two evenings, working on location. She hadn't called Priscilla. To Beatrice, the child was an intrusion, even a threat. To Dalton it was a pleasure. It brought life to the house. It was something that he had avoided, but now, if he wasn't careful, it would be something he'd crave. He'd never admitted it, but he was a big 'softie'. Most men are.

A car pulled up outside. Priscilla saw it from the bedroom window. She hadn't got up, but was sitting on the edge of the bed, staring and thinking. The majority of the time, it was just staring. Jacky was working downstairs. He had a client and the client's car was also parked outside, at the front. Jacky's was in the garage. It was a stoke of luck that hers was secured in the garage at home. Priscilla didn't know much about car makes. There were big ones and small ones. There were ones that were in bad condition and presumably old and those that she presumed were new. The car that was arriving caught her attention because it looked out of place in this environment, and it emitted a throaty sound. In other environments, it was perfect, but Priscilla wasn't to know that. Such circles were almost unknown to her. All of Jacky's clients were private and could afford new cars. This one was a bit scruffy, so she presumed that it fitted into the former category. It did exude power, though. The owner got out. He was scruffy, but exuded the same sort of power as his car. He didn't walk, he strode.

She'd seen him somewhere before. He looked familiar, but she couldn't imagine where. He moved toward the door, a man with a mission. He didn't ring the bell. He walked straight in.

Jacky's client was just leaving. Same routine.

"Yes, I will have your prescription. Have you made an appointment for the patient?" he said to the receptionist.

"Yes, Dr Jones, the prescription will be ready tomorrow and the appointment is next Thursday, ten-o-clock." Dee gave no hint of a look. She was learning fast. This was one client who liked to be called, 'patient', it made her feel like she was being looked after. Not all of them did.

He showed her out of the door and turned to the scruffy man. He was irritated by him. He brought down the tone. The man was now leaning on one elbow, at the reception.

"Doctor Jones," he offered. "Officer Edsell, Patrick Edsell, from the Police Department. Most people call me Pat." He hesitated a moment to let the information sink in and tried to judge the Doctor's reaction. Not that he had any reason. It was just a habit. It's like when you give policemen a lift in your car. They possess natural suspicion. They always check your tyres. The more worn they are, the more often they seem to do it. They never look at the new one that was replaced after a blow-out.

"And what can I do for you, Officer," said Jacky as boldly as he could muster. Police never came unannounced, without a reason, and it was always better to be assertive from the start. A little of his Irish lilt crept in. He'd noticed that the Officer's name was Patrick. He didn't mean it, but there was nothing wrong with having something in common with the law. His reaction had been as automatic as it had been defensive.

"Not a lot Doctor, I have an enquiry that you may be able to help with".

"My office is the place for us then, Patrick". The Irish was out again. He just couldn't help himself. He didn't even look in the direction of the receptionist. She'd just been given enough ammunition for the next month. He hoped it would be quick. It is funny how a policeman can make you nervous. He wondered whether Mother Theresa had had the same feelings. He would have to leave that question open. "Take a seat," and he closed the door behind them.

When Priscilla heard the name, because she did listen, it came back to her. He was the policeman who made the arrest on the Governor. She could hear no more, because the door had been closed, so she lay down on the bed, her dark hair contrasting with her white pyjamas and the pillow . . . and her white face. The question of whether that man was the father of her child began racing around her head once more. Van de Clouet.

"I believe you have a patient staying here by the name of Miss Glover," was his opening line. Jacky stiffened. Patrick noticed.

"Yes."

"Well, I know this is going to sound a bit strange," and he hesitated, not for effect this time, although effect was what it had, but because he didn't know how to word it. "There was a burglary sometime ago at the house of a Mr Dalton Feinnes. I believe Mrs Glover."

"Miss Glover." Jacky corrected. "Miss Glover, is a friend of Mr Feinnes." Although it was not a question and sounded rhetorical, Jacky answered anyway.

"Yes. Her sister, Beatrice, is engaged to be married to Mr Feinnes."

"Quite." He took out his note book. "On the third of October, there was, as I say, a burglary and the motive seems a little unclear. It appears to have been set up by a lady with approximately the same description as Miss Glover. The reasons are not clear, at this stage, but the lady was present. It would certainly help if we could identify this person. Have you any idea where Miss Glover might have been on that particular night? It's a bit of a long shot, I know."

"As it happens, yes I do." Jacky shifted in his seat. "It was my secretary's birthday and we were all here together. That was the date of her birthday, and that is how I know".

"Was?"

"Yes, she passed away almost a year ago, now. Molly, that was her name, would have noted the occasion in her treatment book." And he added, "In her own hand."

"Treatment?"

"Yes, Miss Glover has been a patient of mine for a number of years. Excuse me a minute." Dr Jones got up and walked out of the room, and over to reception. "Could I have the record book containing patient attendances, please, Dee?" For the benefit of the officer, his voice contained a few extra decibels, not enough to be obvious, but they were there all the same. Dee noticed, there was a distinct departure from his dulcet tones. It was an attempt to emphasise his openness. She handed it over. He walked back slowly, whilst he thumbed through the pages to look up the entry. He knew that times were not recorded, only dates, but such was his superstitious nature, he had to make sure. He'd already stepped over a line that was unfamiliar to him. He had to be careful.

"Here we are," he started, even before he'd crossed the threshold. He put the book down, open at the page, on the desk in front of his inquisitor.

"Perfect," was what Pat said, but not what he thought. It was a little more on the vulgar side. Pat was asking himself whether or not he 'protesteth too loudly', but he couldn't decide. Yet. "The guy who I arrested is a real nutter and he would say anything to divert blame, but it was such an unlikely story, I couldn't imagine him making it up. He doesn't have the wit. It was worth a look." He made to get up. "I'm sorry to have disturbed you." Jacky followed suit. He was taller than Jacky, but if he thought that it made the slightest difference, he was wrong. "Perhaps I could have a word with Miss Glover?"

"Miss Glover is probably sleeping. She has been with us a week for recuperation and a week in hospital before that. It's not a good idea." He remained quiet for as long as he dare, then added, "unless you think it wise, of course?"

"It's probably a waste of time anyway. The slime-ball is locked up, that's the main thing. I just don't like loose ends." He turned to the door after shaking the Doctor's hand. He wanted no hard feelings between countrymen. "Donegal was where my lot fled from. Probably horse thieves." He smiled. The smile contained a question.

"Near Tipperary, ourselves," was the reply.

"How many patients do you normally have staying at any one time, Dr Jones?"

"We have just the one room for over-nights. It's rarely used. Emergencies, really" He could have kicked himself a moment later, when they both left the office. The room in question was opposite and the door was wide open. The bed was empty. Jacky muttered the name of his favourite Saint and felt that he had to say something. You didn't need to be a gynaecologist to recognise a pregnant silence. "Miss Glover has taken my apartment, upstairs. She is a family friend and it's quieter. That room is only suitable for over-nights." He paused. "As I said."

If Pat had been down town, he would have rolled his eyes, but he wasn't. The only things that were expected to roll in this neighbourhood, were the lawns. He might well have looked casual, in this environment, and indeed, he was, comparatively, but it just wasn't his scene, he wasn't comfortable, the area was unknown territory and he didn't want to be heavy handed. A complaint to the Commissioner would have been disastrous, he'd broken wind enough recently. Pat was hardly the flavour of the month, down town, especially after beating the hell out of Tom Scott for the second time. But this time, just a little more seriously. He'd been lucky not to be suspended. The accusation that he made against Scott, that he had colluded with criminals and almost fucked up an investigation hadn't stuck. Scott was so badly injured he had to report Pat, from his hospital bed, though he knew better than to press criminal charges. This went in favour of Scott. who came out smelling of roses with a faint whiff of manure. Pat simply ended up smelling of shit. This was the Commissioner's territory and this was where he lived. Pat had to be careful.

Priscilla had picked up on the last part of the conversation. She'd heard the office door open. She moved to the window and held the net curtains back a couple of inches. She'd not picked up the last words of goodbye, but she sensed that the tone was affable enough. Molly was on her mind, right at the front of it.

As Pat Edsell reached out for the handle of his car, which wasn't locked, (it was a game that he played, seeing how long it would be before anyone interfered with it. People didn't interfere with this man, nor his car. There was a running bet down at the precinct on the date of the first incident, but Pat was way ahead) he caught sight of movement of the curtain in the reflection in the wind-shield. He filed it in the computer that possessed the best cross reference system in the world, his head.

Jacky was feeling weak. His last client had left and he was in no mood for more, of anything. He locked the office door behind him and crossed the reception to the lab. He'd recently developed the habit of locking that, too. He hesitated at the door, he wasn't going to enter, but he did, anyway. When he arrived in front of the flasks he stood still and reached out. They were his babies. His livelihood depended on them and they depended on him. The last thing that he always did was to check the temperatures, even though they were automatic, alarmed, and checking themselves. The LEDs winked at him. He winked back. It was another habit. There was so much life in them that he couldn't think of them as cold objects. He often touched them at the end of the day. No matter how many times he did that, he still expected them to be icy cold, but they weren't, they were warm. They were warmer than Molly would ever be again. He couldn't believe it. The irony, and it wasn't lost on him, was that he was the guardian of what he couldn't produce, himself, rather like the eunuch in a harem. If he dwelt on it, he felt sick, but his focus had moved.

He turned and looked at the refrigerator. There was nothing interesting about the plain white door, but he stared anyway. He approached it. Quickly, he opened the door, reached in and took out the ice-cream tub, marked 'pistachio'. He yanked it from the place, where it had welded itself to the shelf, through not being used, held tightly in a growing jacket of ice. His eyes brushed across the second, smaller container, but didn't connect. Holding it in both hands, with reverence, he actually marched across the room. With great deliberation, his right foot put pressure on the pedal of the bin and the lid gaped open at him. Thud. Clump. The container was binned and the lid was down. The ghost of Molly had been exorcised, what they had shared in life was now away. Without looking back, head held high and eyes, level, he returned to the door and locked it behind him.

"I'll be taking no more calls this afternoon, Dee. When you have finished, you may lock the door behind you." He returned her steady smile, as their eyes locked together. Both contained an element of pity. "See you in the morning," and disappeared through the door marked 'private'.

There were questions he needed to ask. He caught sight of Priscilla's legs on the bed, but made straight for the bathroom.

"If you are awake, Priscilla, I'll fetch you some English tea." He sounded like 'Old Mr Dormouse', from Oakingham. His Mother used to read the stories to him and he loved them, even as an adult he loved them. He smiled. Monsieur le Mole was an old friend.

"I am, but could you make it Earl Grey." She waited for the answer, then added, "I'll make it if you want."

It was a kind offer, but it was his pleasure to do things for her. He wanted her to be back to her old-self and brighten up. The awful quandary that faced him was that the sooner she was better, the sooner she would leave. He splashed water on his face, cold water. Could the mirror be telling the truth? It was impossible. He couldn't look that old. The reflection viciously assaulted his hopes of a future with Priscilla.

She didn't really want 'Earl Grey', in preference to 'English Breakfast', but wanted a further opportunity to test his countenance, see if the visit from the policeman had had any effect. She didn't detect anything in his voice, but she was still on guard. She was stirring, coming alive, the adrenaline was there again. She straightened the duvet next to her and pulled her nightie down tightly. It was not to cover herself, but to make a neat appearance, show a little more of her chest, accentuate her bust. She ruffled it slightly. Stomachs, we could do without. She idled away the next few minutes looking at her legs. They were not a disappointment, and she wriggled her toes. She'd paint the nails later. It made her contemplate her fingers. Those nails, were chipped. She wrinkled her nose. She was beginning to take note. The double row of pearls were beside the bed. Whilst both hands were in front of her, she ran them through her hair, pushing it back behind her ears, both ears, exposing her pale throat. Jacky came into view, two china cups in hand, both rattling slightly in their saucers, the nervousness of youth combined with the age of an old Doctor. She ran her tongue over her lips to moisten them.

"And how is the best patient in the clinic this afternoon? Rested are we?"

"You mean the only patient in the clinic." He knew she'd been listening. She smiled. "Thanks, are you going to join me?" and she patted the bed beside her, pulling back the covers.

She didn't ask about the visit. He didn't mention it They both had their reasons. Although he had every intention of doing so, he wouldn't bring it up. He undressed instead. Every article of clothing that dropped to the ground made the possibility of confrontation more remote. By the time that he was naked, there was not a snowball in hell's chance. There was, according to his quick calculation, no likelihood of ever finding another woman like Priscilla. If he looked even remotely ridicules or less than desirable, Priscilla didn't show it. He was very thankful for that.

He climbed into bed and pulled the covers over his modesty. The amount of exposure that a man of his vintage could volunteer, was limited. Priscilla pulled the duvet back down to his waist. Half a century of timidity was difficult to combat, but he felt good and although his chest was soft, it was full.

He half turned toward her and slipped the strap of her top from one shoulder. It was the only garment she wore, the semi-transparent material, possibly silk, delicious whatever it was, hanging loosely, struggling to cover one nipple, but she dislodged it before the thought of helping it on it's way even entered his head. It was swollen. The milk was still very much in evidence as he took her into his mouth and accepted the relieving flow, her hands holding onto the locks of silky white hair behind both ears, Irish ears. The relief was both physical and emotional, the pressure from her long fingers urging him to suck harder. He obliged. He was her baby, and she was in charge. He knew that, they both knew that. She wanted him. She really wanted him. Even if the feeling wasn't reciprocated, and it was, he would have been helpless. Helpless was a good description of his circumstance, resistance was futile.

Alternative positions were an abstract concept to Priscilla, scanty knowledge gleaned from soft literature, but now they became reality. She climbed his comparative bulk and settled down on him, sliding effortlessly over his re-discovered manhood and confidence. She was ready and she surprised herself. Responsibility was snatched from him and he luxuriated under the command, problems and failure melting from his understanding, their bodies and their tongues intertwining. He was the stallion and she, the rider from heaven, milk splashing into his face as she gathered momentum, putty in her hands and a rod in her body. It was the greatest experience of his long life. It was her first, what had gone before was unimportant, nothing. And they were satisfied, as one. Twenty minutes had been erased from time, lost but never to be forgotten, nor regretted. Twenty minutes of heaven on earth. His barren semen was of no consequence, her motherhood was secure, as they rolled onto their sides, bathed in a cocktail of perspiration and scents, falling straight into the arms of Morpheus.

It was dark when they awoke, the time wasn't clear, just silence. Not a word was spoken, the spell was a fragile one. Their bodies were cool, the tea was cold.

"I love you, Priscilla."

Indeed a line had been crossed.

"I'll not be a moment", and he slowly prised himself from her tightening embrace. She relaxed her flickering eyes and lengthened her breaths. His dressing gown on, he went over to the kettle, shook it to test the volume of water and switched it on. "Let's hope that the next cup of tea produces the same results", he said, but she was in another world, a world shared with her baby.

The door marked 'private', re-opened and Jacky appeared, purposefully. He was fiddling with the bunch of keys, but his selection was complete by the time he reached the laboratory door. Priscilla's heavy, regular breathing was all but inaudible from the bedroom. The light was an unnecessary luxury. He knew where he was going. Illumination struck his features, etching the lines deeper, as the refrigerator opened with that universal sound, somewhere between a plump and a rattle. The cooling flesh of his big, soft hands, that not so long ago were almost buried in the luscious heat of the female form, plunged into the icy recess and wrenched out the small, remaining, box. Without a glance or a thought for it's contents, the glass slides nestling in the womb of cotton-wool, it followed the same path as it's larger cousin. Just how closely related the two boxes were, he hoped he would never know, but as Molly had been buried, Priscilla was re-born. When the laboratory door closed behind him, the lock remained open. Jacky followed the Siren sound of the boiling kettle and what he hoped, would be his future.

When he arrived back upstairs, the shower was running, steam issued from the kettle and the bathroom in similar proportions, those automatic kettles were a nuisance when they didn't switch off, they caught you out, because you expected a certain behaviour. "If one was in a certain mood, one would have felt let down," was how Priscilla would have put it. He liked the way she spoke. This was Jacky, though, he hailed from Ireland, not Boston, and although it was only a kettle, had he been alone, he would have sworn out loud. Jacky only ever swore in his own company, "bad enough being a 'bog-hopper' let alone a 'foul-mouthed bog-hopper," was what he used to say to his male colleagues when the subject of the opposite sex came up.

Men who have just had sex with a lady, especially if they had been smitten at the same time, expected a certain behaviour. They could also feel let down, and might even use bad language, if they were disappointed. Contrary to popular belief, the male of the species feels just as vulnerable as the female at times like this, maybe more so. Whether it is revealed or not, is another matter.

This was certainly the case when Priscilla appeared from the bathroom, fully dressed wearing her lipstick and pearls. He didn't swear, he was too shocked, a mixture of shock and disappointment. He had a cup of tea in each hand and although his body was covered, he felt silly.

"Mmm . . . tea," Priscilla said, in an attempt to undo the hurt that she had obviously been responsible for. The 'hurt little boy look, that women could either find appealing or pathetic, depending on their mood, was not going to disappear that easily. As she took hold of one of the saucers, she said, "I'm going round to see Dalton and Beatrice." She stopped for a moment. Beatrice's name had been added to soften the blow. It had little effect on Jacky, but it added a sense of urgency to Priscilla. "I must see how my baby is. I've left him too long." She touched his hand, then received the cup. "Please understand, Jacky."

"You must be feeling a lot better, then?"

"I think you know that already, don't you?" She smiled as warm a smile as she could muster, but there was an urgency that was hard to conceal. Jacky was looking at her face intensely. There was a darkness about her eyes. He wasn't about to miss anything. Every little sign was important to him. He'd exposed himself, his love was on his sleeve and he felt vulnerable. It was his turn.

"Do you want to bring him back here tonight," he said, hopefully, trying not to sound as pathetic as he felt? Priscilla put her hand on his again. It was a technique she had learned from him. Doctors and the clergy are the main exponents. Failure was inevitable. "Can I give you a lift round? I'll get dressed." The hand went out again.

"No Jacky. It's late."

"Not too late."

"No, I'll get a taxi, find out what is going on and give you a ring."

"Will you be coming back here tonight?"

"I'll telephone, Jacky, don't worry, relax, enjoy the rest of the evening."
It was as firm a dismissal as he was ever likely to get, so he left it at that, put on a brave smile and sipped his tea, bravely ignoring the fact that it was too hot and burnt his mouth. It felt right, punishment for expecting too much. He told himself to get a grip, his reaction was getting out of proportion. He blew his tea to cool it.

It was with good grace that he waved her off at the door, as the cab disappeared from view, leaving the awful silence and loneliness that he had grown to hate. He resisted the temptation of the laboratory, as he passed. What had been discarded would remain that way, and moved on, once again, to the quarters that were once again, 'private', but would never again be his own.

Chapter Eighteen

The blue-green numbers on the dashboard of the taxi indicated that it was almost ten p.m. by the time the fare was paid. The ten dollar bill had been in her hand when the vehicle had come to a halt and no change was required. The street was very quiet and certainly deserted. The last time she was here was in very different circumstances and she eyed the patch of shadow where she had so patiently waited for Ian. Now it was the turn of the taxi to wait for Priscilla. She pressed the bell and announced her presence on the intercom. The gates started to open and the taxi moved away. The security lights bathed the short drive and by the time she arrived at the door, there appeared, the beaming Rosario.

"Senorita Priscilla, Senorita Priscilla, adelante, come in, come in." She was pleased to see Priscilla. Priscilla was also pleased to see her. "Mister Dalton and your sister are out, but they will be back soon. Baby is asleep, come and see, come and see." In the nicest possible way, Priscilla was dragged into the house by her arm, and although she wasn't used to physical contact with anyone, let alone comparative strangers, such was the openness of Rosario, she felt at ease. This woman was looking after her baby, after all.

Priscilla felt an overwhelming sense of relief when she caught sight of her baby. Rosario had him neatly bedded and he was sleeping soundly. Priscilla ran the back of her hand over his forehead, lightly, so as not to wake him. He snuffled gently, looking angelic in his little cap and blanket.

"Mister Dalton bought him a cot and all sorts of things", offered

Rosario, proudly. There was a single sized bed next to the new cot. "Maybe you ought to stay the night, here. I think that it is too late to take baby home."

"Do you think that Dalton would mind?"

"Not at all, he already said that it was OK"

"In that case, I will, Rosario, thank you very much."

By the time that Dalton arrived home, Priscilla had been asleep for some time, but was awakened by the front door and the sound of Rosario rushing forward to alert him to Priscilla's presence. She heard her own name mentioned. There were low voices, one of them Beatrice's. She couldn't make out anything specific, but she thought that she could detect a little tension. It could have been her imagination though. She prayed that her son wouldn't wake up until everyone was settled, she could face no-one else, tonight. It had been a long day, making love to Jacky seemed a lifetime away. It is strange how good, important events can recede into history at such a pace. The events were being pushed back by the clamouring problems of the not so distant, future. The identity of the father must now be her priority. When she knew that, she could move forward. Whatever the ills and the repercussions of her conduct, the baby was hers and it made her glad. She would never be alone again. She fingered her pearls, lay on her side and watched her son through the bars of the cot. Yes, she had something to be thankful for.

It was already light when she was awakened by little sobs. Baby was hungry. Mothers rarely sleep through the sounds of a child. Her breasts were as full as ever, after their emptying, the previous night and she put the one that felt the fullest to the baby's searching lips as soon as she had picked him up. The crying stopped like magic. His cheeks felt warm and flushed, next to her skin. They were sitting on the edge of the bed when there was a knock at the door. It was Rosario. She had heard the crying.

"Hello." Priscilla waited for a moment. "Come in." She could tell by the gentleness of the knock, who it would be. Rosario was holding a prepared bottle of milk. She beamed more than usual when she saw that baby was getting real milk.

"Good morning, good morning baby," she sang. More beaming. "I will leave the bottle here in case you need it later," she said. Rosario had slipped gently back into the role of maid. It had been seamless.

The feed was almost over when her sister came in. She was still wearing her robe. Priscilla didn't have one. She had the distinct feeling that Beatrice was purposely marking out her territory, parading openly. Again it could have been Priscilla's imagination. Priscilla felt slightly awkward with one of her breasts out, her nipple engorged and red, she had never been close enough to her sister to flaunt herself. Now she felt naked, exposed. As the baby had finished feeding, she withdrew her breast, the right one, and slipped it back inside her open blouse. Now she felt better. Baby made to cry, but was persuaded not to, by a kind word and a cuddle. Priscilla felt superior, not on her territory, but superior all the same.

"Morning, Priscilla. Are you feeling better, now? Sorry we weren't in when you arrived, but you didn't let us know." Her opening gambit was designed to undermine Priscilla, she couldn't help herself. Reference to being ill would normally have dealt her a blow, but her strength was back, she could take it. It was Beatrice who was feeling delicate, now. The baby was a stark reminder of her inability to conceive. She had spent her life being worried about unwanted pregnancies, she'd always felt that entering a room with a man was enough. Now that she wanted to have a baby, she'd had her chance, but now it was eluding her. Then there was the abortion. She shuddered at the thought. Superstition was barely beneath the surface when subjects like these were raised. Retribution was a word that was never far away. Dalton was besotted with the baby, and Beatrice's conception was mentioned less by the day. It was eating into her soul. Jealousy was taking over from reason.

"Morning girls." They were addressed as one and one of the unit didn't like it at all. "How is my big boy this morning." This was an expression he might well regret in the future. Beatrice didn't like it now. Priscilla shivered in every direction. Dalton's eyes were lit up. Priscilla had never seen him in a robe before. She feasted and hoped. Beatrice made her excuses and left the room, she had to be off for a photo shoot. What she didn't add, was that she had moved to production, time was slipping by for everyone.

"Stay for a few days, will you Priscilla. Beatrice has been a bit strung out, of late. I think that she has been worried about you, and anyway, we've got used to the wee fellow. Rose will help you and you'll get a bit more rest and benefit from the company." He waited for the answer. "The room is yours for as long as you like." Boyish hope was in his eyes.

"If you think that Beatrice won't mind, Dalton, I'd love to."

"Mind? Good heavens, no, she'll be over the moon." They both suspected that that would not be the case, but didn't even admit it to themselves.

Arrangements over, he left to get dressed. There was a smile on the pale lips of Priscilla. There was a grimace on the face of Beatrice. It had been her turn to listen in and she hadn't liked what she had heard.

"You'll be wanting to sleep with her, next, Dalton," was what hit him when he caught up with her in the bedroom.

"What?"

"You heard," she hissed, and she turned on her heals, turned on the shower, followed by the key in the door. It was a new door, this time made of hard wood, solid hardwood. Dalton was left rolling his eyes and shaking his head. He would have stayed still for longer, but the marble under his bare feet was far from warm. When Beatrice came out of the bathroom, she was dressed. He was naked. His colouring wasn't dark, but he was 'Adonis', all the same.

"Save it," was all Beatrice said, as she walked straight by.

"For later?" asked Dalton.

"If you like, but I won't be back until tomorrow." It was obvious what she meant, and it was the first time that the main weapon in his arsenal had let him down. He felt deflated and indeed, he was.

Priscilla watched her leave, from the window. She was going to no shoot with wet hair, unless she was to be behind the camera, for a change. Twenty minutes later, the smiling Dalton said his cheery goodbyes and left the house.

"See you later, make yourself at home. What's mine, etc." And he was gone. Priscilla watched him disappear, with the large iron gates closing quietly behind him, she wouldn't have heard them even if they were noisy. There were two stout pieces of glass between her and the cruel outside world.

She reflected on the irony that she had been outside, once, outside and behind that high wall, plotting. She could so easily be back in that position, this was only a temporary situation. The reason that she was at this side of the wall, was the baby. She longed to call him Dalton, too, but knew that it would be impossible, it might not even be the correct thing to do, if the tests revealed something that she was now dreading. How strange that the baby had been responsible for her position, but not in the way that she had expected. A thing, so small, had opened a door that the woman could not. There were problems ahead and she couldn't rest until they were sorted. She could hardly sleep. This was what was draining her, the uncertainty. She would resolve it today.

Even before she bathed her baby and changed him, she was on the phone. Arrangement made for the afternoon, she settled down and buried herself in the domestic routine that she had surprised herself by enjoying, made better by the open company of Rosario. She had felt aimless, in the past, but now, she was needed. The tasks were as simple as they were necessary, but she felt a whole person, a whole woman.

"I need to go to the lawyers, this afternoon, Rosario." She turned to see what her reaction would be, but those deep brown eyes said it for her.

"No problem, Miss Priscilla." Things were never a problem for Rose. There was not the slightest hint of reproach in the title of 'Miss'.

She took a taxi, again and went by her own house. She needed to change and would pack a small bag. In fact, she needed two bags, one for herself and one for the baby. The house was quiet, now that the cats had been adopted by the neighbours. She missed neither them, nor the house, she had gone down a certain path, made her bed. It would be difficult to return.

She lay a small brown envelope on the kitchen Work top. It contained six very small, fine, brown hairs. On the front of the envelope, she wrote

156

the word, 'BABY'. There were two other envelopes. On the second envelope, she wrote, 'SAMPLE ONE'. From the plastic bag that she had retrieved from her bathroom cabinet, she took out a hair brush. She extracted as many hairs from the bristles as possible. These were longer and thicker, but almost the same shade as the contents of the first envelope. She put them carefully into the second envelope and sealed it. From the second plastic bag, she took out another hairbrush. There were hairs on it, but this time, they were black, and short. She instinctively held these hairs by the tips of her finger and forefinger. They were from Kenichi Kumamoto. Dead man's hairs. She shivered, and closed the envelope quickly. She wet one finger of her opposite hand and rubbed it along the lip of the brown paper, pushing it firmly down, before it dried. She wrote on the front, 'SAMPLE TWO'. She didn't have a third sample. That was to be decided by a process of elimination. She prayed again, that it wouldn't come to pass. The thought turned her stomach. There was a practical consideration in the thought process, though. It was expensive to have a test done, very expensive, and her resources were being stretched. It was whilst she was going over this problem that she decided to have just one tested. No, it would take too long. Better solution. She would take the samples together. She would ask for the test to be done on the first sample, 'SAMPLE ONE', and if it were a match, then there would be no need of the second one. Great. She liked the feeling that she had thought something out herself, especially when she was pleased with the result. She just hoped that she would be pleased with the result of the test.

That done, she put both brushes into one bag. Back upstairs, she reached to the back of her underwear drawer. The weapon that had discharged it's load into her victims with such precision and viciousness, reflected the light from it's steel probes menacingly. She checked that the power was off. She checked again. She ran her finger over each one. Power. She liked it, and was, in a way, sorry to get rid of it, but corrupt power could be dangerous, no, it was time for it to go. The detective was on her mind. She was already nervous, now it was worse. Back down stairs, it joined the hair-brushes, stripped of their evidence, in the plastic bag.

Priscilla's bag, the baby's bag and the plastic bag joined each other in the trunk of the car as she set off down town, reaching the offices in ten minutes and parking in the lot, to the rear. There was a large bin next to the fence, where she could dump the plastic. She was late, it would have to wait. Her large handbag contained the three envelopes as she ran to the front of the building and let herself in. Three steps down and she was at the window that doubled as reception. A large black lady with big hair looked up from her typing and called through to the back office, acknowledging Priscilla with a smile. An untidy door to her left opened noisily and her Lawyer came out grinning.

"Hi Priscilla."

"Hello, Joyce," and she followed her in to the office. She had known Joyce for years, a good, solid, well-respected Lawyer, who was well known for being sympathetic to the plight of single women. She saw it as her duty to protect them from dark forces, which usually meant, men. The other group with which she sympathised, was homosexuals. It sounded a comparison that was as unfair as it was unlikely, but it was true. They went through as much detail as Priscilla wanted to expose and as much detail as Joyce was willing to be a party to. How she came to be pregnant and when was not going to be the issue. This was further than Priscilla wanted to go, and as there were the rights of women to privacy and dignity at stake, then that was all right with Joyce.

"I know that I told you that the DNA profiling would be expensive, Priscilla, and indeed, it is, but the work is done at the university, which is not allowed to charge. It is the police department who pay, but in the form of a grant. The technician who does the work was at college with me and we meet for lunch every month or so, just around the corner as it happens, the place with the massive steaks and the wrought iron railings. You should try it sometime. The bees are a nuisance at this time of year, though, so you would really have to sit indoors. Anyway, I digress," Joyce stretched her arms above her head, and drew breath, "she says that she will slip the work in and do it as a favour". Joyce tended to talk 'at' people, rather than 'to', people.

"Joyce, that is really kind. I'm having a cash crisis at the moment and it was worrying me."

Joyce was feeling better all the time.

"I know, Priscilla. These bastards go around screwing us, then won't stand up to their responsibility. We'll nail him and he'll have no option but to respond." There was a silence. Joyce was on her soap-box and expected little less than a round of applause. A moment later, she was nearly on her face.

"Joyce." She opened her hand bag. She slowly put the three envelopes out on the desk, fanning them like a hand in a card game. She re-arranged them so that the writing was orientated for the Lawyer.

"There were actually two men". The wind was out of Joyce's sails for a moment. Her little grey eyes bore into the darker ones of her client. It was a jolly good job that she had thought of the process of elimination, otherwise she would have had to own up to three men.

"It's not that they won't own up, but they don't know about the baby. At least they, well, one of them knows about the baby, but the possibility of the baby being his, has not been raised as an issue. I don't want to accuse the wrong one." That off her chest, her tightening chest, she sat back and waited for the reaction. There was a certain amount of heat in the region of her temples, her brow was damp

"Mmmm," was what she got. Joyce might not have been so helpful with the cost, had she known that snippet. "So there are two tests?"

"Well, not really, I suppose that by a process of elimination . . ." but she stopped at that. It wouldn't work. She needed both to be eliminated. "I just want to be sure, Joyce, for me and for the baby." She was beginning to wish that she had not applied the lipstick. Joyce wore none, her face was white, not because of what had been said, it was just her normal condition.

"OK, I'll get it round to her by this evening and I'll phone with the results." Priscilla still fell into her category of badly done to, woman, so it wasn't a problem. The man would be at fault, anyway.

Priscilla was eager to get away. What she was doing was bad, she knew that, but she deserved more from life, she'd done her bit and had no reward. She wasn't going to wait any longer

What was she saying? She couldn't have waited any longer. Years had been spent dedicated to a mother who had squandered her resources, money, time, affection on baby sister. Overall, life had treated her with contempt, no reward, no thanks. Her father had left the three of them, Priscilla didn't even have the luxury of him in her memory. Joyce had been right, men had screwed them, screwed the three of them, screwed all women. Her actions had justification, she could not afford the luxury of moral high ground, she had been sitting there all her life, the view was fine, but the rewards were paltry.

Priscilla was just about to get into the car, and had the door open. She remembered the bag in the trunk, containing the hair brushes and the electric gun. Thank God that she had remembered them. She certainly didn't want them left at her house and didn't want them in her car, back at Dalton's. No, the need for them was over. She pushed the button. The trunk opened. The plastic bag that she took out told no obvious story. It was black, with gold letters. One of the two things that it did reveal, was Priscilla's love of shoes, expensive shoes. It was a common trait in women of a middle class background, who were single. Their lifestyle enabled them to sport fine shoes and lavish the time on their trivial preoccupation. Trivial to men, that is. Joyce would agree. She looked around. There was no-one in sight. She tossed it lightly, up and over the lip of the commercial bin. Dirty galvanised steel. A cross between a thump and a clang should have been the end of it. Back to the car. She looked around again, slid into the seat, started the engine and slipped away, back into the anonymity of the traffic, in the direction of the suburbs and the well-manicured lawns. To Dalton's.

To a lady like Priscilla, occupier of moral and social high ground, low life was not a regular preoccupation. The fact that the bin and it's filthy environs could be of any interest to any creature, let alone, it's home, was completely alien to her. The noise of her deposit was meaningless to most. But not all. Behind the bin sat a gentleman of debatable years. The ageing process is not a constant, the gradient is variable. The man in question, widely known as John, in his rarefied circle, might have many physical failings, but his hearing was not one of them. Trash is a relative term, this was why he lived here. Her trash was his opportunity. It was his living. Exploration of the contents, excitement and expectation, surprise and even joy came about as a result of living here. He had heard the noise. It didn't come from old bottles. It wasn't waste paper. A well healed lady and a smart car was the source. He could hardly contain himself, as he peered into the aperture and spotted the smart bag. He kicked a crate roughly and impatiently into position, to gain access, stood on it, reached up and scrambled over the rim, dropping unceremoniously into the garbage. The effort made him wheeze. Coughing up his tubercular phlegm, he deposited it noisily onto the side of the walls, in an attempt to re-oxygenate his heaving chest, before regaining composure and an upright position. He reached out for the bag. A hairbrush. Another hair brush. He put them to his nose and sniffed them like a dog, more for identification than pleasure. It was already a worthwhile foray. Another object, unknown. Shiny, black plastic. A wrist strap. Two metal prongs with an on-off switch. He allowed it to swing from his bony wrist, like a child with a new toy. Alcohol and solvents had long ago simplified his expectations. He pressed the button a couple of times. Nothing happened. He turned it on and was intrigued by the sound. It emitted a prolonged squeak, like the rats who shared his home, but continuous, this was one scavenger that had overlooked the electronic age. The low sound lasted twenty seconds and finished with a whine. John had never heard of a capacitor. Revenge could well be exacted for lacking recognition or respect. Electronics could be a cruel and demanding master. He pressed the button another couple of times. Nothing, not even a repeat of the sound. He couldn't even spell discharge. If he didn't know what it was, how could he sell it? The steel prongs were sharp, but not too sharp. He let it swing from his wrist again, his old back, against the sides of the bin and his legs half submerged in the split bags of garbage. He put the palm of his hand upto the prongs and pressed against them. They were solid. They didn't move. He was running out of ideas. He pressed the button. A man with a heart condition, cirrhosis of the liver, tuberculosis and under nourishment should not subject himself to high voltage electricity. It's dangerous. His head jerked back, contacting the sides of the bin with the force of a bludgeon, whilst his legs simultaneously gave the solitary kick of a mule, his heels digging furrows in the primeval slime at the bottom of this filthy, unwashed vessel. When he rolled onto his side, he was face down. Paralysed and unconscious, his pathetic, diseased lungs quickly lost the battle against plastic and debris. What had once sustained him, now delivered the coup de grace. Ashes to ashes, trash to trash. The prolonged squeak repeated itself, stopping after a further twenty seconds. It was to be the first of many, but the rest of the squeaks would be more familiar to John, had he remained alive. His body was to experience the horror which haunted everyone who shared the domain of the rat.

Chapter Nineteen

The contrast could not be more pronounced. Total luxury. Safety. Priscilla was back at Dalton's house with her baby in her arms. Unconditional love was flowing between the pair. Their needs were comparable, though the reasons were not the same. Baby needed mother and mother needed baby. Priscilla was excited and at the same time, apprehensive. With the baby cradled in one arm, she had put her mobile phone on charge and laid it carefully in view and in earshot. This was one call that she didn't want to miss, and although she knew that the call wouldn't be coming so soon, she couldn't help herself, she kept looking at the phone and willing it to ring. She constantly worried about the signal strength, was it plugged in, the power on. Checking, checking.

As she tried to bury herself in the routine of feeding and cleaning and sleeping the baby, she went from excitement to despair. What would she do if the father were Van De Clouet, ex-governor, now a prisoner of the State? Had she any right to deprive her baby of it's father? Had she any right to lumber the baby with the stigma of her father's crimes? In the face of that, the man's money faded into irrelevance. She tried to imagine the scene, the publicity. Oh God, it would be terrible. How dare she moralise?

Then her mind would drift to Kenichi Kumamoto. He had lived so far away from her and died in the same way. He had died alone. How could anyone be so sure of his reasons for his actions? She could imagine things being out of control. Covering up one mistake after another. The parallel between his circumstance and hers, was clear. She felt sorry for him, but the ramifications and consequences of his actions were rattling around Asia and affecting the whole world. How many millions of people did this man touch? How many did he assault. She felt sorry for herself. How did such a good-looking man exude such confidence whilst under such strain. He must have been tortured, yet she couldn't see it. She devoured all the news about him. She looked into the baby's eyes. They were dark. His hair was dark. How oriental would a baby be. Why hadn't she asked this question before? The evidence was in front of her, yet she had overlooked it, but even now she wasn't sure. God, this was torture. Everything she discovered made things more uncertain, more complicated.

Priscilla almost hoped that it would not be Dalton. He was so nice, so open. She was caught in a cycle of anxiety, first one of the men then another, round and round and round. Beatrice walked straight in the room. Priscilla didn't even know that he was in the house.

"Beatrice, I thought that you were not coming back until tomorrow?" Beatrice looked dark, her eyes were red. She'd had a bad day. Being behind the camera was not as easy as it looked, it was demotion, end of her youth, her fading looks, her bruised ego amongst people who knew. Alcohol was on her breath. Confrontation was on her mind.

"Did you really think that I was stupid enough to leave you and Dalton in the same house. Alone?" she burst out. This full frontal attack hit Priscilla between the eyes. She had thought that Beatrice could be jealous, but had misread the situation. There was craziness in her eyes. Psychotic craziness.

"Beatrice, what are you . . .?"

"Don't come that with me, Priscilla. I know your game, you are trying to get your neat little hands on Dalton, with your girlie tricks and manners and your primmy, prissy ways." Although Priscilla was older, she hadn't been exposed to the attrition of late nights, partying and alcohol. Sun had not weathered her alabaster complexion.

"Beatrice, I'm not . . ."

"You are," she screamed. "You bloody well are. I know you are. He hardly looks at me now." she slapped her hand against the wall. "You've got your baby, you're all right. You've always had everything. Everything." The stinging of her palm gave her no relief, it further aggravated her fragile mood.

"I hardly think you can say that, Beatrice." Priscilla was shielding the baby, holding it tightly. She didn't want this assault and barrage of accusations to reach those delicate ears. Beatrice was ranting, pacing around the room. She slapped the wall twice more. She looked violent. For all her confidence and anger, she looked vulnerable at the same time, there were tears in her eyes. She ran her fingers roughly through her hair, her right hand covering her left breast, breathing deeply and noisily.

"You bastard." Priscilla held her baby even tighter. "You bastard."

"Shut up, just shut up. I can't stand this any more. I hate that language, you know I do. If you want us to go . . ." The shrill ring of her mobile phone cut through the atmosphere like a knife. They both went quiet. It had taken them by surprise. Priscilla put the baby in it's cot, supporting his head as she lay him down. The phone, which had been occupying her every thought, upto now, was out of her head. She answered it wearily and automatically. She almost didn't bother. Beatrice continued to pace, it was a truce but only a short one. The battle was far from over.

"Priscilla?" No answer. "It's Joyce." It took her a moment to focus her thoughts.

"Joyce. There isn't a problem is there?"

"I don't know Priscilla, maybe you will be able to tell me."

"Why?"

"I have your results."

"So soon?" She stepped back and sat down on the chair next to the bed, her eyes meeting those of her baby. She could hardly believe she was about to find out the truth. It was almost a year to the day. This was almost as exciting as having the baby. Trepidation hung over her, however, there was a damn sight less pain. Her knees were actually shaking and her heart was pounding in her chest.

"Well of course, it was easy. What usually takes the time is not the process, but finding the match, hunting through loads of specimens and cross referencing. In this case, she only had to do the one. It stood out like a beacon."

"Dalton. It was Dalton. It really was Dalton," she said to herself. Priscilla had turned her back to Beatrice to exclude her sister from the conversation. She kept her back turned away. She wanted to savour the moment in privacy. She was also grinning.

"Priscilla. Priscilla. Are you there?"

"I'm here, all right, Joyce. Thank you. Just confirm that it was the first envelope, could you?"

"Sample one, was the envelope, all right, Priscilla. Let's hope that it was the one that you wanted. Give us a call, when you are ready and we will talk about the case. Good bye." Priscilla didn't answer immediately, she was in a dream. The phone had gone back to the tone, before she returned to reality with her good byes. "It was, Joyce. It was. That was the one that I wanted." Her voice tailed off, but the phone was dead anyway. She was talking to herself.

"It's late, Beatrice. I don't want to hear this anymore, today. Robert and I will both be going back home tomorrow." The baby's new name came out without thinking, no planning, just a spontaneous decision.

There was the sound of the front door. Rosario had opened it for Dalton. Rosario had heard everything. Beatrice didn't hear the door, her ears were ringing.

"Good evening, Rose. Where is everybody?" Rose pointed to the spare bedroom, not saying a word. She gave her boss a half smile and a shrug.

"Robert. Robert" screamed Beatrice, "since when did you decide to call your little bastard Robert? That's Dalton's middle name." Beatrice's eyes were piercing Priscilla. The name had just come out. Of course, different names had gone around her head, but this had just come out, yes, it was spontaneously. It certainly wasn't pre-planned. She knew it was Dalton's middle name, and now there was confirmation of the father, Robert would be how it would stay.

"I'll call my baby what I want, Beatrice and don't you dare, ever, not ever, use that expression in my presence again. Your chance to be a mother was forfeited when you had your abortion." The last word was shouted, right in her face. A tiny amount of saliva ended up on her chin. It was removed with the back of her hand.

It was at that exact moment that Dalton opened the door. He couldn't stand shouting in the house. He had certainly never heard the word 'abortion', under this roof. The girls were silenced by his unexpected appearance.

"What's all this abortion business?" Now his eyes were blazing. "Well?" His question was ignored.

"Priscilla has called her baby, Robert. That is what we were going to call our baby, Dalton." Beatrice was imposing a calm onto her voice, but it was a clumsy attempt.

"I asked what this abortion business is about. Now answer me." His hands were on his hips, squared to them both. The baby started to cry and broke the silence, in a big way. Dalton turned to the cot. It was both Beatrice's opportunity to leave the room and the final straw. The bedroom door slammed, followed by the front door. It was the back of the white high heels that were the last view the pair got. Rosario was not in evidence, she saw nothing, but her ears gave her all the evidence that she could handle.

"What did she mean, Priscilla?" Priscilla was leaning over the cot, picking the newly named, Robert, from his bed. The noise subsided, and so did the redness in his face. His voice was gentle, measured.

"She had an abortion a few months ago, maybe last year. I thought you would have known. I thought it would have been yours." Priscilla looked at his face. It was in torment. He hadn't known.

"If it was, Priscilla, and had I known, then I would never have allowed it." He looked into her eyes. Her eyes asked a question that was answered. "Really." She believed him. He put out his arms to take hold of the baby. "Come on, Priscilla, come through to the lounge and talk." Nothing was said, but she followed. She would have followed him anywhere. "Robert. So we have called you Robert, eh?" His smile reached both ears and some more. Robert returned the gesture, but with the addition of a healthy dribble . . . and a burp.

Chapter Twenty

"Police entrapment, my arse! No wonder the department doesn't want to go after these bastards with money. Like that bloke with the suitcase full of heroin, yeah, yeah only taking it to see how far the bad men would go. Like he wasn't going to sell it on. Oh, no. Fucking glove doesn't fit so he's let off. Probably been slamming the door on the fucker half the night to make it swell. Gallon of cortisone injections. Fucking ridiculous. Once upon a time circumstantial was enough. Video action doesn't do now. Oh, no. Bastards. No, probably need a full length feature film next, then they'll claim the rights on it. What sort of a name is Van De Clouet anyway? Probably Dutch. Probably from Amsterdam. Other countries collect stamps. Bastards. This stinks. Probably half his mates in city hall are upto the same. 'We're hoping that the case will be dropped, so we would rather leave questioning to a later date. You may find them unnecessary, and we wouldn't like to waste police resources'. Drop the case. He's lucky I didn't drop him." Officer Edsell was in rather a bad mood.

"Kicking the chair across the room in front of his attorney probably didn't help, our case," ventured Pat's partner. It was as much as he dare say. In circumstances like these, it was best to just listen.

"Pat!" he shouted. They were cruising down Boulevard Fifth. Somebody pulled out in front. They had no chance of braking in time. Pat didn't. The accelerator crushed the pile on his carpet as the engine roared a warning to the wheels, which replied with a screaming protest and a puff of blue smoke. Stevie's skull smacked back into the headrest as his eyes compressed, further distorting the image in the side-view mirrors, of the station wagon passing behind them by a slim margin. A very slim margin. Pat cranked on the hand brake, locking the back tyres and spun the wheel. A real protest from the back wheels, as they moved sideways, the second, and the car spun around coming to a halt parallel to the offending vehicle.

Stevie was momentarily disorientated.

The driver was an ape, a big ape, doing an impression of a lumberjack, in an area where the thickest tree was slimmer than a hooker's thigh.

"Hey Shit, what the fuck do you think you're doing?" shouted Officer Edsell. Stevie rolled his eyes. The eyes needed the exercise. Not the sort of greeting to the public that was taught at the 'Academy'. Pat was halfway out of the car. The second cloud of blue smoke in the last fifteen seconds hadn't completely cleared. The car radio rasped. "Control, D Sixteen." A sweet voice, some girl from 'control', totally out of context in this fast-developing context. An alien environment.

Stevie answered it. It was a welcome relief.

"Yeah, D Sixteen, Stevie". Realisation washed through the ape and he took his paw off the door handle. He put both hands into view with his palms out. It was the time honoured greeting to an alien, but this was the first alien to have long hair that was unwashed and a face that was unshaven, at least in the comics that he had read. That was all that he read.

The voice on the radio changed to that of a man. "Stevie. I have something that might interest you and the Monster." There was silence. If the officer in uniform, at the other end of the air-waves, thought that this would elicit a response he was wrong. Pat and Stevie looked at each other. It wouldn't be an invitation for dinner, that was for sure, although an eating experience would figure, but they weren't to know that.

"Yeah, what is it?" Stevie replied after getting the visual go ahead from Pat. The driver of the pick-up was mesmerised. And holding his breath. This was one ape who was hanging, hanging by a thread.

"I have a mangy corpse, half eaten by rats in a big shit heap of garbage." Stevie automatically held up the microphone for Pat.

"Hey, fuck off. Sort out your own shit. We're engaged on an important arrest here on the 'Queen's Highway'." The driver of the pick-up wasn't sure what the last comment meant, but it was bad news for him. He rested his hands on the wheel, in resignation. Pat handed the mike back to Stevie.

"I'll take that as negative, then, should I Officer Edsell?" There was a pause, just long enough for Pat to turn away. He'd no intention of answering the question. The 'Ape' was resigned. "The corpse was wearing an electric stunner dangling from his wrist. Just thought you might be interested." Stevie extended his arm that held the microphone again. Pat grabbed it from him.

"Where is it?"

"Down town, behind the Carmel Buildings, Pacific Avenue, South."

"Ten minutes. We'll be there. Thanks." Stevie re-took possession of the mike. The third cloud of smoke in as many minutes enveloped the offending pick-up as the car shot off, Stevie's neck muscles taking the strain of the acceleration and the driver of the pick-up taking his first breath, even though it was laced with rubber and carbon. It tasted fine by him.

Pat had transformed the ten minutes to eight, by way of the police prerogative. Speeding. When his car grumbled up the lane to the rear, it was waved through the cordon. The handful of uniformed officers nudged each other as he pulled up. The two detectives already there, smirked. Stevie was wishing that he hadn't worn a white shirt to work, today. Pat wasn't wearing a white shirt. "Undercover officers don't want to look too clean," was one of his favourites, "you never fool anyone if you use conditioner on your hair." Pat made the first cut, through the gathering. Stevie followed. The crowd parted and the smirks disappeared.

"Pat."

"Mo." Mo smelt of aftershave. "Nice to see you boys." It was the sort of greeting that was usually reserved for a get-together, after work. "The body was discovered by the garbage guys, who noticed a leg as the bin was tipping. It's a wonder the whole thing or what is left of it, wasn't swallowed by the machine." He waited for a reaction from Pat. Pat's eyes met his, so he carried on. "His name was John."

"How the fuck do you know that?" Pat's eyes re-connected.

"Well, it might not be his correct name, but the bin-guys know all the bums around here. They hang around looking for scraps and anything to sell. This guy wasn't passing by, it was John's home." The detective shrugged, to distance himself from the way of life these people lead. Pat, on the other hand, understood, solving problems demanded understanding. He had been down there.

"And he's in that bin?" It was rhetorical, but the detective nodded anyway.

"Most of him. The rest of him is running round the neighbourhood, care of his four-legged friends, re-cycling him as shit."

"Let's get it tipped over on it's side and have a look anyway, should we?" A wave of disquiet rushed around the assembly at his use of the word, 'we'.

"Has anyone been in?" Stupid question. The others didn't even bother shaking their heads. "Stevie, you push and I'll pull." Stevie was glad to be pushing. He would be upstream when the flood broke. Everyone else parted. It was noticed. Stevie noticed. It was a bitch to work with Pat, but, at the same time, an honour. He was going to dirty his white shirt anyway, so he may as well not flinch, but do it with good grace. He forced a smile.

"On three, Detective." Stevie liked that. "Three." Dong. A dull ring as the bin hit the deck. It was three quarters full. The contents rolled out, at least some of them. More of the contents followed, at a much greater speed, but, again, they were contents of the four legged variety, with thin tails, and dark brown. It would be argued later that there were at least twenty, but Pat would insist that there were only eighteen. Everyone scattered apart from Pat, who stood his ground. The rats scattered, both sides of him. They parted like the Sea of Galilee, squeaking noisily as they went amidst much swearing and cursing. Jesus was mentioned a time or two. Pat strode to his car and took a pair of pink rubber gloves from the compartment of the same name. The group re-assembled, their eyes wandering from the pink gloves to Pat's face and back again. "Fingerprints," was all that he said. The others weren't so sure. They could never be, with Edsell. Washing-up stretched their imaginations.

"Clearing a bin full of rats, garbage and rotting corpse was rather like putting your arm up a cow's bottom," Pat would say, later that day. "The sooner that you get in, the sooner you get out." It was an analogy that would capture the flavour, but leave Stevie with a lingering after-taste. Regardless, straight in, was how he went for it. On it's side, the aperture was about four feet high. At a crouch, Pat moved forward, throwing the black plastic bags, largely intact, and tied at the top, behind him.

"Make two piles, could you, Stevie? Ones that are open, and ones that are closed." The smell was overpowering. There was a line of balance between revulsion and curiosity, where everyone approached, but never crossed, apart from Stevie. Fifteen bags came out, before the body was fully exposed, revulsion getting the edge on curiosity and winning another yard between the crowd and the bin. It was dark inside this foul receptacle and Pat was crouched between them and the corpse. It was a bundle of clothes that had alerted them to the prize. Pat pulled the body out by the shoulders of the filthy coat. It had obviously been filthy, long before death, but this little lot had not helped, one iota. They all noticed that he was holding his breath and was surrounded by a gorging mass of heavy flies. When it came into view, most of them looked away. It was in an horrendous condition, most of the face gone and one hand was stripped to the bone. Degenerating globs of grey slime were what was left of the neck. The rats had been partying and were non too pleased at being disturbed for the second time, many looking on waiting for another opportunity from the safety of the weeds growing along the fence-line. Nobody would have laughed at his rubber gloves now. Nobody would have tackled this, even with, rubber gloves.

Pat pulled the body well clear of the entrance, it helped keep the flies away from the job in progress. There, hanging from what was left of his wrist, was the electric stunner, with the stainless steel tips proudly shining in the afternoon sun. It was easy to imagine why no-one had wanted to remove it, because this was the hand that had been the main course. Not disturbing the evidence was a well used excuse for not dirtying ones hands. With the stub of an old pencil, Pat pushed aside a piece of gunge from the instrument to reveal a small red light. The gunge moved. Maggots. It was still switched on. He pushed the button to turn it off, and out it went. He looked up at his colleagues. A thorough search was hardly a description they could lay claim to.

He went back to the task of clearing the rubbish bags. There were only a half dozen left and he could see that they were securely tied. They were all from the restaurant, next door, or office waste, next door to that. There were two distinct style of bags, the restaurant ones had food scraps and paper table rubbish, the other ones contained office waste in the form of documents. He could tell that much from the half-hearted search that the rats had conducted. The poor John, had been their centre of attention, though. There was a third type of bag, just the one. It was black, with gold lettering, it read, 'Shoes by Ricci'. Pat knew that this was the one. It may as well have read, 'evidence for Pat'. Clues normally stood out, they didn't have to be neon lit. He turned his back on everything else and came out in reverse, pleased to get some air, but certainly not showing it. The sunlight felt great, it did him a power'. It was doing nothing for poor old John.

"Mo, take that thing off John's wrist and put it into an evidence bag". He was referring, of course to the stunner. That was the trouble with getting the best view, you were in line for the worst job. Mo hesitated. "Go on, Mo, he won't bite, you won't even smell it with that aftershave". A titter went around the small crowd. They were pleased that he didn't pick them. Stevie was extra pleased. "Want to borrow my rubber gloves?" he added, to turn the screw a little tighter. Mo didn't answer, but he did put his hand inside the evidence bag and used that, inside out, as a glove. He certainly wasn't going to touch anything like that. He didn't want to destroy any clues. Sales of pink rubber gloves rose in the vicinity of the precinct over the next few days.

Pat moved away, slightly, with Stevie. In a conspiratorial way, they turned their backs on everyone and looked in the bag. It was they who had done the retrieval, and it was they who would be the keepers of the secrets. They had paid the price. There were two hairbrushes in the bag. They were not cheap, nor were they expensive. He picked them out, carefully. They were both clean. There was not a single hair on either of them.

"Curious, no hairs, Stevie."

"One of them has funny writing, maybe Chinese. No, it's Japanese," he said after a little more inspection. Pat was impressed. He didn't show it.

"What the fuck do you know about Japanese? Huh? It could easily be Chinese."

"No, it is definitely Japanese." Pat looked at him, focusing particularly on his smirk. Stevie hesitated just long enough to savour the taste of satisfaction. "It says Tokyo on the other side of the handle."

"Smart git."

"Thank you, Sir," said Stevie. Pat Smiled at him, he really liked that sort of thing, it was a great game. They both did.

"Organise the body. Get finger prints. Oh, and search the clothes," Pat commanded, in the direction of the two remaining detectives, one of whom was the hapless Mo. "I'll take that bag," and he relieved Mo of the stunner, which was swinging at arm's length, in a sheath of clear plastic. "See you down at the station. Come on, Stevie, let's make progress here." And they left the scene, faster than they had arrived, a little protest from the rear wheels.

The speed with which they got into forensics and out again bore a similarity with the DNA procedure. It was the matching of the samples which took the time. In this case, as with Priscilla's samples, there was no matching, because there were no prints, apart from the ones of John, on the hairbrushes. They had been kept clean in the plastic shoe bag, but the stunner had been rolling about in all sorts of unmentionables. They had drawn a blank.

"Well," said Stevie, at least there is something positive that has come from it".

"Oh yeah. And what's that?"

"We can knock off and have a bite and a beer. Not necessarily in that order." Stevie grinned. For a moment.

"Fuck that." This, Stevie knew, was a bad sign. "We'll shoot around to the 'State', see the bold Ian and confront him with the items, get a positive

ID on them both, 'if', they were used in the robbery. Not that it will affect Ian's sentence that much, he'll not be out for a while, anyway". Stevie's stomach was complaining, now that he had thought about food, though he could still taste the garbage. Rotting flesh lingers.

"No, Stevie, there's something stinking about this. I'd like to get to the bottom of it."

"Well you certainly got to the bottom of that bin. Did you see the look on their faces, especially Mo?" They both howled with laughter. They'd be the talk of the 'steamy'. Stevie originated from Glasgow. "Come on then, hit the gas, open the windows and let's blow that shit out of our systems. We'll eat later." That was just exactly what Pat liked about the 'big man'.

The 'State Penitentiary', was thirteen minutes away. It took fifteen. Pat took some ribbing.

"It was the evening traffic."

"Yeah, yeah. I think it was age, and I'm not talking vehicles." He laughed at Pat's expense.

The duo were well known in this establishment. They were responsible for a number of the guests. Several greetings were called out as they were led between the rows of cells. The inmates didn't seem to hold a grudge against Pat. He was well liked, even though he was responsible for their incarceration and even though he only ever addressed them as 'Shit'. They simply, politely, called him Pat.

"Ian Driscoll has a visitor already, Pat," said the warder, great big belt holding up his trousers stretched over an over-sized bum and a big bunch of keys swinging noisily from the same. It was a walk designed to intimidate. It didn't.

"Yeah, and who might that be, his maiden Aunt?" Pat was unhappy at the lack of finger prints. The traffic had added to his burden. He was in no mood for further disappointments.

"Hi, Pat."

"Hi, Shit. You behavin'." The black prisoner grinned. "Sure you are." Pat made an imitation gun with two fingers, took aim and fired. The prisoner ducked and fired back. The warder was on another wavelength, he never picked up the signal.

"No, it's his Lawyer, Ingolson."

"No, shit." Pat nodded to another inmate. They pulled grimaces at each other, but they broke into grins before reception was lost. Stevie peeled off the formation and stopped to talk to a couple of Hispanics. He was amazed that they were in the same cell and would get to the bottom of it, giving Pat space. It is surprising what information you get in prisons. People are desperate to communicate with the outside world, it's a breath of air. Information is light baggage and it does have a value, sometimes high value. They trade, give you the information, you give them air.

There were only two of them, now, when they reached the holding pen at the end of the row of about twenty open cells. This one wasn't open. It was used for single prisoners who were very dangerous, or noisy or for interviews, and the closed wall led to a little more privacy, for questioning, etc. rather than the open bar configuration. The door was locked, and the warder, whose name was unknown to Pat, fumbled through his great collection of keys, probably for a degree of dramatic effect, but it was lost on Pat. Too much time wasting and he would end up being known as 'asshole'.

"Driscoll, I have a visitor for you." No 'Mr' for the prisoner. "I suppose that you will be staying in attendance, Mr Ingolson?". There was a nod from the Lawyer and a scowl from the prisoner. "I shall be outside, be warned, let's behave now, y'all." His charge was given the 'eye', but it didn't intimidate anyone. It was a procedure.

"I hope that you are referring to Officer Edsell and not my client, Sir," said the Lawyer, who had spotted Pat silhouetted in the doorway. "It was he who was responsible for the loss of my client's arm."

"Fuck off! I don't suppose the crashing of an aircraft in an attempt to flee the law, with a bundle of heroin had anything to do with it, did it?" The warder tried to exert his influence.

"Come on Gentlemen, come on. There'll be none of this on my floor, or there'll be no contact from anyone." He stared at the occupants of the cell, but he wouldn't have dared do the same to Pat. Pat pushed by and grabbed a chair, spinning it around and straddling the seat, leaning on the back, his plastic bag on his knees, hidden behind the backrest, tantalising the Lawyer.

It is a fact that the deeper the shit that prisoners are in, the cockier they are. Anything they say has less of an impact on what happens to them, they are upto their necks anyway.

"Brought us a present have you, Officer Edsell? The title was used with a large dose of venom. "Bit early for Christmas." Pat ignored it. The Lawyer, Ingolson, said nothing.

"The wrist watch that you stole from the house of a Mr Dalton Feinnes . . ." The Lawyer sprang from his seat.

"My client did no such thing, Officer."

"He already admitted it, so don't try. . . ."

"He had been speaking under duress, having just lost an arm, was in shock, traumatised and in the process of a brutal arrest. He bought the watch in a bar, paid good American Dollars for it." Pat rolled his eyes. Ian smirked, his short sleeved tee shirt exposing his stump at the elbow, but still sporting a bandage. The damage had been so great, following the original accident, that it had had to be amputated. The lower arm was gone, but it was the equivalent of a battle honour, he may as well wear it openly and gain something from the loss, even if it was only criminal kudos. It was a talking point in here. Pat retorted with a forced smirk, to match the one exhibited by his adversary. The way that he felt, he would dearly love to amputate the other one. At least it was his wanking hand. He nearly said that out loud, but he thoughtfully kept it to himself. Maybe on another occasion. He reached into the bag and whipped out the stun gun.

"Hell." The word blasted out of Ian's mouth. The face paled around his gaping lips.

"Seen this before have we then, Driscoll?" There was a pause, whilst his eyes met those of his Lawyer. Ian's smirk had disappeared.

"Never." Ian's composure was back. He'd been kicked in the ribs, but his balls were still intact. He would swear that he could feel the prongs sending his heart into orbit and back, and his brains into hell. That sort of feeling lingered. Pat carried on regardless. He knew fifty per cent of what he had come for, now. This was the instrument, or at least one like it.

"What about these brushes? Ever seen them before?" It was too late, Ian had put up the shutters. Ian's head was shaking whilst his solicitor answered for him.

"My client has seen none of these items and would not like to answer any more questions, thank you very much." Now Pat gave out a real smirk.

"He's only answered one." Everyone knew what he meant. It wasn't wasted. Pat got up, his eyes fixed on Ian. Ingolson got up in an attempt to emphasise the end of the interview and turned his back to put his papers in his briefcase, further dismissing the inquisitor. Pat took his opportunity for a little fun, he wasn't leaving empty handed, but neither was he satisfied. He made a very small, pretend movement, toward Ian, with the stun gun. Ian's reaction was as classic as it was confirmation. He kicked back in surprise, with his heels, making the legs of the chair squeak loudly. The Lawyer snapped his head around in response, to see what was happening, but his tormentor was still. Quizzical looks got him nowhere and was content to see Pat Edsell march out of the door without a word, the stun gun swinging from his wrist and the plastic bag, containing the brushes, in the other one. It would be more truthful, to say that he was relieved.

Chapter Twenty One

The day had started fairly normally. Dalton had not heard from Beatrice but had spoken to Priscilla a couple of times. Really, there was trouble with the new film and it was fully occupying his mind. The film itself was running smoothly, but there is more to films than filming, there is finance.

Finance was largely contracted up front with the banks and the investors, but it was never paid, up front. It was drawn in stages, and the more problems that the banks or institutions had, the slower the payments came through. This put the film company under great pressure, then this rubbed off onto the cast and this turned into delays and then that turned into more cost, which made the money come even slower and additional money, almost impossible. This was where Dalton was at, at the moment. It wasn't just him, or his film company, or even the industry. It was everything that was experiencing difficulties. Concentric circles were hitting the world of finance and the epicentre was the Far East. Japan.

He was in his dressing gown, a lemon one, his favourite, on the patio. He was drinking fresh orange, iced, on which Rosario was the expert (she crushed the ice in a bag, first) and largely enjoying the sunlight filtering through the leaves of the overhanging trees, although the dappled effect on his morning paper was something that he could do without, but it didn't annoy him enough to force a move. He stayed put. Rose brought him the morning post. There were six letters.

"Thanks, Rose." He smiled.

"Your egg will be cold." He smiled again. He rather liked the gentle scolding. She seemed to know when to do it and when not to. Only when they were alone. The front door bell rang. Rose left, to answer it. Dalton opened the first envelope casually, returning the newspaper to the far edge of the table, folded neatly. He picked up the envelope on the top of the pile. He made it a rule not to sift through them and pick up the most interesting. He always said that they were in an order for a reason and he would take them as they came, in line with his general philosophy. He would soon wish he had eaten his egg before opening the letters, because he certainly wouldn't be eating it afterwards. His appetite would be somewhat diminished.

Joyce Pitrowska, Attorney, Carmel Buildings, Pacific Avenue, South. The name and address went into his head smoothly enough, but the next part came at him in shots. He felt dyslexic. He couldn't focus and it certainly made no sense. Admit paternity. Priscilla Glover. Robert. Baby boy. Arrangements.

"Excuse me Mr Feinnes, but there is an Officer Edsell here to see you. He would like a word." She waited. "I think he is a policeman, the one that came about your break-in." She waited some more. No answer. He was floating.

"Baby. Born on . . ."

"I beg your pardon, Mr Feinnes?" Dalton was still looking at the letter.

"I don't want to see anyone at the moment . . ." He looked around at Rose, but there was the detective in the doorway. Dalton put his elbow on the table and his head in his hand, rubbing his forehead, taking deep breaths. "What's got into her," he thought to himself. He'd had accusations before, not all of them based on fact, but now there were foolproof procedures to check the validity of such claims, they were largely a thing of the past. It was a ridiculous claim.

"I'll only take a minute of your time, Sir." Pat was not going to be able to speak to him unless he pushed. Reticence was not a description normally attributed to his particular character.

"What is it?" Dalton said, testily, after one last rub of the forehead. "I'm

180

sorry." Dalton was never rude, on purpose. " Good morning."

"Sorry for fucking disturbing you," Pat said to himself. The immaculate, crisp yellow dressing gown was the catalyst for his annoyance, his own was old and disgusting by any standards and it was annoying to be reminded. "I've come across these two hair brushes, in the course of my investigation, and I thought perhaps you could identify them." Now both of Dalton's elbows were on the table, all ten fingers were against his brow. He looked at his finger nails. It gave him time to think and exhale all the air in his lungs, slowly. He turned his head and his eyes went from the brushes to Pat and back to the brushes.

"I'm afraid not, Officer." 'Officer', put the distance between them, and Pat knew, from experience, that that was the end of that. He was in no mood at all to argue the point. "Fuck you," was what he would have like to say. "Fuck you, fuck you, fuck you, I hope that you get robbed every day for the next ten years . . . or more."

"Thank you very much for your time," was what he did say and turned on his heels. He would continue the tirade in the privacy of his car, until he reached the 'Station', but then he would elaborate. "Had my arm up a dead cow's arse for that bastard. Those were his brushes all right. Twat." His anger would be seismic and rumble on for more than his colleagues would have preferred. If they were given a choice they wouldn't have heard any of it. They weren't given a choice.

Dalton was far too well brought up and refined for that sort of language although there was a part of him that shared the sentiment. The other part of him, the reasoned part, was perplexed. It was just a nonsense trying to claim this. He had been so good to her. He adored the baby. Maybe she didn't know who the father was and was looking for a substitute. What was the Lawyer thinking, letting the woman make an accusation that was not true and impossible to substantiate?

The time had crept to nine thirty. He should have been at the studios, already. "Don't put this off," he said to himself. "Call the ridiculous Ms Pitrowska." He hated the title, 'Ms'.

"Could I have the cordless phone, please, Rosario?" He had only had to raise his voice slightly. Rose was not far away and she appeared with the phone in a few seconds. She smiled. She knew the atmosphere was not what it should be, sensitivity to changing moods was one of her attributes. "Thanks."

He pulled out the small aerial as he scanned the page once more, dialling the number at the top of the sheet at the same time. Two rings.

"Good morning, Joyce Pitrowska's office. How can I help you?" It was the black lady with the 'big hair'. Her voice was white

"I'd like to speak to Ms Pitrowska, if I may." He anticipated the next question. "It's Dalton Feinnes."

"If you would hold for a moment, I'll try to connect you." Music started playing, light opera.

He idled the next few moments, allowing the bright, dappled light and shade to play on the back of his hand as he drummed his fingers. The music stopped, taking him by surprise. The business-like voice snapped in.

"Joyce Pitrowska, good morning, how can I help?"

'How can she help? Wow, that's a bit thick. The day before, she writes me a letter accusing me of God-knows-what and now she's saying, 'How can I help'. Great."

"This is Dalton, Feinnes." No response. "Dalton Feinnes, to whom you wrote yesterday. I received your letter this morning."

"Yes."

"Well." He hesitated and thought for a moment. He'd expected some sort of apologetic noises, excusing herself. It was the client's wishes. We can sort this out. I hope you are not too offended. I realise that this is a serious allegation to commit to paper, etc. Nothing.

"Well. Do you realise that this is a serious allegation." He would have to point it out to her himself, if nothing was forthcoming. "Although, I know Priscilla Glover, and indeed, was present at the birth, of her son, and indeed, was . . . " he hesitated before he admitted the next part to himself, though he knew that it must be the case, "was, (past tense), engaged to her sister, Beatrice, and the boy was even named after my middle name . . . I have had nothing whatsoever to do with her on a physical level. Never."

"You have dated Miss Glover, though?. . . . Mr Feinnes." Joyce accentuated the title 'Mr', like Dalton had done with her title. He didn't miss the point.

"Now look here." He was losing it. It wasn't going as he had expected. "Now look here. This is a very serious allegation, and although I sympathise with Priscilla's situation, and think a great deal of her, it still remains a very serious allegation. One which I would deny, I might add." His voice had raised slightly. It was unlike him.

"No, Mr Fiennes. You look here. Do you seriously think that I would send a letter out like that without knowing the facts?" His brain went back into 'floating mode', it wasn't making enough sense to formulate an emotional response, let alone a balanced one. "I specialise in this kind of case and we always hear this kind of thing in a paternity case. You men go right upto the line before you finally admit your responsibilities, right upto the line. Why you can't be honest, why can't men in general, be honest? I'll never know, you just belittle yourselves with your pathetic denials, even in the face of irrefutable evidence."

It looked bad and sounded awful. Her tone had too much conviction, too sure of herself, it wasn't sounding right by any means.

"I have never . . ."

"Mr Fiennes. We have tested. We have confirmed the father by DNA profiling. You are the father of this boy and you will have to admit it sooner or later. Sooner would be preferable. Good morning and good bye."

Dalton was left holding the dead phone with a little green light winking at him. His eyes were not focusing as they should be.

He stared ahead, the sunlight, through the leaves flashing into his eyes as the leaves moved in the light airs. He dialled Priscilla's house. The number was in the memory. He would get to the bottom of it. Twenty rings were enough, but he gave it another five. No response. Two more. A blank.

"Damnation," he shouted aloud. All this on top of the problems at the tudio. Just when I thought that things couldn't get worse. He thought he'd better dress.

"More coffee, Mr Feinnes?"

"Thanks, Rose, but no." He would have liked to have told her, confided in someone, but he couldn't. That was one of the problems of keeping everything to yourself, trying to be independent, strong. People confided in you, but you couldn't confide in them. It was mainly women. He wandered through to the bedroom. The door wasn't closed firmly behind him, but Rose would never just enter. He took off his robe, carried it into the bathroom and hung it on the back of the door. The weather was easily warm enough to have no clothes on, the robe was for modesty, only. He'd showered once, when he awoke, but he had to have time to think and he was hot, flushed. It wasn't the facts that annoyed him, he even let the possibility of being the father wash over him to explore the feeling and he rather liked it. It was the injustice that annoyed him. He found Priscilla attractive.

He put on the shower. The stream of water was powerful and hot within seconds. Stepping out of his slippers he glanced at his firm body in the mirror, even as the steam nibbled at the vision. When it had faded into clouds, he stepped inside and let the hot water wash over his head and bounce off his sturdy neck, rivulets running down his flat stomach and flowing across his manhood, leaving as a stream. He had a good body, it felt good when he soaped it, washing away the latest assault. He'd waited too long to be a father, he knew that. He looked so confidant, felt so confidant most of the time, but at the same time, felt vulnerable, afraid of commitment, even a little afraid of the future. An accident in the bedroom department might have been the best policy, there was nothing like being pushed, having the decision taken away from you. It was always something you could hang your blame on.

He also had no idea why he said that the brush was not his. Of course it was his. Was it as simple as not wanting to have any more problems on his plate at the moment, or was there more to it? He couldn't decide, but he had a feeling about it and he felt that he had done the right thing.

He had an idea. There was still soap in his short hair when it came to him. He stepped out of the shower, leaving the water running, billowing steam following in his wake, puddles of water on the marble floor. The idea had grabbed him. He crossed the hall, his genitals heavy and bouncing between his thighs. He made it to what was now known as 'Priscilla and Robert's room'. His body was almost dry, spots of water across his broad shoulders. He brushed his wet hair from his forehead as he reached the side of the baby's cot. He pulled back the covers. The tiny sheets and the pillow case had been changed. He stood up. "Damn." Nothing was going right.

The bedroom door moved, ever so slightly, but noiselessly. Rosario could see Dalton next to the cot. She knew that he hadn't heard him, and knew that she should have stepped back out of sight, and indeed, she did, but not immediately. She should, by rights, have been wondering what he was doing, but it never entered her head. Rose was mesmerised. He looked good. He always looked good. She had seen him in his swimming costume, which were like small shorts, but there was nothing like total nakedness. It was different. His buttocks. Thighs. She stepped back. His form was etched on her memory and would remain there, ready for recall on those lonely nights, flashing back of it's own accord when he was in her view and unaware of her presence. She 'rewound' the picture now to check that it had been retained.

His hand moved over the back of his head and down over his neck in frustration, firmly. Another idea. He pulled the bottom sheet off and lifted the mattress out. It had been new, and he inspected it closely. There were three of them, three tiny dark hairs in total, under where the pillow had been. He held them up by their ends. They had been broken off but he didn't believe that they included follicles. They were too fine to be sure. He stood erect, thinking. He closed his eyes momentarily and smiled to himself. Eureka. It was there, hanging in ront of him. How the hell did he miss it? On the side of the cot, hanging by a blue ribbon, was the dummy, comforter. Comfort indeed. Holding it by the ribbon, in one hand, and the hairs in the other, he slowly made his way back to the bedroom, only now realising that he had been out of the room unclothed, and how awful it would have been, had

Rosario come across him. He liked the feeling of nakedness, always had.

He hung the comforter over the knob of the bathroom door, whilst he pulled off several sheets of toilet paper from the roll. He laid the sheets out in two strips, on the bed, putting the hairs on one, and the comforter on the other. He folded them over, carefully, like a parcel. He stood with his hands on each hip, pleased with himself, pleased with the feeling of the sunlight on his naked back, feeling the caressing rays, down, down over his calves and touching his ankles.

Soft white tennis shirt, flannels, white socks and blazer. Boxers. Rolex. It caught his eye. He ran his thumb over the face as soon as he had his left hand through the strap, and wondered where the instrument had been for all those long months. There was a scratch on the face. He would have the glass replaced when he had time. What he didn't realise, was that this watch had saved a man's life. A shard of aluminium had been deflected from that very face, without which, at subsonic speed, it would have severed the artery and possibly the wrist. Propellers move very quickly, indeed, even when they are disintegrating. If he had known who it was, and was still in this frame of mind, he would have hoped that the worst had happened. Little did he know, that today's predicament was inextricably linked to that event. His theories of pre-ordination might well have more than a grain of truth and gained another degree of credibility.

Packing the two parcels of toilet tissue, in his briefcase, Dalton left the house. He would phone the studios from his car, and tell them that he wouldn't be in, today.

Rosario watched him leave, from the upstairs window. Her heart beat a little faster than normal. There was one fairy that was no longer sleeping. She could feel it. It fluttered.

It didn't take Dalton long to reach the university. It was the parking situation that took the time. He had to drive around for longer than the journey had taken. When he did find a place, it was so tight, that he had to climb over the passenger seat, to get out at the other side. He could hardly open the door and had trouble retrieving his briefcase from the back seat. The edge of the door caught his chin and he let the air out of his lungs quicker than normal, in exasperation.

He had been here before, four times in all. His original contact was through a mutual friend, but he was on good terms with the manager of the particular department that he was striding towards. 'Genetics Straight Ahead'. Why was it that even though you knew where the room was, one couldn't help but read the sign, anyway. Damned annoying, if you were in the sort of mood that Dalton had developed.

He gave a light knock, for politeness, and walked in. The drab green door was half-glazed, with the sort of frosted glass that rattled, no matter how carefully one closed the door. A lady looked up. She was about to smile. Her name was Lauralei, a big girl, pretty, wore glasses and had been a detective, but had transferred, full-time from forensics to represent the Police Department. The police were the biggest client for the division that was responsible for DNA profiling. It was expensive to run the department, and they liked to get grants, or gifts. Dalton's money fell into the last category. It was basically a boring job, and although there were important ramifications, it was still, largely, preparing slides and matching patterns. No, it was research that gave the few people who worked here the kicks, and without the 'bread and butter' jobs, there would be no research. Money was the catalyst.

"Hi," Dalton said, as jovially as he could muster, in the circumstances and to this individual in particular. She knew who he was and knew why he'd been here in the past. Paternity suits weren't her 'poison'.

"Hi," she drawled, the word lasting three times as the identical one that Dalton had just uttered. "If you are looking for Keith, he's through there." She threw her head in the direction of the lab, then caught his eye again, and added, "As usual." Dalton felt bad. It had worked.

Keith heard the footsteps and looked up from his position at the sink.

"Well, we'll be getting you your own desk soon, old buddy."

"Not you as well, I just had to pass the detective from hell. Please." The forehead was rubbed again. "Give us a break."

"How are you doing?" he asked, completely ignoring the plea.

"Fine." Dalton took a deep breath. "But I have a problem."

"Don't we all?" Keith was a really good sort, and didn't mean anything by the comments. He was completely bald. He claimed that the birth of his fourth child had been the cause, but who knows? He had lost the lot in the space of one day, though, not only on his head, but his whole body.

"This time, I promise you that I am as innocent and pure as the driven snow." Dalton put up his hands in submission.

"I think that I have heard that one before in this establishment," said Keith, forefinger on his lip and a mock stare to the heavens. "Yep, think I just might have heard that one before."

"Well this time, it's true. So there." He would have tried to join the banter, but he felt that it was far too serious a problem to joke about. "What the hell is Priscilla playing at?" he said to himself for the twentieth time. He couldn't believe that a mere two and a half hours ago, this kind of thing was furthest from his mind.

"OK, what have you got?" asked Keith, keeping up his mock expression of exasperation. To avoid further exchanges, Dalton put his briefcase onto the bench and took out the two parcels of tissue. When he opened the first one, Keith didn't comment, but switched to 'professional mode'. Profiling was a new science, relatively, and it was a relatively exact science, but extracting the pure DNA without mistakes, took a degree of artistry and interpretation. He shook his head.

"I'm sorry, but I don't think that we will be able to make an extraction in this case, there is no follicle. What else do you have?". He pushed the first package, containing the three hairs, away. Dalton might have been experiencing a feeling of floating, earlier, but now, he was definitely sinking.

The dummy, or comforter provoked a response.

"Things have moved into a serious stage, I see," said Keith, as he held it up by the ribbon, between his fingers and thumb. "Very Serious."

"Quite. But can you do anything?"

"A saliva sample is a possibility, as long as it hasn't been washed". He held it up for scrutiny. "I suppose you mean now?"

"Yep. I'd be grateful." Keith looked at him. "Most grateful." Of course, inside, he was telling himself that there should be no need of this at all. He had nothing to prove, but he didn't like the attitude of the Lawyer, not one little bit. "Do you want a sample again?" His scalp stung at the thought of it.

"No thanks, I kept a copy after the last drama." Keith looked around, when he heard the squeak of chair legs. Dalton was sitting down. "For God's sake. Don't tell me you are going to wait?" Dalton sat down anyway and didn't answer. "I suppose that means 'yes'? And I also suppose that 'right away', means 'at this very second'?"

"Correct. As long as it takes."

Chapter Twenty Two

Several days had passed. Priscilla had lost all track of time. She was in a timeless round of feeding, bathing, and attending to baby Robert. He was gorgeous and she adored him. He was everything that she could have asked, but she would have preferred him to arrive with a father. On her second visit to see her Lawyer, Joyce, it had unnerved her. She felt as though she were being sucked along. Joyce was such a strong character, with such strong convictions, big on morals, big on church. As a recently confirmed sinner, Priscilla couldn't even pretend to be in the same league, and was wracked with guilt. Regret was not part of that process, because Robert was the balance, the bonding between mother and baby more than compensated.

Joyce was determined in her crusade, and, to be fair, had no thought that Priscilla could be anything other than an innocent party, wronged, yet again, by a man who had had his way and gone his own way, in that quick order. Any protest from Priscilla would blow her cover and she would be exposed in a big way. So the letter was composed, typed out by the lady with the 'big hair' and delivered. Priscilla's only real part of it, was a nod of the head and even that was out of her control.

Priscilla had been calculating when the letter would arrive and the dreadful scene that it was to cause. She wasn't to know whether Beatrice had made up or disappeared. One thing was for sure, she certainly dare not go around to her house, until she knew how the land lay. Confrontation would be inevitable, but not just yet.

Then there was Jacky. He had been fussing around, with the best intentions, and professed his love, but she had her doubts. She had noticed that he never asked to hold the baby, unlike Dalton. Perhaps it was because it wasn't his, but there again, Dalton loved to hold the baby and wasn't aware that it was his, either. She had watched him and come to the conclusion that it was a combination of this, his age, and the fact that he couldn't have one of his own, and, on a long term basis, he had come to terms with that state of affairs. He seemed jealous of the attention that she lavished on her son. When the baby was asleep, and they were in bed together, because sleeping together, they were, he seemed more at ease. She had noticed that he had taken to keeping the phone off the hook after office hours. He was still kind and thoughtful, making a real effort to amuse her, but there was something there, something on his mind.

They had made love several times and it had been nice. She had enjoyed the closeness. It enveloped her, took her mind off her own, not inconsiderable problems. It wasn't passionate, but like millions of females the world over, she had known no other. His old problem had returned and he had explained it to her, but his failure to perform was nothing that worried her, and it did improve, after he had admitted it to her, and they had talked. Priscilla hadn't really known what to say, but nobody was in a hurry and she had always been patient. It was closeness that she required, not passion.

When he was in a position to perform, the last thing they wanted, was the baby to cry, and when it did, that was the end of the proceedings for that night, there was no chance of a second attempt. Again, Priscilla wasn't too bothered. The problem was that she didn't love him, she couldn't reciprocate. She certainly couldn't return his more intimate kisses. She didn't know why and never suspected that she was already in love with somebody else. Jacky was trying to fill a vacuum that was already taken.

"That policeman has driven by in his car again, Jacky, today", she said, almost casually. It sounded very casual to Jacky.

"That scruffy detective?" His low voice sounded conspiratorial.

"Yes." They were speaking quietly, because Robert had only just gone to sleep. Jacky had been in the lab for the last hour. Priscilla had caught him there several times, after the clinic had closed, just staring at his precious flasks. They were his real babies. She knew. And his lovers.

He came to bed. He smiled weakly and spoke to Priscilla in a low voice. "Priscilla. You know that I love you." She held his hand in response, always happy to hear it, yet feeling guilty for not responding. 'I love you', always contains as much question as it does, statement. "How do you feel about Ireland?"

"Ireland? I've never been. Never even thought about it, really. Don't they still have those awful troubles there?"

"Not everywhere, they don't, especially in the South. There's a kind of tranquillity there, that Americans don't understand, peace that co-exists with conflict, but I'm really not talking about the troubles, it's life in the slow lane, but by choice. I think you would like it." He looked at her face. There was pleading in his eyes, a sadness. "It would be a new life, a new start for Robert, if you came with me."

"Why, are you thinking of going?"

"Yes, I am, Priscilla. I've decided." He looked away, idly, out of the window, onto the quiet street. "I'm of an age to retire anyway." He lay down next to her and put his arm around her. "I really do want you to come with me, but I have to go, I must."

"Have to go? Why?" Her heart started beating faster in her chest. He blew the air out of his lungs and swallowed deeply, hers was not the only heart that was racing. His casual air was feigned.

"Priscilla, I'm having problems with Molly's relatives, or to be more precise, her Uncle." Now Priscilla's heart was really racing at the mention of Molly. She was hoping that Molly had long been forgotten. The funeral had passed quietly and, of course, she had not attended, she had been in hospital.

Priscilla sat up and looked into his face. It was warm in the bed but now it felt stifling and she kicked the duvet down, to give them some cool air.

"Yes, you see I was the beneficiary to her will and she was rather wealthy. She never spent anything, you see, she'd had several legacies and managed her resources like the 'best of them'. She made far more money from that than ever she did working here. In fact, she made far more money than I ever did. What has made it worse, was that I was the witness to it." He looked at her, "The will that is. I didn't know that she had any relatives, she told me that she hadn't. I believed her". He was talking quickly, now, and he had to force himself to be quieter, so the baby wouldn't wake. The flood gates were well and truly open.

"And I suppose that he has found out and is contesting ?"

"Precisely. Anyway," Jacky was now up on one elbow. "Anyway, I've transferred the whole lot, out of the country, by courier, through Canada. I had known her for years, and she wanted me to have the money." He was blurting out the story as though it was trapped inside and he wanted to confess. It was the Irish way.

"He would, the Uncle that is, have a big problem trying to reverse the will. It would take him years."

"Mmmm, but that's not all." He stopped and looked at her intensely. Now he was begging. "Her uncle wants an investigation into the death and the certification. It was me who signed it, it was also me who signed for her medication, but it was legitimate, Priscilla, it was legitimate". He might as well have stopped talking, because Priscilla wasn't listening, the buzzing in her ears was drowning everything out. "There are things that I don't understand, Priscilla, but I am going, I'm too old for all this". He cupped one of her solid breasts in his hand. She gently removed it.

"I must think, Jacky. Let's sleep on it. I will give you the answer in the morning." She turned out the light. "Go to sleep, Jacky. It will be a lot clearer in the morning". They both lay down, neither of them spoke, but neither of them slept, not a wink.

Now she really was out of her depth and drowning was imminent.

Chapter Twenty Three

When Beatrice arrived at the gates, naturally, they were closed. It had not been too long since she had walked out and, after all, it was the first time that she had done such a thing. She had shouted. She had said some things that she wished that she hadn't, but these were mainly to her sister, not to Dalton and she had deserved it. The only part that she was really worried about was the termination of her unwanted pregnancy, unwanted at that point in time, that is. The truth was, that it could just have been one other person who was the father, but that was something that she had not revealed. Pretence, of that nature, on that scale, for a life-time, was something that she couldn't have carried off, though it was a burden that many females had born through the millennia. These days, it wasn't quite so simple. There are two edges to most swords.

She had had time to cool. In fact, the incident had almost disappeared from her memory. Work had not been a substitute, because she had not been doing what she preferred. There was no glamour at the wrong end of a camera and she wasn't at the rear of the instrument through her own merit. The only thing that people saw when you had your eye to the lens, was your bottom and that was beginning to be a little larger than she would have liked, at least, larger than her younger rivals. Perhaps more hinged on Dalton than she would even care to admit, even to herself. She was also surprised that the phone hadn't rung, no matter how hard she had stared. She dare not phone, herself. Her assets, were more of a visual nature. It was one thing to let the heat of the argument die down, but there was a danger of the fire going out altogether, or even catching hold elsewhere. If Sarah Cobham got wind of it, she'd be around in an instant with her barbed talons out, the bitch. No, she had left it long enough. She fingered her engagement ring nervously. Though she had accused Dalton of having designs on Priscilla, it was based on her own anger and inadequacies. Priscilla had been neither a contender nor a threat. Dalton was well out of her league, she should have realised that, but jealousy had blinded her.

Anyway, the gates looked more imposing than normal. She stepped out of the car, after first looking nervously around the shadows. It was only early evening, but it was a street that was fairly dark and she felt exposed in her own headlights as she waited for an answer on the intercom. She pressed the bell again. There was no ringing sound for the person outside, only a static buzz to indicate life in the system. Three rings and Rosario answered.

"It's Beatrice, Rosario," was her answer to the accented question, but Rose had already known the answer, she'd seen the car arrive.

"Mr Dalton is out, I am afraid." The accent, that was normally quite picturesque, was now grating on her nerves.

"Well, if you just open the gates, then I'll come and wait." There was a pause. A pause that was longer than Beatrice was happy with. Her nerves were pulled tighter. She never thanked her, partly because she felt that the intercom was already closed. She slammed the car door, thankful to be in her own space, the music still caressing her, the smell of the cream leather, a comfort in so much as it was familiar. It might seem a cliché to admit that Leonard Cohen was playing, but it was a fact. She was drawn to the deep, sexy tones of his mystery. And it suited her mood. It was also depressing.

Beatrice never did have a key to the door, it was always opened by the staff of the time. Neither did Dalton. "A key was the sign of unreliable staff, or no staff at all," was what he once quoted his neighbour as saying. Of course, he believed it himself. She could tell by his tone. On this occasion, it was opened, but after a delay, a delay that was noticeable but not large enough to quantify. Beatrice would assert herself.

"And at what time is Mr Feinnes expected back, Rosario?"

"He left this morning, Miss Glover, and didn't say." Two could play at that game.

"I'll wait." And at that, she marched off into the lounge, which looked out onto the patio, and turned on the television, loudly.

Dalton had, indeed left the house in the morning. He had not slept well at all. His wait at the University had been in vain. Keith had had great difficulty in isolating any DNA material from the poor samples with which he had been furnished and complained to the increasingly impatient Dalton, several times, which in turn, made Dalton increasingly impatient.

"Well that's all that we have to work on, so let's try, should we?"

"I am trying. I've been trying."

"Well try a little harder," insisted Dalton. It had actually become a challenge to Keith, something to stretch him. It was what he liked, although he doubted that Dalton could imagine the difficulty and the complexities of the issue. Most people's perception of such procedures was based on what was described in the press and the paying public wanted to hear solutions and success, not difficulties and possibilities.

It was early evening, again, before there was any progress, Dalton was about to give up. He had tried to phone Priscilla a few times, but the phone was just ringing out and he wasn't sure what he would say, even if she answered. He needed to be armed with the evidence first, then he would be able to confront her and the dreadful Ms Pitrowska.

It was a quiet victory. Keith was not prone to premature congratulations or boastful behaviour, science was his domain, and he knew just how many times, things could go wrong at the last minute.

"Dalton, I've managed to isolate part of the gene, we'll develop it and see if we can find a match, but I warn you, there might not be enough. It's like a jigs-saw puzzle with a few of the pieces missing. We don't need them all to recognise the picture, but we do need certain ones and enough of them, at that." He allowed himself the luxury of a grin, in the direction of

Dalton, but only a small one. Dalton was totally focused on the outcome. There was no way that he would be going home or anywhere else, for that matter, until he had that result.

Beatrice was becoming impatient. The television was only on for dramatic effect. She felt tired. Her make-up looked tired. She crossed the hall, to the bedroom. Rosario heard her, but wasn't sure what, if anything, to do. Overstepping her authority would jeopardise her own safety. Beatrice deposited her shoes at the bedroom door. Dalton's rules were hard to break. He hated outdoor shoes in his bedroom. In fact, he hated them in the house. He'd spent time raising money for his films in Japan and that was one habit that he'd returned with and it had stuck.

She crossed the carpet and onto the marble, entered the bathroom and ran some water into the basin. Her hands were hot and sticky. She washed them. It was nerves. She felt like a stranger in her fiancé's house. Her face met her eyes in the mirror. It was drawn and needed the lipstick replenishing. She opened her bag. It was the same shade that Priscilla had taken to applying. It looked better on her own face, Priscilla just didn't suit it.

On the way back across the bedroom, she noticed a letter on the dressing table. It was open, with no attempt to hide it. Dalton had never expected to have anyone in the room. Rosario had already read it.

"Tut, tut, tut, tut, tut."

Dalton looked up from the most boring science journal that he had ever encountered, not that he had encountered many.

"Tut, tut, tut, tut, tut, what?" said Dalton. Keith replied by drawing a long breath of air between his teeth, and then blowing it out again, just as slowly, but even more dramatically, with his cheeks puffed out. He was in danger of impersonating a tradesman who had just been called in to rectify someone else's work. "Who's been a naughty boy then, eh?" Or a policeman.

"I don't get you, Keith," said Dalton. If people are unsure and want sympathy, they always address their tormentors by name.

"I have a match. It fits. You are the father all right."

If Dalton had put a shotgun in his mouth and pulled the trigger with his big toe, the effect would have been less dramatic. Either way, his mind had been well and truly blown.

"You are bloody joking." He shook his head. Vigorously. "You must be bloody joking. You must have made a mistake." He was drowning with nausea.

"Sorry, my friend, there is no mistake. Come and have a look." Sure enough, the lines of varying greys were identical and fitted together. Keith had circled the important ones with a pencil. There was no mistake, even to a layman.

"How could that possibly be?"

"There's only one way that I know, 'Dalton, old boy'," mimicking the sort of accent that he thought that Dalton possessed, when he was in certain company, "And you and I know what that is."

The problem was that Dalton didn't know.

Beatrice wasn't snooping. She was bored and she only picked the letter up idly, not even with any real curiosity. If she had had the will to reason, after reading it, she would probably concluded that she had only picked it up because it was there. Dalton never left papers laying around, not for secrecy, but for tidiness. It was out of character. But reason left her, arguably, for ever. She had reached a water-shed in her power of reasoning. The name of her sister jumped out at her. The combination of sister and Lawyer was unexpected, but add to that, paternity and baby, well that was fantasy. Nightmare. It was Beatrice's turn to feel nauseous. Her legs turned to jelly and collapsed under her, sitting down heavily on the corner of the bed, the bed where such good times had been experienced. It now revolted her.

"That bitch. That bastard. That bleeding bitch," she screamed. One of those names refereed to Dalton.

The last person to touch the letter and, indeed, the person who put it there, heard everything, winced, and crossed herself, simultaneously. Beatrice clenched her fists around the paper and pulled at it, in different directions. It gave up the struggle and parted in the middle. She threw one screwed up half at the bathroom door and one half at the bedroom door, throwing herself, face down, on the bed. The paper wasn't the only thing to be screwed up. She felt the cotton smudge her thick, red, lipstick and felt it's dryness in her open mouth, but snapped herself upright, spitting amateurishly onto the cover, disgusted at the thought of her sister and Dalton satisfying themselves on what she had considered her bed. The smudge of red, in the middle of the pristine cover reminded her of blood, the blood on the sheets where Priscilla had given birth, the smile on Dalton's face as she discovered him with the new born bastard in his arms.

Her head was in her hands as she sobbed in self-pity. She could think of nothing other than the pair of them together, she couldn't shake the image from her mind. She knew that women would do anything to anyone if the result was the man they wanted. Men didn't realise this, they had no idea and women didn't like to admit it, even to themselves, but now, Beatrice was confronted by the truth, it was standing naked, before her, the truth was naked and the images were naked, her sister's skinny, shapeless, pale and pasty body submitting to his desires and entrapping him with her talk of opera and books. Now it was a baby. She understood now, how Priscilla had knowledge, Dalton's likes and dislikes. What a bloody fool she had been. Now it was obvious. She pushed the heavy bed with all her might, her excess energy threatening to burn her up, but it only moved a matter of inches. Her frustration was killing.

"That bastard will pay," was what she shouted. It's not clear quite who she was talking about. It wasn't even clear to Beatrice, but perhaps she had yet to decide. It was clear to Rosario, but Rosario was mistaken.

She rushed from the bedroom. She could stand the place no more. It had become as alien an environment as another planet altogether. The door swung back and crashed into the wall, the antique door knob burying itself into the plaster-work. The outer door moved in the opposite direction and was left gaping in her wake. She fumbled for her car keys through a blur of tears, rummaging frantically through her hand-bag, frustration mounting. Luckily, the only luck she would have, the car fired the first time and she immediately spun the wheels to bring the car facing the closed gates. The engine growled repeatedly under pressure from the accelerator whilst the gates opened of their own accord. Control could only be exercised on the way in, they opened automatically on the way out, but she was being watched. Her tail lights disappeared as the six cylinders pushed her up the road and out of sight, at speed, through a neighbourhood that wasn't used to such behaviour..

Rosario didn't touch the door, she left it as it was. She looked at the two balls of paper at either side of the room and left them alone as well. The envelope was where she had left it. The only thing that she touched, was the drawer that they had come from and she tugged on the handle, until that was open fully, leaving it in that position, like a gaping mouth. Her own face was expressionless, apart from a faint line on her forehead. Now Rosario was worried. The tiniest of sins always found her out, she should never have looked at the letter, nor left it out. She wanted a reaction, but didn't expect an explosion.

Chapter Twenty Four

It wouldn't work. Priscilla knew that, now. She couldn't face the thought of Dalton being angry, being hurt. She was far too close to him. She shuddered at the thought, but The Japanese and Van De Clouet, were further away, there was a distance, she would not have had to face them, and they would have been preferable, even though the thought of them both made her flesh creep, now. But that depended on what she wanted the outcome to be. Her objectives had become indistinct. You see, she never did want the man himself. She wanted the baby, and yes, money, but that was simply a side effect of having the recognition of a named father. It had sounded so simple in the conception. Now, of course, she wanted the man and not the money, but that was a dangerous way to think, it would end in disappointment and her head was already in such a state of disarray, she would be able to take no more. After doing that trick to anyone, there was no hope of the man. She was thinking herself lucky that there was someone who wanted her at all. On any level.

There was a phenomenon that she had not anticipated when the plan had been conceived. Dalton was the father of her child. He had certainly done her no wrong. It would have been different if he had knowingly been involved and, say, abandoned his responsibilities, but he hadn't. Now, she wanted to protect him. There was a bond to him, through Robert.

Jacky half opened his eyes. he had been awake a while.

"Yes, I'll come with you. We'll both come with you. And good morning." His eyes were open now, all right.

"Well top of the morning to you, what a wonderful day it is too."

"It's raining."

"It can shower us with frogs for all I care. It's still a wonderful morning." And with that, they kissed. Jacky's kisses were enthusiastic indeed. She felt obliged to accept the advance, as well, because she had just accepted an invitation for life. She could hardly throw cold water on the enthusiasm now.

When she'd extracted him from her mouth, she jumped out of bed. Robert was in the same room and was stirring. As she got out, at the window side, she parted two of the venetian slats and looked out into the street. They both knew what she was looking for. Her face gave him relief. There were no cars. Both their own cars were at the back, in the double garage.

"I'd like to go as soon as possible, Jacky. If we are going, then let's go."

"I agree." He studied her for a moment. They studied each other. Priscilla walked over to the baby.

"Come on Darling. Up you get. We are going with Dr Jones to Ireland. Now what do you think to that?" Robert replied with a sneeze, a wet one.

"Jacky did look faintly silly as he got out of bed, naked and crossed the room for his gown, but Priscilla thought that she could forgive him for that.

"I am going to make enquiries now, Priscilla, now this minute. Are you sure that you mean straight away?"

"Straight away was what I said, Dr Jones, and straight away is what I mean." Priscilla carried Robert over to the bathroom and started the water running for his morning bath. Jacky went downstairs. The noise of the running water drowned the sound of his footsteps on the bare, wooden stairs. Robert had a bouncy chair, metal frame and cloth cover. Priscilla placed him in the chair and let her gown fall to the floor. She was going to bathe with her boy and kill two birds with the one stone. She needed a clip for her hair, so that she wouldn't wet it, and keep it out of the way when she attended to Robert. It was by the bed. The floor felt cool on her own bare feet, as she crossed the room. Priscilla heard the tiny tinkle on the bedroom extension, as Jacky lifted the downstairs phone. She would have still not thought anything.

"Good morning, it's Dr Jones, I spoke to you yesterday about a flight reservation," The two elements of 'flight' and 'yesterday', caught her mid-step. Had she not been out of the bathroom, she would never have heard a thing. Jacky was speaking in quite a low voice, not whispering, but low.

"When is the next seat available, and could you make that two seats, please?" He paused, then as though an afterthought, but possibly as an omission, "There is a baby also." Another pause. "No, I don't want the flight on Wednesday, I want to cancel that and take those three . . ." Robert started to cry, so Priscilla went back to the bathroom.

She was in the bath, with Robert, when Jacky came back up the stairs. He knocked gently, out of politeness, but didn't wait for an answer. It was the first time that anyone had ever taken that kind of liberty. It wasn't a real big-deal, he seen Priscilla naked before, but that was in bed and sort of, by appointment. This was only a few minutes and two doubts into a new phase of the relationship.

She looked good. The hot water had given her body a little more colour. Her breasts were larger than normal, because Robert had not been fed, yet. He was a little moody because of it, he wanted his breakfast, but the phone call had upset the order of proceedings. She had to think. No time. She wished that she had locked the door.

"There is a flight with British Airways, this evening at ten thirty and I have made a provisional booking." He looked at her and she looked back at him. They were both making an assessment. It was a push. It made decisions much easier.

"That's fine, I'll have to go over to the house and sort some things. I'll need my passport. The last time I was abroad was Europe, France. We can send for the rest, later." She didn't want to expand on her experiences in France. That was where she had bought the stunner. Also, she hardly ever referred to the trip, because it followed her Mother's death and she had worried that it had looked like a celebration of the tragic event. However, it had been liberating.

He held out her hand and she took it for a moment, before he left the room and left her to her thoughts. She was being swept along, she knew, but she had to leave before the storm broke. She hardly dare think of going to the house. She let Robert suck her in the bath, the warm milk soothed him, and she wallowed in the water, feeling what a mother likes best, being wanted and being able to provide.

Dalton had not slept well at all. This was one conundrum that he couldn't crack, nor was he likely to, without more information. When he returned to the house, and was met by the news that Beatrice had been around, he was on edge, further, but that was all the information that was offered. It was only when he was in the bedroom, that he found the drawer open and the two balls of paper at either side of the room. He'd already seen the lipstick in the centre of the ruffled bed. He could just imagine the scene when Beatrice read about Priscilla and Robert. "Jesus." He went back out into the hall and called Rosario, but there was no answer. It was late and she had retired for the night. He hung his clothes neatly, and had a long shower, hotter than normal. There were certain things that he would have liked to wash away. It was a long shot.

It was a warm night, but the things that played on his mind, artificially increased his temperature. He had an idea. Not risking anything, this time, he pulled on a clean pair of silk boxer shorts. He would check the messages on the answer phone, but there were only two, and they were from the studio. They were feeling his absence, but rather than make him feel glad, and wanted, it annoyed him. It made him feel used and hounded. Almost nothing would please him tonight. Sex was the last thing on his mind, the very last thing. He could make a lady pregnant by walking down the same street, by being in the same town, damn it.

Jacky had had two clients all day. He'd been half hearted about them, he couldn't concentrate. They didn't know it, but he would never see them again. An hour was spent, writing a letter to his receptionist, Dee, not explaining much, just that he had to leave and that he was sorry. It was a hard letter to write. There were several attempts. Everything he had worked for was here, but as soon as he had decided to leave, it suddenly looked useless, futile, worthless. All these years for nothing. It had been as though a light were switched off, it was that sudden. The accolades that he had expected had not come, respect was more a fancy than a reality. He was only asked to professional functions because he paid his subscriptions, had he stopped, then they would have stopped. When he had started this work, he was almost considered a magician, getting results for people who had given up hope, but now people expected the result, they were even impatient and complained if things were not as speedy and easy as the press would have them believe. For all that it was commonplace, it was certainly not routine and results were not guaranteed. Creating life was not becoming a right, it was still a gift, and Jacky still believed in the hand of the Almighty.

He had done a good job, a damned good job. The photos on the wall testified to that, but they were curling at the edges. Photos were given less often, now, although numbers of births were actually up. He had made the families possible, but they were not his family. He felt used, almost abused. The pay-off had come, but it had cost the dear Molly, her life. He should never have given her that medication, in those quantities, but she demanded them herself, and she couldn't stop. Her heart attack was inevitable. It had been a lucky escape, for him. If he hadn't known the ambulance crew, and the hospital Doctor had not been busy, they would never have taken his word, skimmed over the procedure and missed the main point, then he would have had some explaining to do. 'Overdose' might not have come to light, but 'dependence and addiction' would have been more than mentioned. That blasted policeman knew something, though, otherwise he would not be around, all the time. No, it was time to leave. Molly's uncle was like a dog with a bone, he wasn't going to let up. The money was Jacky's, now, and he wasn't going to give it up. Never. He was owed it.

He felt like a lone warder in an empty prison. His inmates had been forgotten. He thought that his precious sperm bank would have been used on a regular basis. That's where the profit and the satisfaction would have been, but through all these years, of logging, checking and watching over his charges, the owners never used the facility. He gave them their child, they banked their sperm and forgot about it. The standing order for the facility was largely forgotten, it was so small. A storage facility was never the plan. It was to be used, for life. If he didn't remind them, they would have forgotten that it was there. It was carried on by everybody for wrong reasons, negative reasons, their fear and superstition kept them paying up, just in case something happened to the child that they already had. Jacky had envisaged a positive usage, and that was where his interest lay. It wasn't even giving him the satisfaction of getting rich.

The final straw was when he tried to arrange a reunion party, of all 'his' children. The response was paltry, an insult. The few that did reply and were only coming because he phoned them and they felt obliged, had to be told that it was off. He could sense the relief. It was tangible. The truth was that they didn't want to be reminded of their inadequacies, his part in the proceedings had been put to one side, forgotten. They were stealing his credit. He'd been robbed. Well his turn had come.

The letter finished and sealed in an envelope, he left it behind reception, for Dee to find in the morning. He had let her go early, but had made sure that he wasn't in sight when she left. His face would have told a story. Subterfuge really wasn't his way.

Jacky joined Priscilla behind the closed blinds in the bedroom, and helped her pack. All the things that were in daily use were already at Jacky's house, because she had been there long enough for them to drift in that direction. There were lots to do, and things to get from the house, but she had wanted to go after dark, not letting Jacky know that fact, of course.

"I'll take Robert in the car and get the other things that I need, Jacky. It will take me a while. What time is checking in?"

"Nine thirty, the flight is at ten thirty. It will take you thirty minutes, at that time of night, to the airport. You had better go in your own car and we'll meet at the check-in." All of a sudden, it seemed a big hurry, to Priscilla. She was being pushed again. There was nothing that she could do. It took the decision making away from her and, in a way, she was thankful, but out of control . . . well that was another matter.

"I'll just have to go now, then." She made a point of kissing him on the cheek. She wasn't about to let him set off with any doubts in his mind. It is surprising how much confidence a kiss can transfer.

For the fourth time, that day, a sports coupe passed the clinic. It didn't stop. There were no cars parked outside, but the occupant wasn't to know that there was a garage at the back.

Priscilla turned into 'her' road. There were no other vehicles in sight. The motion of the driving had sent Robert to sleep. That, and the feed he had just consumed, was enough for any exhausted mite with nothing on it's conscience. His mother, on the other hand was exhausted but nothing would make her sleep.

Her own, open plan driveway, was deserted, as she had hoped. She hadn't known what to expect, but the more that she thought about it, the more nervous she became. There was plenty on Priscilla's conscience. She was pleased to be leaving. The unknown was usually worse than reality, but this case might be an exception.

Priscilla nosed the car into her own drive. It didn't look much, when compared to Dalton's, but she knew she would never see that again. She might not even have a drive, in Ireland. The house, of course, was in darkness. Another dark street. Had her driving mirror been inclined another few degrees, to the right, she would have noticed the hood of a sport's coupe protruding a block away just at the junction of South Wesley. She didn't notice.

Priscilla had pulled the car up next to the side door. Robert was asleep, soundly. She decided to lock the doors and pack, not disturbing him, but going outside every so often to check him. It would be a lot easier and it was long past his bed-time.

She made a point of looking around when she stepped out of the car, but the narrow drive restricted her field of vision, substantially. Had it not done so, she would have seen the interior light of the coupe come on as the door opened to discharge the occupant.

Once in the house and the lights on, she felt better. Of course, she didn't lock the door, because Robert was outside, in fact, she left the door open slightly. It was a warm night and she wanted to know if and when he cried. Priscilla started to pack the essentials, starting with her passport. Her mobile phone was where she had left it, fully charged, but switched off. She would need it, so she slipped it in her blazer pocket and phone Joyce, her Lawyer, from the airport. Joyce had given her, her home number. It hadn't seemed to be of any practical use and Joyce never expected it to be used, but it was a good PR exercise, showing that she cared.

Well, now she would get a call. Priscilla had decided to instruct her to send a letter of apology to Dalton and arrange for her house to be sold, if all worked out well, in Europe. She was even feeling quite pleased with herself. The proceeds of her house sale here, would more than keep her in Europe, especially in Ireland, where the house prices were a lot less. This house was a family house and far too big for her now, anyway. That would only have to be the case if she didn't get along with Jacky. He had come into all that money and he would keep them both. From what he had told her, it was an awful lot of money. In the long term, she, might even get the lot. At least now, she had a future. The future excited her. It even seemed right that she should have a share, after all, she was the instrument that brought about her demise, although Jacky imagined it to be his own doing. There was a symmetry there, somewhere.

She had two bags ready to go into the car when she thought that she had heard a noise in the kitchen. She hoped that it wasn't the cats. She should never have left the door open, because the cats were only next door with their new family and they might think that they could come home and enter the house. When she left, they would be locked in and that would be terrible. It was a good job that she had heard the noise.

"Tommy. Tabs." No sound. She stopped short of calling, 'come to mummy', because her affections were now elsewhere. Priscilla stepped outside. Robert was still asleep, though the interior of the car was dark and unless you knew he was there, he would be invisible. They were the last two major items of luggage, so she put them into the trunk.

"Right, those cats," she said, out loud. "Come on, I know that you are in there." She was at ease, now. It was her own house. She turned on the kitchen light, noticing that the drawer next to the sink was open slightly. It shouldn't have been, but her thoughts never crystallised. She closed it.

Slam. The front door banged closed. There wasn't a breath of wind and it should never have happened. She almost jumped out of her skin, and it left her shaking. But it wasn't the door that she saw, when she swung her head around. It was Beatrice. Her heart had been dumped on, by her adrenal gland.

"And just where the fucking hell do you think that you are going, Sister?" Beatrice hadn't shouted it, but it was in loud and measured tones that were frightening. She was dressed in white trainers and black, tight leggings, that made the tops of her thighs look lumpy, the Nike tee-shirt was heaving as she struggled to control her rate of breathing. That made two of them. She would remember those details for a long time. Priscilla couldn't answer, immediately.

"Well? . . . I suppose that you are going off with my Dalton, you sneaky bitch, you and that little bastarding love child of yours . . . eh?"

"Beatrice, you have it wrong, you . . ."

"Don't give me that crap, just don't give me that. I've seen the Lawyer's letter that you sent. What a fool I've been, even getting engaged to the rat whilst you were having his baby." There was no possibility of getting past Beatrice, Beatrice was raging, there were demons in her head. Priscilla had hardly ever seen her without make-up and now, her white face looked awful, swollen with aggression and over-indulgence. Beatrice had been attending the gym for ages in an attempt to halt the decline. It had made her muscles bigger, but couldn't mask the ageing process. Now her anger made her look stronger and more menacing than ever.

The only thing that Priscilla could do, was hit her with her accent, it normally struck fear into most, and had always worked with Beatrice. It had been cultivated just as surely as a muscular frame.

"Now just you look here, Beatrice, I think . . . ," but she didn't finish. Beatrice was angered by the attempt, more than cowed. The hand that was out of view, came into sight and Priscilla was forced to focus her attention on the largest kitchen knife out of her drawer, she recognised it at once and realised why the drawer had been open in the first place.

"Beatrice." But the protest fell on deaf ears. Her sister was crazed and lashed out with the blade, more as a gesture, at first, rather than a specified intention of harm. However, that was just a pre-cursor. It missed her by inches and she thought she was going to faint there and then. It might have been easier. The kitchen was walk-through, so it was open at both ends. It was fortuitous to say the least, otherwise it would have been the end of her. As Beatrice was recovering from her lunge, Priscilla turned, and with one hand on the corner of the entrance, pulled herself around, momentarily out of sight, pushing one of the chairs out of her way and behind her, with the other hand. It was the living room and the lights were off there, in preparation for her departure. Beatrice lashed out again, taking a sizeable chunk out of the woodwork, causing the knife to vibrate in her hand, sending painful shocks through her wrist. Priscilla had a small start on her, but had to pass the other, open end of the kitchen. If Beatrice had anticipated her direction, again it would have been 'curtains', but she followed and crashed into the upturned chair, sprawling across the floor. One of her shins was badly bruised by the impact taking off a length of tanned skin.

"I'll kill you, you bastard, I'll kill you." Priscilla's legs had never had to do so much work, and yet had never felt as tired. She made huge demands on them as she strode up the stairs, whilst her sister recovered her feet, turning to kick the offending chair across the room. The din was tremendous and served to frighten the victim further.

The bathroom was the only room with a lock on it, so that was the option that she took. It was lucky that she had that little foresight, or it would have been the end of her, there and then, for not a moment after she had fumbled the lock closed, with it's big, old fashioned key, her sister's frame hit the door. It was only the centre of the door, where the lock was located, that was still touching the surrounding woodwork as she repeatedly threw her weight against it.

"Beatrice, stop, for God's sake stop!" But it was no use whatsoever, Beatrice heard nothing. She was attacking the door with the blade, now, trying to cut her way through. There was no defence, nothing in the bathroom that Priscilla could use.

The window. Priscilla threw it open. Not enough. The banging on the door saved her. Beatrice heard nothing. It was an old sash window and was stiff, and panic set in. Now it was the turn of her arms to feel the strain. It took every ounce of strength to open it far enough to scramble through, one leg out first and then her head. It was unladylike but effective. Just. Priscilla half fell, half slid out onto the garage roof, as her sister redoubled her efforts at smashing down the door. The lack of further protest from her quarry, subconsciously encouraged her, something wasn't right. Her weak little sister would never be able to effect an escape. The lock gave out, at the same time that Priscilla dropped the two metres from the garage roof, in front of the car. Her tights were in tatters with sliding across the roof tiles and the back of her skirt was around her waist, but it was no time for niceties. Priscilla fumbled for a second time, retrieved her keys from her pocket and pressed the button for the doors to open. The lights from the car's security system flashed as all four locks popped up. Beatrice just caught sight of those amber flashes, reflecting off the neighbours garage and knew what had happened, instantly. She turned on her trainers, which were now a great advantage and flew down the stairs, straight through the front door as the engine fired. Priscilla saw her coming and pressed the central locking. All four doors locked again, simultaneously. It was to save her life. Beatrice had her hand on the handle as Priscilla slung the gear lever into reverse and spun the back wheels. In turn, Beatrice had the handle forced out of her grip as the car shot backwards, spinning her onto the ground. Never great at reversing, Priscilla shot off the driveway and mounted the lawn, taking several shrubs as she went. At least she had cleared the garden and was out on the pavement. Beatrice Sprinted towards the car, but was left standing as the car accelerated noisily away, the rear of the car snaking after the front wheels. Robert slept on.

Dalton had had enough. He had just decided that phoning was going to get him nowhere. He had tried the house number, but Priscilla must have been away. She must be at the clinic. That phone must be off the hook, it couldn't be engaged for that long. He would go and see for himself. He left the security of his house, the gates closing behind him. He was feeling frantic, now. Perhaps Priscilla had done something to hurt herself. Why didn't she answer? His mobile phone was on the seat beside him, with the numbers that he needed, stored within. He clicked in the cruise control at just below the limit, and settled back uneasily, to cross town, the quietness of his Mercedes allowing him the luxury of concentration on his dilemma, whilst the reflections of the street lights crossed his white hood, rhythmically. He ran everything through his mind, but couldn't come up with any answer or conclusion. He must be missing something.

Jacky was at the airport. He had collected the three tickets and had checked his luggage in. Whatever happened, he thought, he was going, now. He had a nagging doubt about Priscilla, but he tried to shake it out of his mind. He looked about him, wondering whether it would be the last time that he would see his adopted country. Could he learn to love Ireland again? Had it ever been any other way, or were Irish immigrants just deluding themselves? Could he ever learn to love Robert? He thought that he loved Priscilla, but maybe it could have been any woman who would reciprocate.

His mind was back at the clinic. Yes, the phone was off the hook. He hadn't wanted any disturbance whilst he had said his farewells. It was with a heavy heart that he had gone into the lab for the last time. It was a full ten minutes that he had stood in front of his two beloved flasks, their lights winking at him brightly, always nudging up and down, jostling to keep at their exact temperatures, competing. He'd always thought of them as his family, living things. Twins. There was more individual life in these two flasks than there were inhabitants in the whole of the San Francisco Bay area. It was a sobering thought. But what was the quality of life? He'd accepted, now, that they were kept here without reason, abandoned by their makers. No, this was wrong, it was an aberration.

He turned his back on them. Two paces and he was facing the console on the wall. He was glad that his back was turned. He pulled the two fuses that fed them, out together. They lived together and they would die together. There was a small blue spark as the circuits broke, followed by a deadly scream from behind. The back up batteries had kicked in. These were not to power the flasks themselves, they were for the alarms. Screaming and wailing, screaming and wailing. It was awful. It ripped him apart, but once it had been done, he somehow felt cleansed and a little relieved. A climax. The figures in the panels, one on each flask, started winding up. Slowly at first, a headlong race to destruction. It might take an hour, naturally, and upto a day for his charges to come up to room temperature and maybe even back to life, but that would be followed by a slow and tortured death. No, he couldn't stand that.

Dr Jones took a single, very deep breath and turned. For the last time, he put on the thick, white, gloves. Through the noise of the ear-splitting alarms, he broke both the seals and, one at a time, put the lids carefully to one side. The liquid nitrogen boiled like the cauldrons from hell, heavy vapour pouring onto the floor like some cheap and crazy floor show. It would be all over soon. That was all that it took, all those years and that was all that it took. His head shook from side to side. He turned on his heels, switched out the light and left them to die in peace.

It was nine p.m. Priscilla was still shaking. There were tear stains down her face, which was paler than ever. What lip stick that she had been wearing, was long gone. She had to get out of this crazy town, and was glad that she was leaving. This crazy town and this crazy family. It occurred to her that she was the instigator, but everyone who did wrong could always find justification, and hers was strapped into the back seat, sleeping the sleep of the innocent.

She was about half way to the airport, in the direction of the clinic. She would never see that place again. With one hand, she took her mobile phone from her blazer pocket and checked that it was on. It winked at her. She thought about making a call, but she would wait until she was at the airport. Time was running out. Her tights were a mess. She couldn't go into the terminal in that state. At the next lights, she put on the hand brake and began to wriggle out of them. It was difficult, with the seat belt, but she eventually got her thumbs into the elastic of the waist and pulled them down. She was glad that it was dark. She was still shaky and fumbling, because she expected the lights to change any minute. As she freed both feet from the tattered nylon, and went to replace her shoes, she noticed the lights go green. Her foot wasn't in one of the shoes properly her bare heal made it harder to push in against the leather. A car, waiting to cross in front of her, blasted it's horn, impatiently. Hand brake off, she jabbed the pedal and shot forward. Nerves had knocked the smooth edges from her driving. She had not looked in the mirror, behind her. Had she done so, she would have glimpsed a black sports coupe hurtling in her direction, hiding behind the glaring beams. As it was, the first thing that she felt, was her head being snapped backwards and to the side, the car spinning forty-five degrees and the crunching of compressing metal.

Beatrice had imagined Priscilla would be going back to the clinic, at least it was the only thing that she could think of. In the darkness, at the house, she hadn't seen Robert, asleep on the back seat, and by the time that Beatrice had reached her own car, Priscilla was long gone. She wasn't to know that her sister was going to the airport, and that she had to pass the area that the clinic was situated. She had spotted the compact sedan waiting at the lights, with one car behind it, so had to steer around the other car for a side impact. She would stop her sister's car at all costs. The other car was now in deep shock, the occupants, frozen with terror. When the sedan containing her sister had shot forward, it was too late to correct her line of attack and Beatrice just clipped the rear wing on the driver's side and was spun around, herself, the rear of her car taking out the passenger side headlight of the innocent party, waiting behind Priscilla. The two cars were metres apart, for an instant, not parallel, but almost. Robert was crying, it was to be the rudest awakening of his life. In that split second, the eyes of the sisters met, Priscilla's were pleading, Beatrice's, blazing. It was an information superhighway for that moment. More information passed between them in that short period than the internet could have managed.

Priscilla never let her foot relax, just kept up the pressure, as the rear wheels fought for traction and screamed their protest. Beatrice had been in third gear, on impact. It was a stick-shift car, considered to be the more sporty. On this occasion, it failed her miserably and the engine stalled with the sudden stop. She had failed to depress the clutch. She fought with the keys to restart, but they needed to go back a notch, before they would allow such a manoeuvre. They were precious seconds that left her glancing up at the disappearing tail lights and down into the gloom at the dangling bunch of keys. Amongst the keys, there hung a small doll with long hair and a funny Scandinavian face. Far from being the amusing mascot intended, it stared back with an evil defiance, daring her to continue. She took up the challenge and gunned the six cylinders back to life. The lights changed to red. No-one moved. They were all mesmerised by the activity, caught like moths in the flickering lights. It couldn't be happening to them. The car that was hit, sat silently, one head lamp out, like a stunned Cyclops, as Beatrice spun her front wheels in pursuit of the car that had spun it's rear wheels.

Priscilla was hyperventilating. Her knuckles competed with her face for whiteness. Her face won by a whisker. The sound of Robert crying, followed her like a banshee. It was nine-ten. A confusing, swirling, pattern of headlights behind her gave her no clue as to the whereabouts of her insane sister as she pressed on amongst the torrents of cars which swept her along, like mechanical flotsam. The next lights just changed in front of her. There were twenty metres to go.

"Oh God. Oh Robert!". She relaxed the pressure on the pedal and went for the brake.

Thump! She changed her mind and slammed the accelerator to the floor. The lights were red when she passed through and the other cars had started to move. She had to take evasive action and swerve. The gap between the crossing cars was closing, and she did mount the curb with a jolt, but retrieved the situation, releasing a cacophonous row in her wake. It was a chorus from the 'horns of Jericho'. She sped off again, taking advantage of the path kept cleared by the traffic lights.

Priscilla was exposed by her isolation. Why she didn't make any turns, was a mystery, but she had a deadline and time was running out. Time was also running out for Beatrice. She had ten cars in front of her at the red light, all of which were stationary. Without a thought, she overtook. It was a gamble. There were no oncoming cars, and if none were to turn down here, towards her, from the junction, then she would be all right. Six cylinders roared, twenty four valves spat out the rich exhaust created by the impossible demand made upon the fourth gear, and the front suspension rode high. Beatrice's eyes were fixed on the tail lights of that puny sedan, not to the left, not to the right. As she crossed the intersection, her sister's car disappeared from view, hidden behind the towering mass of a goods lorry. 'Supplies', was the only word that she had time to read. It would be her last. Blackness.

The car that had belonged to the young woman known as Beatrice folded. The front suspension was forced down, and the back suspension reared up like the bronco from hell. By the time that it had flopped back down limply to the surface of the road, there was no sign of life from either the car nor it's occupant, both backs were broken.

Chapter Twenty Five

One hand on the steering wheel and one hand holding the mobile phone, Dalton pressed the memory button. It was the third time that he had tried it, but Priscilla wasn't answering. He was nearing the clinic of Dr Jones. That number was still replying with an engaged signal. He tried Priscilla's 'mobile', again.

Cars pulled over to let vehicles pass, with their sirens wailing and flashing lights. Dalton had to kick off the cruise control, but re-instated it when the posse was clear.

The answer took him by surprise as it was muffled by the racket, in fact he almost put the phone back on to the passenger seat, had he not picked up the faintest of replies.

"Priscilla? Priscilla? Is that you?" He thought he had been mistaken when there was no sound. Eventually, there was an answer.

"Yes, Dalton, it's me. I'm so sorry, forgive me, I'm so sorry." She was shocked to have Dalton on the phone and was not in control of her knees. Her legs were having difficulty functioning. Priscilla was surprised that she had even made the airport. Her bags were on the side walk, with Robert under one arm. A porter was dispatched for a trolley. It was nine-thirty.

"We need to talk, Priscilla." There was no answer, this time. He repeated himself. "We need to talk Priscilla, where are you." Again no answer, but this time there was not silence. The outside public address system was giving instructions for not leaving baggage unattended, otherwise it may well be removed and even destroyed. This was obviously not the local supermarket. "Priscilla, I must see you, now tell me where you are."

The porter arrived for the luggage. She was being pushed again.

"I'm sorry for everything, Dalton, we are leaving. Good bye." She was too shocked for tears, her eyes were dry. Everything was dry.

"Priscilla . . . Priscilla." The phone went dead. "Blast. Blast it." Dalton slammed the instrument down on to the leather seat at his side, and looked in to the mirror. There was nobody behind him. He was two blocks past the turning to the airport. That was where she was, and that must be where she was leaving from with Robert. He must get to the bottom of this. He had to. He had no idea how, but he must be there. He touched the brake to disengage cruise and spun the wheel, turning through one hundred and eighty degrees without so much as a murmur of protest from the tyres.

Cruising was no longer on his mind. Speed was. He was at the intersection in under a minute and made a right, not jumping the lights, but sailing close to the wind. The difference between this and his ex-fiancee, now deceased, was that he had his wits about him and he was sober. There was an accident up ahead, before he turned, and it looked rather nasty, but luckily, the traffic was still flowing and he pressed on. He estimated the airport in eight minutes. It was now nine thirty five.

Jacky couldn't believe his eyes when he spotted Priscilla. She looked in a state. She had bare legs and no make up. She was pushing her hair behind one ear, trying to make the best of a bad job and straightening her skirt beneath her blazer. He was relieved to see her.

"Will any remaining passengers for the flight to Shannon please make your way . . ." went the announcement. The trolley, Robert and Priscilla arrived at the desk at the same time. The porter left them too it.

"Priscilla." He kissed her on the cheek, without commenting on her appearance. "I was getting worried, there for a moment."

"I've had an awful time, Jacky. I nearly didn't make it."

"Mr Powell. Are these ,your companions?" said the girl behind the desk, smiling as she spoke, through her perfectly painted lips. "You really do need to check in, now." Her impatience was invisible.

Priscilla half turned. She thought that the girl was speaking to someone next to her, but there was no-one. It was Jacky whom she had addressed.

"Powell?" Priscilla looked at them both quizzically. Jacky ignored the second question. The girl did the same, but only just. An hour earlier, and she would have picked up on it. There was a wide-bodied jet sitting on the stand burning oil.

"Yes, they are," replied Jacky. She realised he was travelling under a false name. It had come out of the 'blue' and wrong-footed her. "Your passport, dear." There was a semi-tone of patronisation that she had never noticed, in the past, but then she realised that she had never been in public with him before. He'd never actually taken her anywhere at all.

Priscilla fumbled through her hand bag and obeyed the request. The ticket girl eyed both her and Robert. Robert was blameless and got a smile and a couple of 'baby talk' words for his trouble. And he was a 'cutie'.

"Smoking or non?" Back to business.

"Non." Jacky answered for her. Priscilla's face didn't take up the challenge.

"You will be able to sit together after take-off. The flight isn't full." The luggage check followed, before it went off along the conveyor, bouncing around the corner, out of sight. "Enjoy your flight." A tilt of the head and a broad smile concluded the transaction and Priscilla was left holding the tickets for Robert and herself.

"We need to hurry," said Jacky, who looked slightly agitated and not a little nervous. "Come on," and he led the way, joining the queue for passport control. He got a few yards ahead and handed his passport over, looking back as he retrieved it. Priscilla adjusted the position of Robert, and changed arms. Babies can weigh a lot for their size. A group of four men were in front of her. Jacky looked on from the opposite side of the barrier.

"Priscilla." Hearing the name was unexpected, especially from behind and at some volume. Dalton was approaching at a half run. "Priscilla, wait."

Priscilla waited, all right. She had no option. She couldn't move. She was rooted to the spot. This was one shock too many. Jacky could only look on. The barrier really had been crossed. Dalton was up to her and an arm went around her shoulder. The queue sensed that the hold-up was going to be a protracted affair and started to shuffle around the newly-formed trio.

"Priscilla. Robert. Where are you going?" Before he got an answer, he looked at the departure board, flashing the destination, 'Shannon', and in the same instant, he took in the form of Jacky. It was Dalton's turn for the colour to drain away.

"Please, Priscilla. Don't go." He touched her hand. There was warmth there. "I love you. This is my son. I love you both. I know that. I don't know how, but I do know that, now."

There was a burst of loud crying followed by pouring tears. They weren't from Robert. He was fast asleep. It was way past his bed-time. It was ten fifteen.

It was the first time that Priscilla had cried openly and freely since she was a small girl, maybe not even then. It had never been her way. She cried because she was happy. Dalton's other arm mimicked the first and they both embraced.

"This is the final call for flight BA 235 to Shannon." The call wasn't aimed at Jacky Powell, he was already through. As he handed in his boarding pass for checking, his eyes fell on the scar on the palm of his hand. He rubbed it automatically with his thumb and shook his head in the way that only the Irish know how, stepping forward, and not looking back, to all intents and purposes, he'd left American soil. He'd made it, freedom, but at a price.

There was one more passenger to have his passport checked and his boarding pass taken. He'd been hanging back, loitering, and was a scruffy individual, scruffy but not dirty, dark glasses and his hair tied back in a pony tale, blue jeans, 'Harley Davidson Motorcycles', written across his back. He was well shaven, though. His wife had insisted. He'd never been back to the 'old country', and there were limits to what a wife could stand.

It was his one concession. Concessions never came easy to him, they were against his religion. He looked back one more time, at the trio and walked through.

"Have a good journey, Mr Edsell".

"Thank you, I will", and he was gone, filling the vacuum left by the Irish man and being sucked through departures in his wake.

Chapter Twenty Six

There was a Mercedes saloon abandoned on the pavement in front of departures. Vapour curled lazily from the twin exhausts, indicating that the engine was still running. It was the only clue, because the background noise more than masked the purr from the great, white, cat. The ignition keys still swung where they had been abandoned. So much had changed since they were charged with energy from the departing driver, but there was movement in them yet. The gaping door, in contrast, was motionless, straddling the sidewalk, welcoming them, but Dalton led his family to the rear.

"Sit in the back with Robert, and I'll take you home. My house is your house, from now on, Priscilla. 'Watashi-no monwa subete, anata-no mono', what's mine is yours". Priscilla was unaware that he was almost fluent in Japanese.

Her eyes were as red as red can be and his were full of water. Before she stepped in, he gave her a last kiss, on the forehead, and one more hug. Her head fell on to his chest, as he pushed her hair behind one ear exposing her graceful neck.

He pushed papers out of the way on the back seat. 'Fiennes for Governor'. Election clutter. She never even noticed.

"I'll retrieve the luggage," he whispered.

The perfume around her ears was as natural as it was heady and his hands were loathe to let her go as his fingers played over the double row of pearls and the antique silver clasp that held them in place. The clasp was

222

unique. There had never been another one like it.

Made for his great Aunt, Dalton would have recognised it anywhere.